I0764308

Taming Julia

Jodie Wolfe

This is a work of fiction. Names, characters, places, and incidents either are the product of the author's imagination or are used fictitiously, and any resemblance to actual persons living or dead, business establishments, events, or locales, is entirely coincidental.

Taming Julia

Contact Information: titleadmin@pelicanbookgroup.com

Scripture quotations, unless otherwise indicated are taken from the King James translation, public domain.

Cover Art by *Nicola Martinez*

White Rose Publishing, a division of Pelican Ventures, LLC
www.pelicanbookgroup.com PO Box 1738 *Aztec, NM * 87410

Publishing History
First White Rose Edition, 2020
Hardback Edition ISBN 978-1-5223-0272-8
Electronic Edition ISBN 978-1-5223-0271-1
Published in the United States of America

Dedication

My first praise goes to my Lord and Savior who instilled in me a desire to share stories.

To my dear, sweet husband who encourages me daily to fulfill this calling. Thanks for being my biggest cheerleader.

To my friend, Joy. Thank you for all your helpful edits and insights.

To my fellow Scribes. Thank you for your help during the early stages of this project.

To Uncle Robert and Aunt Nickie. Thanks for helping with my Texas research.

To Nicola and Jamie. Thank you for your help in bringing this story to completion.

Finally, for my mom, for always believing I had a gift and pushing me toward using it.

What People are Saying

Taming Julia is the charming tale of an unconventional heroine who longs for a home and family and the reluctant hero who fears he's made a dreadful mistake by marrying her. Jodie Wolfe has skillfully penned a fascinating debut novel with colorful characters and an interesting plot that celebrates friendship, family, and faith.

~ Vickie McDonough, award-winning author of 27 books, including Whispers on the Prairie, a Romantic Times recommended inspirational read July, 2013.

Hear my cry, O God; attend unto my prayer. From the end of the earth will I cry unto thee, when my heart is overwhelmed: lead me to the rock that is higher than I.
Psalm 61:1-2(KJV)

1

Matrimony News, February 6, 1875 edition

Minister bachelor aged 27, height 5 feet 10 inches seeks genteel, honest and first-rate homemaker with a desire to serve God. Must be willing to marry by proxy and arrive in Burrton Springs, Kansas by May 1.

~*~

Burrton Springs, Kansas, Saturday, May 1, 1875

Dear Lord, please don't let that creature be my new wife. Drew Montgomery swiped the sweat trickling a path down his neck and shoved the new hat back on his head. He squinted, taking in the lone passenger stepping from the stagecoach. At least, he thought it was a woman. He shielded his eyes from the sun, taking in the britches.

Britches? A gun belt strapped to a slim waist. He gulped. A rifle rested on her shoulder, and she wore a Stetson situated low on her brow. The figure shifted sideways, and Drew groaned, fearing his proxy mail-order bride had arrived by the look of all the curves. He squared his shoulders and crossed the street.

"Are you Montgomery?" Her coffee-brown gaze seared through him.

He snapped his gaping mouth shut and nodded. "Y-yes."

"Name's Jules Walker." She shoved her hand into his and shook it so hard his teeth clattered. "I reckon, Jules Montgomery since we're hitched." She waved a slip of paper in his face. "Got the paper here to prove it. So are you my husband or not?"

Drew caught a whiff of dirt. He coughed and cleared his throat.

She peered at him as if he were a chicken with one leg.

"I'm Drew." He managed to choke the words out. "Isn't your name Julia?"

She scrunched her face, pushed her Stetson from her head, and allowed it to dangle from the string around her neck. Her brown hair scattered in disarray, slipping from a shoulder-length braid. "I can't remember the last time I've been called Julia. Like I said, name's Jules."

"But..." Drew let the word hang between them. No matter. "Where're your things?"

"Got my knapsack and that there." She pointed to the top of the stagecoach. He expected to see a trunk, but a saddle rested there instead. What kind of woman brought a saddle into a marriage? What kind of woman showed up dressed like a man? *No. No.* Something was terribly wrong.

"I reckon you'll need to sign this here paper to make it all proper like. I already signed my name, and there's the judge's signature." She poked at the words on the page.

"Yes, I'll inscribe it when we reach our home." Drew shouldered the knapsack, hefted the saddle, and headed in the direction of the parsonage.

"Home. I like the sound of that." Jules smiled, a dimple flickered in each cheek, giving him the first hint that she was truly a female. She studied him for a moment then slanted her gaze to their surroundings.

"This is a town, huh? A heap of buildings tossed in one place." She gawked at each structure they passed.

Nothing seemed to escape her notice. The sun beat down with no mercy as they meandered along the street. He wished she'd hurry before anyone spotted her. What type of character had he agreed to marry? She didn't appear at all like the woman for whom he'd advertised, but now there was no way to change things. He forced his choppy breathing to slow. No avoiding it. He needed a wife by the next day, and his lone alternative, the one he'd chosen in order to keep his job, hiked along behind him. Drew cast a glance over his shoulder, moaned, and came to a halt. His bride plowed into him, causing him to stumble and fall to his knees.

"Sorry." She dusted him off with her hat and offered a hand.

"What'd you stop for?"

"Did you bring a horse?" He brushed at the dirt on his pants and picked up the saddle. His gaze drifted toward the stagecoach.

"Nah, Josh made me sell him afore I came here. Almost the worst thing I ever done." She knocked the dirt from her hat before returning it to her head. "Here. There's no reason to tote everything by yerself. Let me help."

"No." He shifted her belongings to a more comfortable position. "I've got it."

"Don't have to get testy."

"I'm *not* testy." A sigh hissed from his lips. *Give me patience, Lord.* He'd met his wife all of two minutes ago, and they already were having difficulty communicating. Had he been too hasty? *I must not have been thinking straight to order a woman sight unseen.* He shook his head. "A gentleman helps a lady."

She snickered, and then her eyes narrowed. "Not goin' back on yer word, are you?"

He gulped. Surely she couldn't read his mind?

"I guess it won't be bindin' until you sign this." She waved the document.

Drew pulled a shallow breath into his lungs, thankful she hadn't pursued her question. "As I…I said, I'll pen my name when we get to my place." He took advantage of his long strides, and hurried along the street, grateful nobody milled around.

"What's yer hurry?" Jules jogged to keep up with him.

Drew slowed his pace. "I assumed you'd be anxious to rest after the long trip. Where exactly in Texas did you reside? I don't remember any mention of it."

Her eyebrow lifted. "Seein' as we just met, I don't suspect I told you, but I last came from the Blanco area."

"I've never been to Texas." His arms perspired beneath the load of gear.

Jules moved the rifle to her opposite shoulder while marching along like a toy soldier. "Is yer place in town?"

"On the outskirts." Drew nodded in the direction of his home, which was nestled beside the building that served as the schoolhouse during the week and church on Sundays. Beyond it stretched a fallow field that met the horizon. He didn't want her to explore. He wanted to get to his house, hustle her inside, and close the door against any busybodies.

Jules scrutinized the homes and businesses, stopping every few steps to stare at them. "Guess it will take some gettin' used to."

"What will?" He tried to peer into her eyes, but she had shielded them with her hat.

"Livin' in a town."

"It's not much of a town yet, but perhaps we'll compare to Hutchinson before too long. Here we are." Drew swung the door open and moved aside, allowing her to enter the kitchen. "It's kind of small, but I hope you'll like it."

~*~

Jules scanned the room. Blue wildflowers sat in the center of a table, their scent wafting. "What's the big thing there?"

"A cook stove." His hazel eyes surveyed her.

How should she know what it was? She snapped her mouth shut. Better to not ask too much afore he signed the paper. Her brother had told her the marriage wouldn't be official-like until then. Josh hadn't said why she needed to come here and take a husband, but she trusted him. She sensed his decision had something to do with her safety. He'd told her returning to Texas wasn't possible.

Her new husband set the saddle near the door and motioned her toward the rest of the house. "Here's the sitting room."

Jules 'sposed it had the name because the thing in the center of the room was something a person sat on. Probably more comfortable than anything she'd ever been on along the trail. There were frilly things on the arms of the chair. She knew better than to ask.

Next they breezed by a small room. "That's my study."

"I ain't sure what a study is. Can't say I've ever seen one." She craned her neck as they passed the room.

Drew stopped short.

"Whoa there." She stumbled into him. "Wasn't expectin' you to hold up so fast."

His face got as red as a berry. He moved aside and allowed her to enter the last room.

She managed to contain a squeal when she saw the bed. Jules couldn't remember the last time she'd slept in one. Another large piece of furniture stood along the opposite wall. She walked over and ran her fingers along the smooth top. "It's right cold. What do you call it?"

"A marble-top dresser," he replied. "It arrived last week. I thought you might want to have something special for dresses and..."

Warmth climbed into her face and neck while a swarm of bees took up residence in her gut.

The man's face darkened again.

She hoped he didn't have something wrong with him to make his face change like that each time they talked. "Feeling all right?"

"Yes." He gulped, taking on the likeness of a cornered critter. "Why?"

Jules wrangled how to answer. She stepped forward and removed his hat. The golden hair at his temples held a crease. For a few seconds, she fanned at his face to cool him off. A whiff of manly scent teased her senses.

He blinked rapidly and licked his lips. He captured her hand in his warm grip. "How about I endorse our marriage certificate?" Drew yanked her toward the kitchen. He shoved her into a chair and ran to the small room he'd called his study. He tripped and almost dropped the pen and jar of ink as he entered.

"I guess yer in a mighty big hurry to get hitched." Jules smiled, not sure why his face immediately repeated that cornered likeness. Her stomach did a funny flop, while her heart thudded in her ears.

He uncapped the jar and dipped the pen. With quick scratching, he made his mark on the paper and blew on it. "There, it's legitimate and right on time."

What did he mean? Jules puffed out a breath and stood up. It'd take a heap of patience to make sense of the man. Knocking her hat off, she let it dangle between her shoulders. A lump twisted in her throat. Her thoughts hadn't gone beyond arriving and meeting her new husband. Straining to recall memories of how her parents had acted, she came up with nothing. What 'xactly did a married couple do together? Warmth flooded her cheeks when she remembered the lone thing her brother had advised her concernin' the situation. "Josh said couples kiss after they're hitched. Should we try it? I've never done it afore, but I reckon we could give it a shot." She puckered her lips and waited.

Drew took a big step backward.

Had she used the wrong word? Jules wrinkled her brow, trying to recollect what her brother had said. Had he called it a peck? *Nah, couldn't be.* That's what prairie chickens did when they found a tasty bug.

Her new husband sputtered.

She whacked him hard on the back. The poor man must still have something caught in his throat. "Got any willow bark?"

He shook his head.

"You keep havin' those coughing fits. Guess I need to get you healthy. You seem a might unfit."

"Unfit?" His eyes darted side-to-side.

"Easy there." She patted his arm. "I'm not gonna to hurt you."

~*~

Tempted to yank his arm away, Drew withstood her soothing. Unfit, indeed! Should we kiss? *Really, Lord? What kind of brazen woman is she?* Jules had sounded so sweet in her letters, but obviously there'd been some sort of miscommunication. How could he bring it up when he'd just made their marriage legal? His thoughts skipped to what would become their first night together. He'd been so busy trying to plan a way around the elders' stipulation to marry, he hadn't considered it. A bead of sweat pooled on his forehead. Would people talk if he started sleeping in the barn? His chest constricted.

"You sick or somethin'? Got all pale around the cheek bones." She motioned to his face. "Seen a doc lately?"

He tried to answer, but his lunch took up sudden residence in his throat. "Excuse me." Drew didn't wait for her reply. He clamped a hand over his mouth and dashed for the door, running toward the outhouse.

He breathed a sigh of relief when he entered the house a few minutes later and couldn't find Jules. Maybe he'd experienced a nightmare. Or he needed to accept his fate and make the best of it. *Give me strength for what's ahead, Lord.* His hand shook as he drank a glass of water. Setting it down, Drew went in search of his new bride. He found her kneeling just beyond the schoolhouse, beside a small campfire with a pot of water hanging above it.

Jules glanced his way.

Drew scraped his knuckles across his forehead.

She frowned, studying him. "Is yer head hurting too? Land's sake. Guess I got here just in time."

The woman has no idea. His *bride* stood and grazed her fingertips across his brow.

"Hope you're not coming down with something. Sure didn't expect to spend my first day with my husband losing his food everywhere." She placed her hands on her hips. "It's a good thing Josh didn't know you were sick, or he would've never agreed to us marrying up."

It took sheer will power to keep his stomach under control and his feet from rushing for the little building behind the house a second time. His thoughts fuzzed and blurred. Jules had been spouting words about being sick and something concerning some man. *Josh?* She hadn't mentioned a last name, had she? A former beau? He racked his brain, trying to remember what she'd said in her letters. Nothing came to mind.

"Here, sit down." Jules pushed him on the grass and tried to press his head between his knees. She quirked an eyebrow. "Feeling puny, still? The tea will be ready in a bit. Rest a spell, and I'll fix you up right quick." She bent and stirred the pot with a stick.

He peered at her, motioning toward the house. "You could have prepared this inside."

"It's so much nicer out here." She shaded her eyes from the setting sun. "Besides, it don't take me long, and once you drink my willow bark tea, it'll help your gut." Her gaze darted about as if checking the perimeter.

If he'd known her better, he'd guess her nerves were drawn tight. His face warmed, and he ran his tongue across his lips. "Did you say willow bark?"

She examined him momentarily. "Yes, it's good for what ails a body. Josh and me use it all the time along the trail when one of us is feeling poorly. Glad I had some in my bag, or it would've taken me a heap longer to fix it. 'Course it'd taste better if I had some whiskey and honey. Don't s'pose you have any? Any willow trees around here? Sure is awful flat and not many trees. How do you stand it? Texas don't have a lot of trees neither, depends which part you're travelin' through. I guess each place has a beauty all its own. Sure do miss trees, though. The wind always blow like this? Might take some gettin' used to." She took a breath, "Don't say a whole lot, do you? Josh gets tired of me talking too. 'Course it's always worse when I'm nervous. Not that I'm nervous. Have you lived here long?"

Drew wasn't sure which question to answer first.

"Tea's almost ready. I'll fetch a mug from my pack. Hold on."

He opened his mouth to respond, but she'd taken off at a run, her lithe form covering the distance and returning in record time.

"Here we go." She used the edge of her jacket to grab the pan, poured the contents into a tin cup, and handed it to him. "Should I keep the fire going so I can cook us up some grub in a bit?"

A waft of the bitter brew accosted his nose. "No. Yes. I mean, our dinner's in the warming pan. I imagined you'd be weary from the trip, and I didn't want cooking a meal to be a concern on your first night here."

"That's right thoughtful, Drew. I 'preciate it. Josh would've never done something so proper. His gut always came first."

Drew formed the words to inquire concerning the elusive Josh. She startled him by bussing his cheeks with her lips. He refrained from placing his fingers where her lips had been.

Jules extinguished the flames and helped him to his feet. She was strong in spite of her petite frame.

"Say, you haven't drunk any tea yet."

Drew blew on the hot liquid then took a sip. He grimaced and shivered involuntarily.

"I reckon it don't taste the best, but sure does the body good. Makes one feel perky in no time. Let's go find some grub. I'm starving."

He allowed himself to be led to the house.

Jules kept after him until he drank the tea. He fought not to make a face as he handed the cup to her. "Thanks."

"You're welcome. Better?" Her intense stare made him want to squirm.

He lowered his eyes, surprised to discover his stomach *had* improved. "Yes, I appreciate it, Jules. I believe I feel up to eating some supper after all."

A smile crossed her tanned face. "Knew it would help. Glad I could lend a hand right away. You won't be sorry for marryin' me."

Her chattering followed him as he crossed to the cook stove, gathered their meal, and placed it on the small table. "There're cloth napkins and flatware in the drawer," he said motioning to one. He pulled out glasses and poured water into them.

"Aren't these fine." Jules ran her fingers across the fabric. "I've never seen nothing like it afore. What're they called, and what're they for?"

"Napkins. For wiping a mouth during the meal." His heart

pounded.

"Whoever thought to have a slip of material to swab yer mouth when food slopped on it? I thought that's what sleeves were for." She inhaled deeply. "Sure smells good in here. I'm hungrier than a hog at feeding time."

What sort of ruffian had he married? Drew held her chair, waiting for her to sit then found his own seat.

"What a gentleman."

A lump formed in his throat as he grasped her hand.

Jules blushed and interlaced her fingers with his.

He bowed his head and prayed, stumbling over the words. Her hand seared a permanent brand in his. The steady ticking of the clock brought him to the present.

"Did'ya want to hold hands all through the meal?"

"Amen." He hastily snatched his hand free and dug into the food. "No, just when we pray."

They ate in mutual silence, but Drew's mind was far from quiet.

Jules snagged his plate. "I'll wash these up right quick. We can do some kissing tomorrow." She yawned. "I'm plain tuckered out and need some sleep."

2

Jules stretched as dawn lit the sky and filtered through the window. She hadn't slept a wink in the big bed despite its softness. She was too used to her camp roll and ground sheet. Josh had let her sleep at a no longer used stage station once and she'd hollered with joy over the bed and the bedding before settlin' down. The sheets on this bed were now tangled in a heap. She rolled over and rested her palm where she'd expected her husband to sleep.

Drew had insisted on making a pallet on the sitting room floor. She didn't think it normal behavior for a husband and wife, but she hadn't questioned him. He'd been mighty edgy, and she didn't want to cause more bother for him.

Although he'd slept in a separate room, every deep breath or soft snore that had escaped Drew had kept her wide awake. Jules hadn't been that aware at night since the time her brother had spotted cougar tracks near their campsite a few years ago. Her heart galloped like Josh's gelding. She'd never minded hearing her brother's breathing or snores. What made her man any different? Body protesting, Jules slipped from the bed. While tempted to stay under the quilt longer, she reckoned Drew would hanker waking to a hot meal instead of a loafing wife.

She retrieved her clothes where she'd dropped them before slipping under the covers, ears alert to any sounds coming from the other room. On tiptoe, Jules edged past Drew. In the kitchen, she swung the door wide, stepped outside and closed it without a sound.

Jules inhaled the morning air as she tramped to the nearby stream. She filled a bucket with water, splashed her face, enjoying the familiar coolness. Moments later, she headed to the spot of yesterday's campfire. It took no time to have the wood blazing. She hurried to the house to drop off the water and withdrew a small frying pan from her pack, making a special effort not to awaken Drew. Outdoors again, Jules noticed a small henhouse and headed toward it. After gathering eggs, she cracked them into the skillet, preparing breakfast for her new husband.

"Wish I had something more than eggs to make." There hadn't been enough room in her bag. "He's sure to have an appetite after feeling puny last night and just pickin' at his supper."

She set a pot near the fire for coffee, using her last supply. Once breakfast was over, she'd poke around in the kitchen to see what kind of food there was to work with in the days ahead. She hoped he didn't mind trail food. If they were hurting for meat, she could go hunting later that day, unless Drew had something else in mind.

The food prepared, she went inside to set the table. She peeked into the sitting room, but Drew didn't twitch. *He must've been run to ground.* She gathered some wildflowers and replaced the wilted ones. Maybe she should let him doze, especially after those coughing fits he had. *Yes.* She'd better eat without him. Rest was good for a body. Jules placed enough food for Drew in the thing he'd called a warming pan and sat down to her cooling eggs. She chewed, spitting out eggshells. "Shouldn't have been distracted this morning. Can't remember the last time I was so sloppy with my cooking. Josh would never let me forget it." She clamped a hand to her mouth. *Best not to wake Drew.* Her heart clenched with thoughts of her brother. Had she seen him for the last time? Belly full, she washed the few items in the nearby stream.

Jules stole through the house, stepping into the study for the first time. *Oh, my.* Books lined two walls of the small room. She ran her fingers along the spines. A whistle escaped. She'd never seen so many books in all her life. Growing up, she'd devoured the handful of McGuffey readers they'd owned until they'd finally fallen apart from use. Jules scanned the shelf in front of her. One book caught her eye and she withdrew it. Sitting in the chair by the desk she got caught up in the story.

The sound of a throat clearing pulled her from the tale. Her husband filled the doorway.

"Why didn't you awaken me? We'll be late for services." A scowl filled Drew's face.

Jules stood. "Late? I didn't reckon we had anything planned today. Figured you needed rest. I've been up for hours. There's some food in the warmin' pan. I'll fetch it while you wash up." She put the book on the shelf and scurried to the kitchen.

A line from the novel played through her mind. 'An elephant! An elephant that belongs to an Indian but a hundred steps from here.' She'd dealt with many Indians throughout the years but didn't recall ever seeing an elephant. Maybe her husband knew about them.

Drew entered the kitchen, jamming the tails of his shirt into a pair of fancy britches. He shrugged into a jacket then sat at the table and bowed his head.

Jules poured him some piping hot coffee, thankful she'd kept the campfire burning. She smiled. Her fingers itching to smooth a piece of his hair, which stood on end. *Where had that thought come from?*

"Ugh! These eggs are cold. You said they were in the warming pan." He grimaced and placed a piece of an eggshell on the edge of his plate.

"They were."

Drew shoved his chair, stood, and crossed the room. "How do you expect it to keep my food warm when the stove isn't lit?"

"Light it?"

"Yes, light it. Honestly."

Jules shrugged. She'd have to learn his peculiar ways.

~*~

Of all the mornings, Lord. Why did I have to oversleep this Sunday? Drew raked his fingers through his hair. He regained his seat to eat his cold breakfast and took a sip of the coffee, nearly spitting it. The bitter brew almost curled his toes.

"Need me to whack yer back again?" Jules hovered by his chair.

He held his hand up to stop her. "No, I could use some cream and sugar though."

"I reckon I've gotten used to strong coffee." She grinned. "Uh, I don't know where the cream and sugar is."

"Never mind, I'll get it. Go on back and change your clothing."

She opened her mouth, closed it, spun on her heel, and headed to the bedroom.

I surely am going to need patience today, Lord. Drew stirred his beverage and nearly inhaled it. The coffee burnt his tongue, blazing a fire down his throat.

The dishes clanked together when he placed them on the dry sink a moment later. He rushed into the study to collect his sermon notes, shoving them into his Bible. Drew hesitated, swallowed hard, and knocked on the bedroom door. At her response, he crossed the threshold.

Jules sat on the bed, dressed in the shabbiest garments he'd ever seen, running a comb through her brown hair.

His jaw dropped, and he struggled to cool the ire igniting in his belly. The rustic woman tried his restraint like none other. Yet, he couldn't take his gaze from her river of shimmering hair.

Her shirt billowed around her shoulders, appearing to be at least two sizes too big. She'd rolled the sleeves, but her hands were barely visible. The pants swam around her waist cinched by what looked like a length of horse harness. An unsure smile played at the corner of her lips.

"Weren't sure why you wanted me to swap my clothes. We fixin' to go huntin'?" She picked at a small hole in the knee of her britches.

"What? No. Why would you say something so absurd?"

"On account of you askin' me to switch my duds. Figured my others were too fancy." She frowned.

"No, apparently there's a misunderstanding here." He clenched his teeth tight. What was it about the woman that caused him to lose his ability to communicate?

"You're sure hard to read." She stood and clumped closer, her lips pressed together, eyes blazing fire. "I reckon my attire may not be to yer liking, but yer *stuck* with me." She stabbed her finger in his chest. "Sure didn't figure on my man being the type to look down on someone on account of how they're dressed. I don't know 'xactly how *you* are, maybe you *do* judge folks."

He barely managed to keep his mouth from gaping open. How had their conversation got so twisted? Had she accused *him* of being judgmental? He'd only meant for her to change into a dress, but perhaps his wishes should've been made clearer. He hadn't asked her to do anything out of character for a woman.

"Please change into something more sensible." *Like something more appropriate for church.* "I, we need to hurry." He bit his tongue, refusing to stir an argument on the Lord's Day. Drew shifted his Bible and pages of notes slipped and fluttered to the floor. He bent to retrieve them, peering up at Jules. Roses bloomed in her tanned cheeks. What thoughts were fluttering through her head? He didn't stay to discover them.

He paced the tiny kitchen, lifted the curtain at the window, and cringed when he saw the churchyard filling up with buggies and buckboards. Drew breathed a prayer of thanksgiving when he heard his wife enter the room.

"I'm ready."

"Good." He turned toward her. "B-but, you're wearing the same clothes from yesterday. Where's your dress? I thought I made it clear to change to your *best* outfit." Drew wanted to shake her slim shoulders. What should he do with her? He wished he could leave her home, but he couldn't show up without a wife when today was the deadline.

Her eyes blazed. "This *is* my best set of britches and shirt, which is why I wore it when we met. I don't own a dress. Can't say I remember ever ownin' one, although I guess I might have as a young tyke. It'll have to do. It's all I have except for Josh's clothes, and those didn't meet your likin'."

"There's nothing we can do now. Most of the congregation is already there. I'll never hear the end of this," he grumbled, opening the door. It couldn't be avoided. She'd have to come along.

~*~

Jules glared at Drew's retreating back. What had he found wrong with her clothing? The only other piece in her wardrobe was her union suit, and she refused to strip down to that. Confounded man. She tried to calm her thudding heart. She'd thought being married would be the same as spending time with her brother, but this man completely befuddled her. She sighed and strapped on her gun belt.

Drew hoofed a full two strides ahead of her. She caught up and stared ahead at the clapboard building nestled in a small grove of trees. Her heart pained at the sight of tethered horses munching on grass. Should've kept her mount. She swiped her moist hands on her britches, while he yanked the door open.

Older women swarmed and clucked about like mother hens, pushing their daughters forward.

Drew sputtered as if he had something stuck in his throat.

Jules gave him a firm whack between his shoulders to get his lungs working. She'd have to make him more tea later, once they finished up at the school. There must be a special program because the bell was ringing.

"I reckon we find a perch, sugar." Jules nearly shouted the

words, so she could be heard over the cackling womenfolk. She'd remembered how a young married couple she and Josh had met on the trail last year had used the word when they talked to each other. Maybe using it would help calm his dander.

Drew's ears and face turned bright red. He yanked her toward the front of the building and sat her on a bench, then went behind a funny shaped box on top of a table. He cleared his throat and bowed his head. "Dear God, we pray for Your presence at our service this morning. May our hearts and minds be attuned to what You desire to show us today."

Jules could feel eyes boring into her head. Maybe she should've braided her hair instead of shoving it under her hat.

A small hand rested on her arm. A young woman with kind eyes smiled and offered an open book with words and some strange markings running across it. Jules opened her mouth to thank the lady, but the folks were already singing.

"'Bringing in the sheaves, bringing in the sheaves, we shall come rejoicing, bringing in the sheaves.'"

What were sheaves and why were the people rejoicing about bringing them? Jules surveyed the room but didn't see anything peculiar. She opened her mouth to ask the woman beside her when the next song began. This song told about soldiers marching off to war. The war had ended. She waited to see what happened next.

Jules hoped Drew would sit beside her once he finished his announcing, but he didn't. Instead, he opened a book and removed a stack of papers. Did he plan on giving a speech? Her brother had told her sometimes that happened when a town held a special celebration. Not that he had ever let her get close enough to hear one.

"Turn to Genesis 2:7-25. Let's stand while we read God's Word." Drew's gaze shifted to hers.

Jules caught most of what he said, although her mind tended to wander. She stared at her husband.

He finished with the line, "'And they were both naked, the man and his wife, and were not ashamed.'" His face went bright red. He ran his finger between the collar of his shirt and his neck.

Maybe she should fetch the poor man a cup of water. Too bad the twosome next to her were so close to her side. Jules decided to stay put and keep an eye on her man. If he had another coughing fit, she'd stomp over them to get him a drink.

~*~

Drew's collar tightened it seemed. He could kick himself for choosing that passage. Somehow, earlier in the week it'd been a good idea since he would have a new bride to show off. What better way to share his news to the congregation than to talk on marriage? His thoughts rambled, and his gaze bounced to the previous verse. *'Therefore shall a man leave his father and his mother, and shall cleave unto his wife: and they shall be one flesh.'*

The room grew at least ten degrees hotter. What would people say if he opened a window and thrust his head outside? They'd probably think he'd lost his mind. He'd probably wind up with apoplexy.

His voice shook as he spoke the first line of his message. How could he talk on the topic of marriage when he hadn't been married for one full day yet? Sweat poured down his sides, and he debated whether he should change his epistle midstream. Would anybody notice?

Drew thumbed through his Bible, trying to find something else to present. The words from a passage in the book of Judges leaped at him. *'And he found a new jawbone of an ass, and put forth his hand, and took it, and slew a thousand men therewith.' Definitely not appropriate.* Resigned, he closed his eyes and decided to proceed with the original discourse.

Each tick of the clock reverberated. He stumbled his way through his notes, not sure if he made any sense. He breathed a sigh when he could finally sit while the congregation sang the closing hymn. Drew kept his head bowed in prayer throughout the singing, not wanting to see any questioning stares. When the music finished, he struggled to his feet, feeling like he'd run a long distance.

"Let us pray. Dear God, thank You for this glimpse of marriage from Your word. Help us to be ever mindful of how we can follow and serve You in our homes and families. May we desire to spread Your word to the lost world. Help us not to judge others without first taking the beam from our own eye. May we be ever attentive to Your presence in our lives. In Jesus' name, amen."

The congregation drew to its feet.

Erma Miller made a beeline to the front of the church.

It was now or never. "Excuse me. Before everyone heads out this morning, I want to introduce you to this wonderful woman on the front pew. I'd like you to meet Mrs. Julia Montgomery, my wife."

3

A hush fell over the crowd.

Jules beamed at her handsome husband.

The murmuring voices rose to a thunderous level.

The woman beside Jules yanked her into a quick hug and squealed.

"The old rascal finally did it." The man on their bench laughed.

"Oh, forgive me." The woman stepped to the side. "I'm Sarah Brown, and this is my husband, David." She motioned to the man who had chuckled. "I'm Drew's sister, so I guess you're my sister-in-law."

"Pleased to meet you both." Jules tilted her hat and surveyed the room of people. Some surged forward while others lingered in small groups talking behind their hands, pointing in her direction. "Guess we caused quite a stir this morning." She grinned.

"How did you meet? When did the two of you get married?" Sarah's blue eyes darted between Jules and her brother, who had a gaggle of women flocked around him.

"We met yesterday, but for yer other question it's kind of hard to say. We married by proxy, so we were already hitched when I arrived yesterday on the stagecoach. Drew finalized it when he added his name. I don't know if it counts the time the judge and I signed it, or yesterday. Hmm. I'll have to ask yer brother."

"I'm surprised, but also excited to have a sister." Sarah drew her into another hug. "What a wonderful day to have such news." Her eyes twinkled. "Please join us for dinner after church."

"I'm not so sure." She cupped her hand and hollered above the noise of the crowd. "Drew, sugar, come over here a minute."

The room grew quiet.

Drew's face blazed when he joined them.

Jules ran her fingertips across his forehead. "Feeling all right, husband?" She touched his cheek. "Why does yer face keep changing colors? I sure hope sickness ain't creepin' at yer door. Here, best sit down." She shoved him onto the bench even as he fought to stay upright. "Move over and give him room to breathe."

Folks jumped away and stared at them.

"Not going to spew, are you?" Jules snagged his hand and patted it, clicking her tongue. "Yessiree. My brother would be having a fit if he knew what kind of husband you've turned out to be."

~*~

Drew wanted to drop to his knees and crawl under the bench. *Lord, shoot me and put me out of my misery.* It'd been bad enough to be cornered by Erma Miller and her daughter Gertrude and barraged with questions, but to have his bride ordering him around after he'd given a message on marriage was *too* much.

"David, go get some water for Drew," Jules bellowed, and then sat beside him. "You'll feel better in a few minutes, sugar. I best make some more of my tea. Good thing I kept the fire going."

"Fire? But the stove wasn't lit." Drew rubbed his temples.

"I didn't realize we'd be coming to the school, or I would've put it out aforehand. It's probably embers anyway. Maybe I should go check on it and start the water heating." She sprang to her feet.

Drew grabbed her hand and held fast, not giving her the opportunity to disappear and further embarrass him. "I'm fine, Julia, really. Let's visit with the congregation before they leave."

"I don't know..."

He stood, keeping a firm grip on Jules's arm. Maybe he could control her better if he didn't let her move from his side. He prayed it would help.

David rushed into the room and handed a glass of water to Drew.

Drew drained the glass and nodded his appreciation.

"Sly old dog." David clapped him on the shoulder. "I cannot believe you'd go off and get married and not tell anybody. Your mother will have a conniption."

Drew cringed. He hadn't allowed himself to contemplate *her* reaction. He wondered why she hadn't attended the church service. Waves of thankfulness swept over him, followed by guilt.

"I guess we'll see at dinner today, won't we?" Sarah stepped forward and kissed his cheek. "Julia's wonderful and exactly what you need." The whispered words tickled his ear. She moved out of the way to allow others to express their congratulations.

After ten minutes of well wishes, Drew longed for a break from the constant questions concerning the specifics of their marriage, which he had no inclination to share. So far, his wife hadn't said anything further to embarrass him, but she hadn't really spoken either.

"The women in this town must have some sort of disease or something." Jules gazed around the church.

He flinched. "What's that?" Drew lowered his voice, praying she'd take the hint and do the same.

"They all have something wrong with their backsides. They're huge." Jules spread her arms apart. She'd spoken in a low tone but loud enough for several women to hear.

Drew prayed the Lord would see fit to nail her mouth shut and searched for any excuse which demanded his attention elsewhere.

Erma Miller gasped and dragged her daughter from the church.

Sarah giggled and put a hand on Jules's elbow. "Come with me, Julia, and I'll inform you on the matter." Sarah smiled, leading his wife away.

Drew exhaled heavily. Weight fell from his shoulders as the door closed behind the pair. He hoped his sister could talk sense into his bride.

~*~

"Actually, I prefer to be called Jules." She paced the tiny room like a caged animal.

"What a beautiful nickname." Sarah lifted her dress to her waist. Some sort of wire contraption bounced around her.

Jules stared, her mouth dropping open, and then frowned. "There *is* something wrong with the women here."

"No, silly, it's called a bustle." Sarah allowed the garment to fall into place. "It's the latest fashion. You've never seen one?"

"I haven't set eyes upon many women in my life."

"Why not? I can't imagine not being exposed to the latest fashions, even here on the prairie. How'd you end up becoming a mail-order bride?" Sarah guided her to two chairs against the wall.

Jules stared at her new sister-in-law.

Somehow Sarah managed to sit. It had to be a might uncomfortable. She couldn't imagine wearing such a rig.

"I last lived in Blanco, Texas, or at least in the country. My brother Josh never allowed me to go into town on account of our parents. I tried sneakin' to one once, but he caught me afore I made it and tanned me something fierce, so it weren't worth the effort."

"Why doesn't he approve of towns?"

"My ma, pa, and sister died of cholera in Illinois when I was three years old." She scratched her earlobe. "Josh must've been sixteen at the time, and he raised me ever since. We didn't have any other family. He never liked getting too close to big herds of folks. Whenever we needed supplies *he* headed into town to tote them. I guess he feared I'd get a sickness or something."

"You've never been in a town before yesterday?" Sarah slipped to the edge of her seat and grasped Jules's hands.

"Nope. 'Course, I've met plenty of people along the trail, mostly men though." She shook her head. "I've never seen a *burstle* afore."

"Bustle." Sarah chuckled. "What did your brother do? How did he support you both? How old are you?" The questions fell over one another like tumbleweeds.

"I'll be twenty-three on the first of June."

"We're the same age then." Sarah leaned forward. "At least for now. Tell me how your brother took care of you."

"We've lived along the trail, long as I can recollect. In the early years, Josh took jobs wherever he could. Drivin' cattle to market, fixing fences, anythin' that paid. Most times he found somewhere for me to hide whilst he worked. We'd live in an abandoned cabin or cave. The past ten years or so, he's been a deputy with the U.S. Marshals. He tracks and catches outlaws."

Sarah's eyes widened. "Incredible, but how'd you end up as a mail-order bride?"

"Don't know what a mail-order bride is. My brother saw an advertisement in a newspaper one day and decided I should come here and marry yer brother. Actually, I married him afore I came, like I said." Jules removed her hat, letting her hair tumble around her shoulders. She scratched her head. She couldn't remember the last time she'd been able to scrub it good. "I reckon I never did get to see the notice and not sure why Josh didn't show me."

"I can't imagine leaving everything I've known to marry a man I never met. Why'd you do it?" Sarah's brow furrowed.

"Because I trust my brother. He's watched over me all these years, and I learned not to question him. One way or another he's always tried to keep me safe. I may not reckon what's in his head most times, but he wants what's best for me." Jules slapped her Stetson against her clad leg sending up a cloud of dust. She hefted a sigh. *Somehow, I have to get through this mess.*

"With never being in a town, is this your first time to attend a church service?"

"When I first heard the bell, I figured there was a special school meeting today. Josh told me about school an' I seen one once. Josh told me about preachers and church, too. He didn't have much use for neither." Jules chuckled. "As for marryin', never figured it'd be a preacher. 'Course, I never *planned* on marryin'."

"Never marrying? I can't imagine." Sarah lifted an eyebrow and motioned toward Jules's waist. "I'm surprised Drew let you bring those weapons to church."

"I didn't bring *all* of 'em. Left my rifle behind. I reckon it would've caused more of a stir if I hadn't."

Sarah's mouth dropped open wide enough to catch flies. "Rifle?"

Jules rested her hands on her gun belt. "Yes, I feel naked without that." She bent over and removed a knife from her boot. "'Course I always have this, and most times I carry a derringer in my hat, but I plumb forgot it. Drew had me a bit fired up afore we left."

"Yes, um..." Sarah's face became bright red.

Did all his family have the same sickness?

"We probably should meet up with our men. I'll need to check on the fire and rustle up some grub."

"Don't forget the invitation to come home with us. Drew usually dines with us unless he's been asked by one of the other parishioners. Our mother is supposed to be there too. At least I assume so. I'm not sure why she didn't attend today. I wonder if she's ill." Sarah stood.

"Maybe I should make her some willow bark tea. Sure helped Drew last night when he felt puny. Might be enough left for a few more doses." Jules held the door for Sarah.

"Drew's been sick?"

"He were, but I fixed him up good enough so he could eat his supper. I didn't want an ailing husb—" Jules halted when Drew's sister's cheeks grew red.

Something *must* be going on with his family. She'd have to keep an eye on the mother whenever they met. Jules hoped they didn't have the cholera or some other sickness.

The main room was empty when they reentered, so they passed through it and stepped outside. Their husbands waited by the remaining buggy. *The herd sure cleared quick.*

"We were on our way to find you." David guided his wife to the buggy.

Jules looped her arm through Drew's. "Howdy, sugar. You got plans for the afternoon?"

He edged away. "We'll be eating with Sarah, David, and Mother, if she's feeling up to it. Perhaps we should stop by and check on her on the way."

"We'll do it." David helped his wife onto the seat. "Unless we can offer a ride?"

"No, I need to check on the fire afore we come. Is it a far piece to travel?" Her finger brushed Drew's knuckles. A tremor shot through her body.

"We're on the other side of town, on a small farm. Until then." Sarah waved until they reached a bend in the road.

"We need to talk." Drew pulled her aside once the couple left. "It's not appropriate to show public displays of affection like earlier this morning."

"Huh?" *Like what?* Had he felt the lightning blast between them too? She'd better not ask. It might rile him more.

"It means you can't be calling me terms of endearment in polite society."

Jules wasn't quite sure what that phrase meant either. He seemed mighty peculiar of the things he liked and didn't like. It'd take some getting used to being hitched to another human. Maybe she ought to change the subject. She said the first thing that came to mind. "I've been wanting to ask what an elephant is."

"Are we clear on the other topic first?"

"I reckon so. I shouldn't speak e-endear-ments to you." Jules peered at his face, not sure if she'd even said the word right.

His face took on that funny color again. "Ahem, yes. What's this about an elephant?"

"While you were sleeping, I started reading one of the books on yer shelves. Hope you don't mind. It's by somebody named Jules too."

"*His* name is Jules Verne."

"The book's about going 'round the world in eighty days, and they're in this place where they travel by elephant. What does one look like?" Jules matched her pace with his. If she caught ahold of his hand would the same jolt sizzle through her? She sighed and tried to concentrate on what he'd been saying.

"I've never seen one myself, but I heard in '55, an elephant walked a tightrope in Dan Rice's Circus. Father showed me the advertisement in the newspaper. He told me elephants are massive creatures which usually live in another country. I also heard a place in Philadelphia opened last summer, and they had a slew of animals, including an elephant." Drew took her arm.

She smiled. It felt right fine to have him beside her.

"The book is one of my favorites Verne wrote." His fingers burned through the fabric of her shirt.

She swallowed, struggling to concentrate. "You mean there're other ones? You have more of 'em?"

"I also have his *Twenty Thousand Leagues under the Sea*. He's written additional titles, but I don't have copies."

"What's a league?"

"It's a form of measurement, usually undersea."

"I've never seen the ocean, but I read about it. What's it like?"

"Don't know. I've spent most of my life in Kansas, except when I went to seminary. My family started this town."

"What's sem-in-ary?"

Drew raised his eyebrows. "It's a special school to become a minister."

"It must be wonderful to go for schooling. I've always wanted to have more book learnin' but never had a chance. Can't remember the last I owned a book other than when I was a young'un."

They neared the house, and she stopped.

"Not even a Bible?" Drew opened the door for her.

"Nope, no books other than a couple McGuffey's. We always had to travel light. I'll be with you in two shakes after I go check the fire." Jules took off at a sprint. A few bright embers remained. She kicked dirt onto them and hurried to the house. Might better comb her hair afore they went to dinner.

"Where'd you disappear to?" Drew's question stopped her in her tracks.

"Like I said. To douse the fire."

"But the stove's cold." He shook his head. "How'd you cook our breakfast?"

"Out in the field like I did yesterday when I made the willow bark tea." Jules pointed in the direction. She couldn't guess why it mattered.

"Next time I expect you to prepare our meals inside."

Jules scanned the room. It wouldn't be too smart to start a blaze in the house. How would she stop it from spreading? He'd maybe change his mind afore she fixed his supper.

She headed to the bedroom and pulled a brush from her knapsack. It was the one thing of Ma's she owned. Somehow, using it always provided a sort of comfort.

Drew followed her, gawking while she tamed the snarls and braided her hair. Jules rummaged for a few hairpins, cinched her wayward strands, and reached for her hat.

His hand stopped her. "Leave it. You're much prettier without it."

Her stomach did a wiggle, and her finger itched to trace his rugged jaw line. She swallowed. Could he hear the thudding in her chest?

"We'd better get going, or Sarah will worry." He snagged her hand and placed it in the bend of his arm.

"I thought maybe we'd walk." Drew closed the door behind them. "It's such a beautiful day."

"Sounds good to me although I sure do miss my horse." Jules tried to settle her pounding heart. Her face warmed right quick. Was she catching whatever he had? Her gaze darted all around, taking in every sight. They passed a place called General Store and a few other shops. One had fancy hats in the window. She'd been tempted to shove her nose against the glass, but Drew insisted they hurry.

The sun had moved some by the time they got to the farm. Heads of wheat waved in the breeze. A dog barked when he saw them.

Jules bent to pet the wiggly bunch of fur and laughed when a wet tongue licked her face. "I've always wanted a dog." She chuckled when the mutt rolled over to have its belly rubbed. "What's his name?"

"He is actually a she, and her name is Joyful. She had some pups a few weeks ago. Would you like to see them later?"

"Sure. How'd she get to be called Joyful? Never heard a name like that afore."

"David let Sarah name her as a puppy. She said her bark always sounded joyful. The name stuck."

Jules grinned as the front door of the farmhouse opened. An older version of Sarah stepped onto the porch.

"I see it's true."

"What, Mother?" Drew's arm grew stiff under Jules's.

"I hear you have taken a wife, if you can call *her* that." She sniffed, holding a piece of cloth to her nose. "Is *this* the best you could do?"

4

Jules waited for Drew to say something. The confounded man remained stony quiet.

His ma spun and clomped inside.

"There you two are. I worried something happened." Sarah smiled and held the door. Studying her brother's expression, her grin slipped. "What's wrong? What did Mother say *this* time?"

"Nothing." Drew spit out the word as if it were something foul tasting.

Sarah's head swiveled to Jules and back to Drew. She opened her mouth then clamped it shut.

Drew led Jules up the steps, waiting for the women to go in the house.

"The food's ready. Wash up so we can eat," Sarah said.

Her new sister squeezed Jules's hand, tugging her to the side. She waited until Drew trotted off, then she whispered, "I wanted to warn you, Mother can be difficult at times."

"Already saw firsthand."

"Why? What did she say?"

David stepped into the room. "Coming, honey?"

"Yes, we're on our way." Sarah's gaze darted to her husband. "We'll talk more later," she whispered to Jules.

Jules followed. She feared it might be a long meal filled with plenty of ruckus. *If only I could go for a long ride on Blue.* Her brother had always teased her about her much-loved horse's name. Bluebonnets had covered the Texas fields that spring when Jules was ten years old and she'd named her mare for them. She escaped in her mind to the many enjoyable hours in the saddle. She missed how Blue calmed her and wished he was there.

"Julia… Julia."

A woman's voice got between her and Blue. "What?"

"Is she a halfwit as well?" Drew's ma huffed.

Her face burning fiercely, Jules shoved away the temptation to go dip her head in a bucket of cold water. No sense proving the woman right. Jules frowned at Drew.

He glanced down and scurried ahead.

"Mother, please." Sarah plunked a fist on her waist. "That's very unkind, and I won't stand for you treating a guest in my home in such a way."

"Then take a seat," his mother murmured.

Jules rushed forward, ready to slap the mean woman.

Drew's hand stayed her. He shook his head, his eyes begging.

It was contrary to everything in her, but she buried her anger for Drew's sake. Going to the washbasin, she lathered her hands. Dreams of using the soap to wash the inside of Mrs. Montgomery's mouth danced afore her eyes. It's what Josh would've done to her. She snorted.

"Really." Her mother-in-law sniffed and held the scrap of cloth to her nose.

Maybe napkins had many different things they were used for. She'd have to ask Sarah later.

Sarah motioned to a chair, and Jules sat. She startled when Drew stretched for her hand. Across the table she spied each person had joined hands. Maybe they were going to do the funny talking Drew did afore meals. She put her other hand towards Drew's mother, but the woman just stared at it. Jules wiped the moisture the towel had missed onto her pant leg. "I don't bite ma'am." *At least not often.* She almost giggled.

The woman placed a lone finger on the edge of Jules's palm.

She wanted to squeeze it hard but stopped herself.

"We thank You, Lord, for this day and for this food. May You bless it and nourish our bodies. Guide our conversations. In Jesus' name, amen," David said.

Drew gripped her hand twice and then released it. A short smile flashed across his face so fast she wasn't sure if it'd been there or not. It would take a lot more than the strange talking for Jules to keep a lid on her steaming temper.

"We're blessed to have everyone here." Sarah kept hold of David's hand. "What a marvelous day to include a new family member." She smiled at Jules. "We're so happy to have *you* in our home for our announcement. We'll be adding our own family member later this year."

"Wonderful." Drew jumped up and wrapped his sister in a big hug. "Oh, I'm sorry. I didn't hurt the baby, did I?"

"No, silly." Sarah laughed, wiping tears from her eyes.

Jules shoved her chair. "Ain't that something?" She thumped David's arm then embraced her sister-in-law. "When's the baby gettin' here?"

"We're guessing around the week of Christmas or near then." David beamed at his wife.

"What a nice gift." Jules hugged Sarah a second time. She and Josh had celebrated Christmas in their early years on the trail. He'd told her about Jesus being born, and then taught her about exchangin' gifts. When she'd asked why Jesus didn't get presents since it was His birthday, Josh had told her about His death. Her brother had gotten that faraway look he wore when he thought about their parents and times past. She figured this Jesus fella was someone Josh knew back then and her brother was most likely missin' Him something fierce. She'd stopped askin' questions so Josh wouldn't be sad no more. They'd grown out of the habit of givin' gifts after that. A thought occurred. How did Drew's family know about Jesus? Had they known him, too? But how? She'd have to ask later. Jules shot a sideways glance at Drew's mother.

The woman gave her daughter a short squeeze. "How lovely, dear. We will need to start preparing a layette for the infant. I do not suppose you knit, Julia?"

Jules scratched her head, sucked in a breath and released it. "I guess I don't rightly know what a *lay-ette* is or how you *knit*, though I have a hankering to learn if some person teached me."

"Taught." Mrs. Montgomery sniffed. "I doubt it is possible."

"Mother." Sarah frowned at her ma and turned toward Jules. "A layette is all the clothes and bedding I'll need for a newborn."

"How do you guess how big to make it?"

Sarah chuckled. "We'll get together sometime soon, and I'll show you how to knit and what size things will need to be. Have you ever seen a baby?"

She shook her head. "Seen cattle give birth, so I guess it ain't a whole lot different."

"I believe my headache is returning." The bit of fabric came out again, the woman waving it like a flag.

"Perhaps lying down would be best, Mother." Drew shoved his chair and went to her side. "Let me help you to the bed."

"No, I would prefer to go home. Drew will be a dear and take me." She fluttered her eyes like she had a mess of dirt in them.

Drew peeked in Jules's direction and shrugged his shoulders.

"Go ahead and see yer ma home," Jules said. "I'll wait here for you."

"Might as well take my buggy." David wiped his hands and stood. "I'll go hitch the horses."

~*~

Drew helped Mother into the conveyance and snapped the reins. *Dear Lord, please help these five minutes pass by quickly.*

The elders' proclamation earlier that morning continued to ring in his ears. "We're not impressed with your hasty choice of a wife. If you can't make her into a suitable lady, then we'll be searching for another candidate to fill the preaching position."

"Honestly, Andrew, I cannot believe what enticed you to do such a foolish thing. What possible value could come from *that* uncouth creature? She obviously is beneath your social stature. To degrade yourself and send for a mail-order bride. Honestly. Sometimes I question your sanity. There are plenty of fine families in our community who are much more suitable. It is a good thing your father is not here. God rest his soul. He would be horrified with the current shift of events. What a stew you have gotten yourself into. Do not worry. I will ponder further and come up with something to eradicate the predicament. I am acquainted with a fine lawyer in Hutchinson. I will send a wire to him first thing in the morning. Do *not* do anything else stupid, like you usually do."

"It's too late, Mother. What's done is done." Drew refused to convey to her he had no other option, if he wanted to keep his job.

"Do not tell me you *desire* to stay married to that *barbarian*. Never mind, I am sure we can find a way around this sticky situation. We could say she coerced a marriage proposal from you, that it was under duress. Who performed the ceremony?"

His head ached even as his body stiffened. "We were married by proxy."

"Certainly, we can get off on a technicality then. It will not hold up in court. I am sure of it." Her ever-present handkerchief fluttered in her hand. "Leave it to me, son, and I will find a way to solve the conundrum."

The elaborate home of his childhood was never a more welcome sight. He couldn't help her into the house fast enough. Once inside, he motioned for her maid to assist. "Please, help her to her room. She's having a sick headache. Goodbye, Mother. I'll be praying for the return of good health." He hurried away, so she had no opportunity to respond. "Thank You, Lord." Drew muttered the words, grateful he'd managed to leave without another battery of questions.

Could Mother be right? Had he rushed into things too fast? He couldn't renege on his marriage to Jules, but perhaps he needed time to court his new wife, especially since they'd shared very few letters over the past months. It would take some doing to train her to be the minister's wife he needed, *but* he didn't have a lot of time. He *had* to find a way to persuade her to start changing and soon.

But how could he go about it? Drew scratched his temple and smiled. What woman wouldn't like a new hat and a reticule, or whatever they called it? He'd walk with Jules into town and buy her a dress or two the next day and spare no expense. *Yes.* Surely, she'd welcome the opportunity to have feminine attire. He couldn't wait to see her pleased expression when he told her his plan.

~*~

Jules stared at the lane from the window, but Drew still hadn't arrived from taking his ma home.

"Don't take what Mother said too seriously." Sarah handed her a dish to dry. "She's a lot of bark."

Snarl's more like it. Jules had been tempted to punch the woman in the nose for how hurtful she'd been to them, especially the way she'd treated her son. Drew's ma didn't scare her. After all, her brother *had* taught her to defend herself.

The door opened, interrupting her thoughts of getting even.

Drew came in with a hand behind him. She curled her fingers into her palms, keeping herself from grabbing his arm to make sure his ma hadn't injured him. Somehow, Jules needed to be close to him. Things loomed all topsy-turvy since her first time away from her brother's protection.

"I picked these for you, Jules." He handed her a bunch of white daisies. "I thought of you when I saw them. Considering the unusual wedding we had, the least I can do is provide a bouquet of flowers."

"They're right purdy. Thank you." Tears blurred her vision.

"How romantic, Drew." Sarah touched his arm. "I kept a plate of food warm."

Jules startled. She'd forgotten his sister was there.

Sarah removed a dish from the same kind of box Drew had on top of the stove in his kitchen. She couldn't figure how it kept the food warm for Sarah, but it didn't work when she'd tried.

"I appreciate it." Drew accepted the plate and sat.

"Mother feeling any better once you got her home?" Sarah wiped the crumbs from the table.

Brother and sister exchanged a glance.

"She didn't give me a moment's peace the entire trip." Drew ate the rest of his meal in silence before wiping his mouth with one of those napkins. "How about we go check on those puppies?"

"Can we?" Jules fisted some of his shirt in her eagerness.

"Certainly." He smiled, reaching for her hand.

David strolled into the kitchen. "What's the excitement?"

"We're going to see the puppies, if you don't have no complaint." Jules searched David's face, hoping he wouldn't say no.

"Come along, Sarah. Let's go see how Joyful's litter is doing today." David held the door.

They stepped onto the porch, and Jules ran ahead of them toward the barn.

Sarah giggled. "Any idea where you're going, Jules?"

She ground to a halt. "No, I guess I don't. I reckoned they're in the barn though?"

Drew chuckled, tucking her arm in his. "I'm guessing someone's excited."

Jules jumped up and down, making them all laugh. "I can't help myself. Never seen baby dogs afore." Jules lowered her voice. "Will they be asleep?"

When they entered the barn, David led the way to a stall. "Possibly, but we don't need to whisper." He lit a lantern and brought it nearer. The light shone on Joyful and six furry bodies snuggled next to her.

"They're cute." Jules bent to pet them, her heart melting as it did when she was riding Blue. "Can I hold one?"

"Yes, but let me hand it to you." David transferred a sleeping puppy into her arms. "Joyful can be pretty protective of her brood."

She held her breath when a tiny tongue licked her hand. Jules giggled and drew the bundle closer to her body.

"Their eyes opened a couple weeks ago." Sarah patted the pup.

"Never seen such a beauty. What's his name?" Jules placed her finger near the dog's mouth, and it started to suckle.

"We haven't named them." David leaned against a post. "It'll be another month before they can be separated from their mother. We'll let the new owners decide on names."

"You aren't keepin' 'em?"

"No, I'd love to, but we don't have room for seven dogs running around the farm. I'll put a notice at the general store when they're weaned." Sarah's finger traced the pup's silky ears. "They'll provide an extra income. People like having a dog to stand guard on their property."

"Don't s'pose you could use one, Drew?" Jules waited for his answer. *Say yes, say yes, say yes.*

"I don't know, Jules. Things are usually pretty quiet at the parsonage, and with the school next door, a dog would bark all day with children's shenanigans." Drew picked up a pup, scratching it behind its ears. "They're loveable, though."

Jules dipped her head to hide the let-down that washed over her. She buried her nose into the wriggling mass. Maybe she couldn't have one, but he couldn't stop her from coming to see them until they sold.

"I suppose we should be heading home." Drew placed his pup with the mother and snagged the one she held.

A sense of loss chilled her chest as soon as the pup left her arms. She squared her shoulders. Best not get too stuck on the little critter. Longing for Josh and their life filled her.

"Jules? What's wrong?" Sarah came and looped her arm through hers while they walked to the house.

The men didn't follow right away.

"Thinkin' on my brother."

"You must miss him, terribly." Sarah hugged Jules's waist. "I can't imagine not living near Drew. I grieved the two years during his schooling. We were so glad he returned home."

"This is the first I've been away from Josh, and I do pine for him. Guess I need to start gettin' used to my new life." Jules patted Sarah's hand. "Happy to have a sister and can't wait to see yer baby."

"Why didn't you tell Drew about wanting a puppy?"

"H-how'd you know?" Jules shot a glance over her shoulder at her husband, but he was too busy talking to David.

"Because the craving was written all over your face. I almost cried when I saw it." Moisture glistened on Sarah's cheeks. "I don't see how Drew refused."

"Didn't 'xactly say no, though, did he? Reckon I could maybe find a way to keep that pup quiet while school's going on." Jules knew a plan would work one way or another.

5

"Why are we totin' all these books into the other room?" Jules wiped the sweat from her face with her sleeve.

"I explained I didn't need assistance with this manual labor." Drew grunted and shoved the last bookcase along one wall in the sitting room.

"Why wouldn't I help? It's what a husband and wife do, right? Work together?"

Color filled her man's neck and cheeks. "Yes, uh. I appreciate it. I wouldn't usually work on the Lord's Day, but I wanted to get things situated before evening."

"What things?"

"With the bookcases in here, it will allow extra room for a bed in my study." He set the books on the shelf while Jules handed them to him.

"Reckon you don't need a spare bed." She placed the rest of the books on the floor and crossed to the large piece of furniture he'd pushed next to the other wall. "I could use this sittin' thing, if I scrunch up a bit."

"Hmm? What did you say? Sitting thing? Oh, you mean the settee."

Jules sat on it and bounced. "'Sides, it's more comfortable than most things I've slept on. I don't care, honest."

"No."

She huffed. Why wouldn't the man spit out what ailed him? He hadn't said much since they came from visiting his family, only mentioning about moving the furniture but not why the sudden change. *Being married sure is harder than I thought.* Jules rubbed the blue flowered fabric of the settee. "*I* can sleep in the study, and you can have your old room. Ain't used to much and am thankful to have a roof over my head."

"No."

She gritted her teeth. How could she change their talk to something more pleasant? "Where're you gettin' another bed?" She wanted to ask why he *needed* one but didn't guess she should. Too bad Josh weren't there, or she'd ask him if married folks slept in the same room. Maybe they didn't. When she got more easy 'round Sarah, she'd ask what her tight-lipped husband wouldn't tell her.

~*~

Drew ran a hand across his brow. Would Jules ever tire of her persistent questions? His head hammered with each one. The theme of his earlier sermon mocked him as well.

Lord, in Your eyes Jules and I are one, but I need more time to get to know this stranger. I can't handle another night on the floor, but I'm surely not ready to share a bed with her. How do I express to her that neither of us can sleep in the sitting room? Someone would likely learn of it. He sighed. What had she last asked him? Drew couldn't remember. He stared out the window. Dusk shadowed the sky. Good. When full darkness fell, he'd carry in the necessary supplies without being noticed.

"Drew?" His wife's lower lip trembled.

Botheration. What had he done? He'd better not inquire, or like most other women—except for Mother—tears would follow. Perhaps Jules had a stronger constitution and wouldn't be one of those weeping women he'd heard about from local townsmen. He'd need to distract her. Drew cleared his throat. "Jules, please assist me here."

Her big brown eyes blinked. Once. Twice. Her mouth sagged open.

He tamped his frustration.

"'C-course. What d'you need?"

"The supplies for the rope bed are in the barn. Would you be willing to fill the cover slip with clean straw while I work on assembling it?"

"Why sure." A smile softened her face, and a dimple played across her cheeks. "Tell me where to find the slip thing, and I'll get right on it."

"Bottom drawer in the dresser." Drew motioned toward the bedroom. "I'll join you in the barn in a short while."

Moments later, he carried in the required materials. If all went well, he'd have the bed assembled before Jules completed her task.

"It didn't take me long to chuck the thing full of straw." She struggled through the doorway with the mattress. "It's right heavy, though."

He relieved her of the burden, propping it along the wall. "I didn't mean for *you* to carry it in here."

"Weren't no trouble. Don't know nothing about how the ropes are put on that rig, but I'd be glad to help. Just tell me what to do."

Drew scowled and bit back a retort. His wife's *helping* would take him twice as long.

"Don't see why you're gettin' so testy." Jules stood with hands on her slim hips. "I have quite a bit of knowhow of ropes."

Yeah, probably only roping cattle. Lord, help me. Drew pinched the bridge of his nose and recited the alphabet in his head. He would *not* respond in anger—on the Lord's Day—if it killed him.

They struggled to assemble the bed. Jules hindered the process by directing him, even though she admittedly had no idea how to build it. His decision to not lash out was tested multiple times. "We're almost finished here. Why don't you bring me the extra sheets and blanket from the dresser? It's late, and I don't want to keep you up any longer than necessary."

Jules turned on her heel and left him in peace.

~*~

How dare Drew treat her like a child! Jules ripped the bedding from the drawer, slamming it shut. Tears threatened at the corner of her eyes. She hadn't pictured her marriage to be like this. *What were you thinking, Josh, sending me away to be hitched to a complete stranger?*

She swiped at the wetness, stiffened her shoulders, and stomped to the study.

"Here." Jules shoved the bedclothes into his hands. She didn't wait for an answer but clomped off, kicking the bedroom door closed behind her.

Her fingers fumbled with the buttons of her shirt as she stripped to her union suit. She scooped up her hairbrush and yanked it through her mass of tangled hair then winced when the bristles pierced her scalp. Wanting to throw the grooming tool across the room, instead she *thunked* it onto the bureau. She grumbled under her breath, flipping the covers before settling onto the mattress. *Alone.*

Sleep took its time coming. She tossed and turned on the big bed, her thoughts straying to the study. Was Drew awake too? She bashed her fist into the pillow. Let him be the first to say sorry. She hadn't done nothing wrong. So why did her innards tell her otherwise?

~*~

Drew rolled over and banged his head on the corner of the desk for the fifth time. He rubbed the small lump, wincing at its tenderness. Maybe he should've set up the rope bed in the sitting room, instead of the enclosed space of his study. He stared at the ceiling. Guests wouldn't question extra bookcases in there, but they would have a hard time understanding a bed in that room.

He punched his pillow and rolled to his side. Sleep continued to elude him. His conscience ate at his gut, causing it to twist and roil. He knew better than to go to bed angry, but it hadn't stopped him from doing it. *Enough*. Drew rolled to the opposite side. His apology would have to wait until morning.

Better concentrate on something else… like how to get to know his wife better and tame the wildness out of her in the process. How could he encourage her interest in womanly things? Would the elders give him time to accomplish the task? What if she changed and he didn't like it? He groaned and switched positions. For the sixth time.

A whimpered cry snagged his attention. *Jules*. Dare he check on her? His throat constricted as he strained to hear if she needed him. Another muffled moan and Drew found himself in the hallway, standing in front of the closed bedroom door. He held his breath and pushed it open. His wife thrashed on the bed, kicking at the covers. What should he do? He tiptoed forward and perched on the edge.

Jules's arm shot out and pressed his back against the mattress. A tremor ran through him.

"Get down, Josh, or they'll kill you."

Sweat drenched her body. Should he awaken her? Obviously she was dreaming, likely reliving something in her past. She moved into a crouched position, drawing a protective arm around his shoulders.

"I see them. Beyond the ridge there. They're probably making for the cave over yonder. I'll take the left flank." Tousled hair fell across her face. She shoved it away and reached for something.

Drew guessed she searched for her Stetson. Should he get up and retrieve it for her? It wouldn't be easy with her holding him against the bed. He decided to wait and see what happened.

"Careful, Josh. Burt and his brother have killed more than one man afore. I won't let him touch you, I promise." She shifted her hands in front of her as if ready to fire a rifle.

"I believe I shot him, Josh."

Shot him? Shot who? Had he married an outlaw? With no warning, tears streamed down her cheeks and sobs shook her small frame. He sat up, wrapping his arms around her slim shoulders, tucking her close to his side.

"Shh, Jules. You're safe with me." He patted her cheek, but the crying continued. Drew shook her, trying to awaken her from the nightmare. Her whimpering stirred him in a way he'd never experienced. He had to do something to comfort her. Without taking time to consider his actions, he claimed her lips. She instantly calmed. Blood roared in his ears when she started to reciprocate his administrations. Breaking away, he high-tailed it to his bed in the study.

An hour later he still lay awake, his heart racing. Had she ever fully wakened? He wasn't sure if he wanted to discover the answer to his question. He hefted a sigh. *Lord, be with her.* His hands clenched while the scenario replayed in his mind. Who were Burt and Josh? Why hadn't he asked her who Josh was when his name first came up? A rock weighed his stomach. When she kissed him, had she been dreaming it was Josh? *Stop.* He couldn't learn anything more until morning, but he'd be sure to learn the truth no matter what it cost him.

~*~

Jules yawned, stretched, and then pulled on her britches. She hauled on her shirt. Her nose wrinkled at the smell. Time to do some washing. She finger-combed and braided her hair, securing it to her head.

The sun shimmered when Jules stepped outdoors. She squinted and made a beeline for the small building with a crescent moon carved on the door. Her business finished, she headed toward the hen house. As she gathered eggs, she spoke to each hen first, so they wouldn't peck at her.

Jules had forgotten to ask Drew if he had any other provisions she could use. Back inside, she poked through the cupboards. She discovered the ingredients needed to whip up some fry bread. Too bad she didn't have any bacon to go along with it. It'd be mighty tasty.

She toted all the items outside plopping them on the ground and stooped to start a fire. In no time the blaze burned. She cracked eggs into the pan and mixed a batch of trail bread. Her eyes darted back and forth. Had she heard something? Her hand rested on her six-shooter. She hesitated, but nothing appeared out of place. Satisfied with spotting no potential danger, she trotted back to the house. Jules snagged the coffee pot and another pan. Would Drew be pleased with her meal, or would he still be upset from last night?

An hour or so later, the food sat on the table. She wanted to wait but didn't want to further upset her man by repeating yesterday's cold meal. Sucking in a breath, she knocked on the door to his study. Jules pressed her ear to the wood. Nothing. Her fingers trembled. She opened the door a crack and peered inside. His large frame sprawled across the small bed, and a soft snore sounded.

"Drew?"

She crept closer to the bed and touched his shoulder. Muscles corded beneath the fabric of his shirt but no signs he'd awakened. She leaned over, and his lips parted. Wonder what they tasted like. She shook her head and cleared her throat.

"Good morning, Drew. Breakfast is ready."

Jules didn't wait for his response. She scurried from the room, closing the door behind her. Her pulse threaded in her neck. She poured coffee into his mug and laid the strip of cloth he called a napkin beside his heaping plate.

"Wonder how often he washes these things."

He stepped into the kitchen and leaned his tall frame against the doorway. "Jules, there's something I need to say."

Her heart thudded.

"I wanted to apologize for last evening." He licked his lips. "I didn't respond very well to the situation and should have said something sooner. Forgive me?"

Situation? "Uh, I forgive you." Jules stumbled over the words, wanting to ask what had made him all-fired mad in the first place. "Breakfast is ready."

Drew's fingers shook when he held her hand a moment later. "Did you want to pray today?"

So that was what that funny talking was called. "No. I mean, you're the one who has more experience with praying speeches."

His gaze remained fixed on her with an odd expression lining his face.

She hoped he didn't repeat his question.

"I wouldn't say I have more experience. Talking to God is the same as talking to you, Jules." Drew smiled.

Except He and I aren't rightly friends. Good thing Drew couldn't hear her thoughts. She bowed her head hoping to end any further discussion on the matter, waiting for him to start the pray-thing he did. Josh had told her about God, but only enough for her to know He'd created the world and them, and she had to respect that.

"Dear Lord, I thank You for a beautiful day and my beautiful wife. Thank You for forgiving us when we fail. May we desire to serve You together and to bring others to You. I praise You for the meal and the hands who provided it. Amen." Drew dropped the napkin into his lap. He took a bite of egg and chewed. "Do you happen to remember anything from your dream last night?"

"What dream?"

He swallowed hard and swiped his lips with the napkin. "I'm guessing it was a nightmare."

"Really? I don't remember a thing, but I've always slept pretty sound. Josh would say a herd of cattle could be stampedin' two feet from me, and I wouldn't hear it." Jules picked up the bread and tore off a bite.

"I've been meaning to ask, who is the Josh you keep mentioning?" Drew's gaze bored into hers.

"Why, he's my older brother. I'm sure I said somethin' about him."

"No, I don't recall you ever mentioning his connection. Are you two close?" Something crossed his face she couldn't identify.

"I'd say as close as a baby critter and its mama. Josh pretty much raised me since I was three. He's all I've ever had my whole life. Least what I recall."

~*~

Drew took a sip of his coffee, remembering to sweeten it beforehand. Her brother. So could he assume she kissed *him* last night and not someone else from her dream? Steel bands tightened his chest. His heartbeat increased, remembering the sweetness of her lips. What a pity she didn't have a memory of their kiss. He shoved the thought aside. Time to dwell on other things. Should he confront her in regard to Burt? How did one ask a wife if she'd shot a man?

"You're awful quiet this morning. You feeling puny?" Jules touched his hand.

"What? No, I'm fine. I'm merely thinking we should head into town together today." Drew took a bite of his eggs. They were much tastier than the last time she'd fixed them. He sighed, wishing he could think of a way to broach the topic of her apparel without getting her hackles up.

"As much as I'd love the chance to see some of the shops and all, first thing I need to get working on is the washin'. It's been a coon's age since I scrubbed my clothes. I reckon you have some things needing washed too." Something flashed in her eyes.

"If you wanted something special, slip out and get it while I do the washin'. We can walk into town tomorrow, but I'm not going nowhere until I get myself some clean clothes. These smell to high heaven."

"Perhaps we could get rid of your old things and purchase something new." Like a dress.

"Don't need nothin'."

Now what? He'd have to tread carefully.

"After breakfast, I'll get the fire started and help with filling the pot with water." Drew scraped his plate.

"No need. I already have the fire going from breakfast. I hope you don't mind. I found yer pot and have it heating the water." Jules shoved the last bite of egg into her mouth. "I reckon I'll need some soap though, if you have some to spare." She mumbled the words around her food.

"No need to ask, Jules. Whatever is mine is yours, now that we're married." Drew pushed his chair and stood.

"I reckon I might like being hitched." She scooped up his plate and gave him a wink.

~*~

The poor man's face changed colors. Funny, she didn't remember seeing his ma having the problem. Some sickness ailed him for sure.

He coughed and couldn't catch his breath.

She ran over to thump him on the back, but he held his hand up to stop her.

"No thanks, I'm fine. I'll be in my study." He scurried away from the kitchen as if a mountain lion was chasing him.

She decided to let the dishes sit until later. Jules went into the bedroom and closed the door. She ran her hand over the surface of the wardrobe before opening a drawer. "He's got to have an extra set of clothes somewhere in here." She searched until she found a clean pair of britches and a shirt. Her clothes lay in a pile on the floor as she stepped into Drew's garb. She breathed deep of his musky scent.

The pants swam around her waist. Jules searched for a piece of rope but couldn't find anything suitable to keep them from falling around her ankles. She buckled her gun belt over the pants, hoping they'd stay in place. She shoved the Stetson on her head, slung the rifle over her shoulder and stooped to pick up the clothes. The door to the study stood closed. Should she bother him? She knocked.

"Come in."

The door flew open, and she stumbled into the room. Her rifle fell forward and knocked Drew in the head.

"I'm so sorry. Here, you'd better sit down." Jules yanked a chair from behind the desk. She dropped the clothes and guided him to his seat. "Let me have a gander."

He shoved her hands away. "There's no need."

"You're not bleedin', but a goose egg's already growin'."

"What were you doing carrying that fool thing around anyway?" Drew growled. "There's no need to be hauling a gun everywhere you go. What are people going to think of the minister's wife being fully armed?"

"Nobody said nothin' yesterday." Jules squared her shoulders.

"Yesterday?"

He jumped up and the chair tipped over. He gaped like a fish and his face went all white. "Please don't tell me you wore those to church yesterday…" He motioned toward her gun belt.

"Yessiree. I don't go nowhere without them. I didn't have time to take my rifle yesterday or my derringer, but I had my six-shooter and knife. If there'd been any trouble, I'd have been able to protect you, sugar." She patted his hand. The word slipped out before she could catch it back. She held her breath, but he didn't say anything about it. Maybe she could call him the nickname at home.

He righted the chair and slumped into it. His hand shook as he rubbed it across his eyes. "What have I done?"

"Feeling puny again? You aren't making much sense. I'll be back in two shakes." Jules propped the rifle by the desk, ran to the kitchen and gathered up one of the napkins. She jogged to the stream to dip the cloth in the cool water.

When she entered the study again, Drew hadn't budged.

"Here." She ran the slip of fabric across his forehead and along the nape of his neck. "It'll take away the sick feelin' and bring some color back to yer face."

He squeezed her hand and stopped her movements. "Promise me you won't ever take your rifle or six-shooter to church again."

She pulled her hand from his. "What if there's some sort of problem? How am I gonna protect you?" Jules brushed a blond curl from his forehead and readjusted the slip of fabric.

Drew snagged her hand. "I'm the one who would be sheltering *you*, Jules. And besides, no harm will come to either of us while we're attending church or in town either. There's no need to be hiding behind your guns. This is a safe town. There's nothing to be anxious about. I'm not sure what you've experienced in the past, but this is a peaceable place. There's no need to worry."

"I'm not worryin'." Jules touched the guns strapped to her waist. "I can protect myself, and I'm not afraid."

"Promise me not to take those guns to church anymore." Drew hauled her close to his side, searching deep into her eyes.

She squirmed, having difficulty thinking clearly with her leg pressed into his. Jules refused to leave herself unprotected. Who knew what trouble lurked nearby he wasn't aware of? She'd found danger to be a distant companion. Josh raised her to always be on the lookout for it.

How could she appease the man without bringing trouble to them? She smiled. He hadn't said anything about her derringer or knife, so those must be acceptable. "I promise I won't take my rifle or six-shooter to church no more." She squatted in front of him.

Drew leaned closer, peering into her eyes.

Her breath hitched in her throat.

His gaze flickered to her lips. The loud drumming of her heart echoed in her head. Why did being in his presence fluster her so? It never happened with Josh. Maybe she'd caught some type of sickness on her trip from Texas. What else could it be? She closed her eyes and puckered her lips. This must be time for the kissing her brother told her would happen. Her chest heaved in anticipation.

"There you two are. I knocked on the door and called, but nobody answered." Mrs. Montgomery bustled into the small room. Her gaze flitted from her son to Jules. His ma's face turned the shade Drew's had been earlier.

6

That confirmed it. Their faces changing colors had to be something wrong with Drew's family. *I wonder if there's any elixir I can find to help them with the problem?*

"Hump, I never. It is a sad state of affairs when a preacher cannot control his carnal desires." Drew's ma huffed, waving her flag as she retreated to the kitchen.

Drew touched Jules's face with the back of his finger, running it along her cheek. She trembled under his gentle strokes. His gaze traveled to her lips. Her heart fluttered.

"Drew! Confound it, son." Mrs. Montgomery whirled into the room, shoved her way in between them and yanked her son toward the kitchen.

Jules took a moment to compose herself before she picked up the laundry and headed outside. Why did her mother-in-law have such a hatred for her? She dropped each piece of clothing into the boiling water and envisioned dipping Drew's ma into the pot instead of the fabric. Why did he allow the woman to bully him? Why didn't he stand up for himself? If he couldn't find a way to do it, she'd gladly aid him.

After swirling the clothes for a few moments with a branch, Jules headed to the house to face the woman. She also had to remind Drew of her need for soap. Too bad she'd left her rifle inside. Some target practice in the field would've helped to ease her nerves. Instead, she gritted her teeth and walked toward the lair, picturing herself like the knights and dragons Josh used to tell her about when she was a young girl. The old woman reminded her of a fire-breathing dragon with her angry speech and that hankie waving she seemed to do too often.

Jules stepped into the kitchen and their talking stopped. Jules stared the monster down, not batting an eye under her examination.

Josh had trained her not to flinch a single muscle when hunting, and she applied her learning to this situation. The woman wouldn't be given the upper hand in anything if she could prevent it.

"I imagine Sarah has an old dress she could spare." Mrs. Montgomery sniffed and raised her nose as if she caught a whiff of something unpleasant.

"Don't know what could be affecting yer smeller, but the only thing with an odor in here is—"

"Jules."

Drew cut off her sharp retort.

She huffed and folded her arms across her chest. Throwing water on the old beast would better dispel the fire of her arrows.

"Never had a need for dresses and don't see any reason to change either. I reckon I haven't worn one since my parents died of the cholera. With livin' on the trail, it's much handier being free of skirts. They tangle and trip you. Besides, most men folk stayed away since I've been wearin' men's britches. They couldn't tell from a distance I was a woman, and Josh didn't allow many to get close enough to notice."

~*~

A man had to be blind *not* to notice his wife's figure. Drew shoved the thought from his mind. He was in deep trouble if she refused to wear dresses. What could he possibly say to persuade her to give them a try? He ran his hands through his hair. His wife continued to ramble. Drew's mouth went dry as the earlier scene flashed before his eyes. Leave it to Mother to interrupt at the worst possible moment.

"Drew."

Mother's grating voice brought him back to reality.

The two women stood toe-to-toe. Jules had her hand clenched in a fist. He'd better intervene before she decided to slug somebody, especially when it would probably be his obstinate and interfering mother.

"Ladies, please. I believe we've gotten off to a bad start." He grasped Jules's wrist and gathered her to his side.

She leaned into him.

He couldn't think straight or breathe with her proximity. What had he planned to say?

"I may not have a whole lot of book learnin', but my brother sure enough taught me manners." Her arm stiffened beneath his.

He held fast to her fist, just in case.

"It is obvious you have not been properly educated." Mother purred the words like the kitten he'd smuggled into his room after his father died. "Your hoyden ways are evidence of it." So the claws were exposed.

Jules's eyebrows lifted. If he'd been a betting man, he'd guess she didn't have any idea what the word meant. He choked back his laughter. She sure was cute when riled though. A quick perusal of her face also showed uncertainty.

"My wife may not have had the privilege of a fine education like I've had, but it doesn't mean she's ignorant either, Mother, and I'd appreciate it if you'd treat Jules with kindness."

Jules's eyes shone. She squeezed his hand. Her smile made up for any words of condemnation sure to be flung from Mother's mouth at any given moment in the future.

"I still say it is not too late to annul the marriage."

"What's annul mean?" Jules's nose wrinkled.

He refrained from tweaking it.

"It means to void the agreement." Mother patted a bead of moisture from her lips with her ever-present handkerchief.

"Void? I'm guessing that means to put a stop to?" Her gaze sought out his. "Why would we want to cancel the agreement?"

He swallowed and ran a finger along his too tight collar.

She scowled. "I don't reckon I fully understand what you two are talking about, but if you hadn't interrupted us, Mrs. Montgomery, I think yer son finally had enough gumption to try the kissin' activity." Jules clamped her hands over her mouth, and her eyes took on a wild expression.

Drew sputtered. He hadn't really been going to kiss her, *had he?* His gaze flitted to Mother. So far no fit of apoplexy. Instead, all color left her cheeks, and her body started to sway. He groaned and lunged for her before her frame hit the floor.

"What happened?" Jules followed him into the sitting room, where he eased Mother onto the settee.

"Get her reticule." He pointed in the direction of the kitchen.

"What?"

"A small bag or purse. She must've left it in the kitchen."

When she handed him the item, he dug inside its depths and withdrew a small vile. He opened it, waving it under Mother's nose.

"What's it for?"

"Smelling salts. She's fainted, and this should help to waken her." He moved it back and forth one more time until Mother sputtered and coughed. Drew pushed her shoulders gently against the couch. "Easy, Mother. How're you feeling?"

"Better." Her lip quivered. "Can you not see how unsuitable this match is?"

"Like it or not, Mrs. Montgomery, yer son chose me, and we ain't gettin' unhitched if it's what you've been trying to say. You're stuck with me, so get used to the idea. I'm not goin' nowhere."

Jules's finger waved in Mother's face. He feared she might poke her in the process.

"Yes, uh, let's give her space." Drew tugged on his wife's arm. "Did you want to ask me something when you came in a while ago?" He prayed he could deflate the volatile situation between the two women.

"Hmm?" Her deep, brown eyes batted once, twice. "Yes, I need some soap shavings for the washin'."

"Out on the shelf above the dry sink is a new bar of soap." Drew pushed her in the direction of the kitchen. He'd better separate the two spitting cats before someone got bit.

~*~

Jules stomped her way to the kitchen, muttering all the way. What she wouldn't do to get her hands around the woman's neck and squeeze...hard. What made her mother-in-law think she had the right to break up their marriage? Jules snorted and couldn't contain a guffaw. She'd defended her marriage and fought against the woman who blasted into her home when she'd been with Drew for only two days. Those days had been teeming with all sorts of feelings, good and bad. He'd made her innards tremble like they never had up until now. She couldn't tell why he differed from her brother, but he somehow made her more alive. Except for the times when Jules couldn't figure what made the man tick. She stepped outside and sucked in the morning air.

"Lord, we aren't rightly acquainted, but Drew said I can talk to

You. I wanted to thank You kindly for bringing such a fine man into my life. I guess I pined and didn't know it. I reckon I don't have anything else to say, Lord. I'll let You get back to whatever it is You do." *No, Drew had ended his special talks another way.* She scrunched her face. *What was it?* "Amen." *It sounded much better.*

With a lighter heart, she hummed while she shaved slivers from the soap bar into the bubbling water, stirring it with a sturdy branch. Next she took several trips to the stream to fill the other large pot with water to rinse their clothes. After a brief trip to the house to scrounge up a washboard, she set to work scrubbing their clothes until her hands were raw.

"Whatcha doing?" A small voice interrupted her visions of lathering her mother-in-law's mouth with the strong lye soap.

A little boy and girl stood side-by-side while she worked. How long had they been standing there? It wasn't like her to be woolgathering so much she'd missed their approach.

"Silly, its washing day, what else would she be doing?" The girl twisted her blonde braid between her fingers. "Can't you see she's scrubbing her clothes?"

"How can you tell she's a girl?"

Both studied her for a minute. The girl blinked bright blue eyes and a small smile creased her face. "Because of her eyes, she's a girl."

"Is that a real gun?" The boy edged closer, stretching his hand toward the six-shooter.

Jules took a step back. "It is, but you have to be mighty careful-like when around one."

"Can I hold it?"

"I guess it wouldn't hurt for a minute." Jules slid the weapon from its holster and removed the bullets before handing it to the young boy. "Be careful. It's not loaded, but you always need to be mindful when handlin' one."

The lad took the six-shooter and grasped two hands around the handle. He pointed it at his sister. "Hands up, you're under arrest."

Jules snagged it and jammed it back into her belt, pocketing the bullets to reload later. "Son, you don't never point a gun at someone unless you're ready to shoot."

"Aww, I weren't going to hurt her."

"A gun ain't a play thing."

"Why do you have one?" The small girl edged closer to Jules, batting her eyes like she had dirt in them.

"I've used it to protect myself."

"Have you shot anyone? Ever killed a man?" The boy fired off his questions in rapid succession.

Jules licked her lips, unsure how to answer him. Josh had told her many times about innocent little children and how they didn't need to know some things. Of course, he was usually referring to her.

The school bell rang.

"Children." A voice called in the distance.

"Come on." The boy yanked on the girl's arm. "We can't be late again, or Pa will tan our hides."

The girl gave Jules a quick squeeze around her legs, and then took off in the direction of the schoolyard. She stopped for an instant, smiled and waved before continuing on her path.

Jules chuckled and swirled the clothes with a stick. Try as she might, she couldn't forget the boy's questions. Sweat beaded on her brow and ran a steady stream down her neck as her thoughts took her back six months when she and her brother had been tracking the Thomas brothers on the bank of the Blanco River. The afternoon replayed in her mind. She shuddered, hearing the gunfire, and smelling the smoke once more. The stained ground. No escape.

Someone grabbed her wrist.

In a second, she had her weapon trained on the man holding her.

"Jules, it's me, Drew." He gave her a gentle shake.

She blinked. Her focus shifted and cleared.

He inched closer. "You're trembling." His hand shifted toward her six-shooter.

"Don't come a step closer." Her voice warbled. Jules cleared her throat and tried again. "Don't never sneak up on a body."

"I'm sorry. I thought you heard me coming. Hey, you've gone all pale. Let's go inside." Drew studied her.

Jules swallowed. He couldn't tell what crossed her mind, could he? Had she called Burt's name or mentioned anything about...? She tried to lick her lips, but her mouth felt as dry as dust. What would she do if Drew ever learned her secret? She shuddered.

"Something *is* wrong. Let's head inside so we can talk. Here, hold onto me. I'll finish the washing later." Drew slid his arm under hers and guided her to the house.

Jules dug her heels into the dirt. The last thing she intended to do involved going inside to talk over the situation. No siree. He couldn't pull it from her, no matter how much he tried to sweet talk her. "I'm fine, Drew, really. I'll finish up these clothes here. Don't suppose there's anywhere to hang them once they're all clean?"

He stared at her. "Are you sure nothing's wrong?"

She forced herself not to blink and to return his glare without flinching. "I'm right as a possum. Point me in the direction of where I should hang these once they're wrung."

Drew finally motioned toward the side of the house where a line stretched from the house to a small building.

How had she missed it? "What's in there?"

"I guess I've never officially given the tour, have I? I'll have to do so once the washing is finished. First, I need to take my mother home. Care to ride along?"

Jules shook her head. "No thanks, I'd better finish up with my chores. How're you gettin' there?"

"I'll hitch my horse to the buggy."

"A horse?" Jules couldn't contain her excitement. Best news she'd heard all day.

"I guess it never came up in conversation before now, has it?"

"No siree. I'd have remembered." Jules matched his stride as they strolled to the barn.

Drew opened the door, and she stepped into its darkened interior. It took a few moments for her eyes to adjust, but the familiar smells and soft nickers from a horse guided her in the direction of the stall. How had she missed seeing it too? Maybe the horse had been in a side pasture. A brown face with a white blaze between the eyes nodded in welcome. She rubbed his neck. "What's yer name, big fella?"

"He's Champ." Drew took a bridle from a hook on the wall.

"Hello there, Champ. I'm pleased to make yer acquaintance." She ran her hand along the length of his face. "Ever ride him much?"

"Not as often as I'd like to. Most times he pulls the buggy when I make calls on my parishioners."

"What's a parishio-ner?"

Drew gave her a funny look. "They're the people who attend my church. Surely you're familiar with the term."

"Nope." Jules slipped the halter over Champ's head and guided him from the stall.

"I don't recall mention of the church you attended. In Blanco, right?" Drew considered her.

She ducked her head, avoiding his eyes and swallowed hard.

Jules wiped her sweaty hands along the side of her trousers. "I never attended a church in Blanco."

"Oh, where did you frequent?"

Silence stretched between them. Her mind flitted on possible topics she could switch to distract him. Josh had told her some people were right firm about churching although he hadn't said why.

"Jules?"

The barn suddenly grew too warm. Seemed a briar bush must've twisted in her mouth when she tried to talk. She refused to lie to the man. Jules squared her shoulders. "Yesterday was my first time." She fiddled with Champ's halter.

"What?" He loomed closer.

"I said, I mean, I've never been in a church until we went yesterday."

7

Drew scrutinized his wife. What did she mean by her comment? If he knew her better he'd guess she withheld something. Problem was, he didn't know her at all. He rubbed a hand along the back of his neck. Had Jules been exposed to outdoor services, or perhaps she'd lived where a circuit preacher had sporadic care for his flock? Funny, she'd never mentioned it in her letters. In the three months of their correspondence, they'd only exchanged a total of four missives.

"We'll talk more concerning this when I return from taking Mother home."

"Yes, Drew."

She wouldn't meet his eyes. He bent to check the harness but when he straightened, she'd disappeared. His chest heaved as their shared kiss flashed in his mind... the one she didn't remember. "Come on, Champ." He led the horse to the front door and tied him off. With a sigh, he headed indoors.

Mother stamped her foot as he approached. "Finally, Drew. Honestly, I do not understand why you kept me waiting so long. So like your father with no consideration for others. It is probably why you did such a fool thing as running off and marrying a woman who is quite beneath your stand in society—if one can call her a woman."

"The buggy's ready, Mother." He guided her outdoors and helped her into the conveyance.

"Where is the whelp? She does not have the decency to come and say goodbye to her mother-in-law? It does not surprise me." Her handkerchief flickered back and forth.

"I'd appreciate it, Mother, if you don't compare my wife to a dog." Drew ground his teeth and slapped the reins across Champ's back. *Sorry, boy.*

"What caused the sudden need to marry? A mail-order bride, of all things." She sniffed. "How distasteful. What could you have possibly learned about her by exchanging letters? We have so many delightful young ladies to choose from in Burrton Springs. I thought you would take pride in the town your father started and choose someone to marry who resides here."

As if he'd ever be allowed to forget his father's accomplishments.

"Erma Miller's daughter, Gertrude, would have been a wonderful match."

Quiet, mousy, boring. Drew didn't think he'd ever heard her say more than a handful of words, unlike her overbearing mother who couldn't keep her mouth shut. Kind of like his own mother. Besides, he could use some excitement in his life, providing he'd be able to guide Jules into becoming more ladylike. He needed to find the proper balance to make the elders happy and also keep the spark alive in Jules.

"Then there's Betty Smith's daughter. What's her name?"

"Beatrice."

"Yes, Beatrice. Another fine example of the lovely women we have in town."

Loud, obnoxious, and lazy.

Mother rambled on citing the wonderful characteristics of the girl.

If he'd wanted to choose a wife from here he could have. None of the specimens had been right for him though. He'd considered and rejected each when the elders gave him the ultimatum in February to marry or seek employment elsewhere. Drew shook the reins, remembering the meeting.

It had been a rough day, and the men had almost seemed apologetic when they'd issued the demand.

Drew suspected the idea had been initiated by the wives who had eligible daughters at home. Thankfully, word hadn't reached the congregation's ears concerning the leaders' decision. If it had, the endless parade of marriageable women would've never stopped knocking on his door. That was why he'd opted for a mail-order bride instead.

"Have you heard what I said?" She shook his arm.

"Yes, Mother."

"Are you sure you will not consider annulment?"

"I'm positive." The back of his neck grew warm.

"Then, we need to attack this in a different way. What all have you learned about Julia?"

Not much. The image of her dressed in his clothes bounced in his thoughts.

"Son." His mother swatted his arm. "This is a *serious* problem. You cannot be joined to a woman who is so uncouth. Who knows, she could have done something horrible before she came here."

Jules's dream stirred in his mind. She'd never told him who Burt was. Could she have shot a man? There had to be a reason why she always had a weapon of some sort strapped to her body or hoisted over her shoulder. Maybe he shouldn't brush off Mother's concerns.

"What type of lady refuses to wear a dress? It is as though she has never been around genteel society. Why would you want a wife who is part barbarian? Is she on the run from the law? There must be something wrong with her. I believe there is more to her story than you realize, Drew, and if I had to wager a guess, you will not like what we discover. Leave it up to me, son, and I will find a way out. One of your *many* messes I have had to clean up over the years."

Mother's words weighed heavily on his heart. Had he been a fool to rush into marriage? Jules's letters were a lot different than what he'd witnessed in person. Had she deliberately deceived him? He slapped the reins with an urgency to return Mother to his childhood home. Once he was rid of her, he could return to his house and discover the truth in his unfinished conversation with his wife. He had to unearth why she didn't match up with the woman in the letters. He couldn't get home soon enough to satisfy himself.

~*~

Jules stalked back and forth through the length of the house awaiting Drew. Why had his mother shown up when she had? Things were going fine between them until then—except for how he'd acted the night before.

In the midst of her pacing, she scooped up her rifle and had it at the ready. If his mother insisted on a fight, Jules would give her one. She wouldn't give up her chance for a home and family, not after all these years of waiting. A chuckle gurgled in her throat. Shooting Drew's ma probably wouldn't earn favor in her man's eyes.

The kitchen door flew open, slamming against the wall with the force. Drew stood rigid, glaring at her. He raked his hands through his hair, causing it to stand on end. A frown marred his face.

Jules pasted on what she hoped was a smile, the fingers of her free hand itching to smooth his mane despite his bad mood. She clasped the rifle tighter when his eyes snapped fire, searing the depths of her soul.

He yanked the gun from her hand and set it down. "Why'd you agree to marry me? You aren't at all like the letters. You didn't deliberately deceive me to get married, did you? Maybe dressing like a man didn't snag a man's interest. Lord, forgive me for not seeing through your lies and falling—" He bit off the last words, his voice shaking. He hadn't planned to say in love, had he? He slammed his hand on the table, sending the dishes to clattering.

Jules jumped. "W-what letters? I didn't ever write to you."

"You deny writing to me? Unbelievable!" Drew stormed from the room and returned a minute later with a small stack of envelopes, waving them under her nose. "How could you forget these?" He ripped one open and began reading.

"'My dearest Drew, I long for the day we wed and can serve the Lord together. I can't wait to be by your side, helping in the church and ministering to those in the community. I'm eager to live as man and wife and pray we're soon blessed with a family.'"

Jules sputtered, unable to give voice to her roiling thoughts.

"Here's another one. 'I've always pined for a home and family. I'm tired of living along the trail and am excited to be settling in one place. I know the Lord has caused our paths to cross for a reason. May I be a noble woman who will bring you good and not evil all the days of your life.'" He sneered. "Won't happen, will it? You've been nothing but trouble. Do you even know the Lord?"

"Uh, we aren't 'xactly on speakin' terms." Jules gulped. What she wouldn't do for some water to wet her dry mouth. "I don't get what it's about." Jules paced the tiny kitchen.

Drew's hand brought her to an abrupt standstill.

"No, I'm the one who doesn't understand how you can trounce on my heart and not think anything of it." He ground the words through clenched teeth, turned his back to her, and stalked out the back door, slamming it behind him.

The room echoed with silence and aloneness.

A tear trickled down her cheek. Would he come back, or had she lost him forever? She flicked the tear away. *The letters.* What made her brother do such a thing and not say a word? Their last conversation echoed in her head.

"I have something difficult I need you to do, Jules."

"Josh, I'd do anything for you."

He remained quiet for a few minutes before he spoke again. "I need you to go to Kansas and get married."

"Married? You're foolin' me."

"No."

She formulated a thousand reasons why she couldn't go and marry a complete stranger. She'd been ready to state each one, but her brother had interrupted her thoughts.

"Jules, do you trust me?"

"Yes, Josh, I do."

"Then do this without questions. You haven't been the same since December, and I've been worried. Trust that I'm looking out for what's best for you."

Her brain had screamed for answers, but she remembered all the times her brother had kept her safe and taken care of her needs. She didn't recall him ever asking anything from her. Not once, until now. Surely she could obey him. She had so wanted to argue and tell him why it wouldn't work, but she'd thought over the twenty years he'd given of his life—raising, feeding, and protecting her without one single complaint. He'd always been there for her.

"I can't figure it, Josh. Why would you write these letters and not tell me?" Jules bent to pick up the paper on the floor. She settled into the chair in the study, reading each word. Pages and pages were filled with her hopes and dreams of having a husband, family, and a home. While the words were penned by her brother, he had somehow captured her true heart. How had he known? She'd never told her longings to him.

She held the letters close to her chest. What should she do? Her eyes lit on a well-read book on Drew's desk. Her fingers rubbed across the worn cover. It must be a book he loved. She opened its pages and thumbed through until a slip of paper caught her attention. An underlined portion in the book jumped out. Curious, she read the words aloud.

"'Hear my cry, O God; attend unto my prayer. From the end of the earth will I cry unto thee, when my heart is overwhelmed: lead me to the rock that is higher than I.'" The words were a balm for her aching heart. It must be his Bible.

A word from the slip of paper snagged her attention. It must be the advertisement Drew had written in his search for a wife. Why had he needed her to arrive by May first? *'Genteel, honest, and first-rate homemaker with a desire to serve God.'*

She could be those things. Jules searched the list a second time. "I can learn how to be more genteel and good with things in the home, and I'm already honest. These other things can't be so hard to learn, and I reckon I can figure what a desire to serve God means, after all, I don't have anythin' against Him. I'll show Drew how good I am with my weapons. Maybe I can take him target practicin' or huntin', so he can see how useful I am. I'll make sure you won't be sorry for marryin' me, Drew Montgomery." She pounded her fist on the desk.

~*~

Drew vaulted onto Champ, threading his fingers through the thick mane. He kicked Champ's flank hard, urging the horse to run faster. The sights of town whipped past in a blur of colors. Within a half hour he stopped beside the Little Arkansas River. Drew dismounted and patted his horse's heaving side.

"Sorry, boy. I shouldn't have ridden you so hard." He tugged on the reins, allowing Champ to cool a bit before the horse drank his fill. Drew ground-tied him and dipped into the river to quench his own. He wet his handkerchief and ran it along his face and neck, reveling in its coolness.

"Lord, what am I going to do with the confounded wife You've given me? An unbeliever, of all things. What will my congregation say? I'll surely lose my job after all." Drew shuddered. *What will Mother say?* "I thought for sure You led me to correspond with Jules. Did I hear wrong?"

No earth-shattering answer or response came, only the sound of katydids buzzing in the trees above his head. He plucked a blade of grass and rubbed it between his fingers.

"Are You testing me, Lord? I can't go back on my word. Jules is my wife, whether I like it or not. Somehow I need to find a way to make things work." He sighed and tossed the frayed stalk onto the ground. "There has to be a way to tame that wildness in her though. To make her into a respectable pastor's wife." He snapped his fingers. "I've got it. Mother had a book years ago called *The Improved Housewife.* Surely there will be something of use for Jules in its pages. And I'll pick up *The Family Medical Guide* at the general store, so I won't have to deal with willow bark tea anymore." He grimaced.

"Perhaps some evening Bible lessons are in order too, and I'm sure I can convince Sarah to teach Jules how to do various types of needlework, since I'm in need of a new suit coat." He rubbed his chin. "Yes, it's a good start, but how will I convince her to start dressing like a woman? Then there's her insistence on carrying weapons. Father, I'll need Your help in the days ahead to make Jules into the woman she should be. I'm afraid it'll take a lot of patience on my part. I'm confident with the three of us working on her, Lord, she'll soon turn into the proper wife I need and want."

8

Jules ran her hand across the cover of *The Improved Housewife* and snorted. "It's gonna take more than a book to make me into a good housewife." She sighed and flipped through the pages. "Here's one I can try... excellent family bread. I reckon we aren't 'xactly a family yet but maybe I could surprise Drew with some baking when he gets back from his visitin'."

She crossed the room and plunked the mixing bowl onto the table. If Josh could see her now he'd think for sure she'd lost her ability to ponder. Somehow talking to herself helped to fill the hours when Drew had responsibilities elsewhere.

"Let's see. 'Take a peck of sifted flour, half a pint of family yeast.'" She scratched her head. "What is sifted flour? Maybe it means to check and make sure there aren't any bugs in it."

She tilted the flour tin but didn't see any crawling critters. "I reckon it's fine. One peck. Sure seems like a mighty heapful, but I guess the book knows what it's talking about." Jules snatched an empty basket from a corner in the barn and sprinted back to the house.

Flour covered her shirt and the table by the time she'd poured it out, and it took an additional mixing bowl and three pots to contain all of it. She opened the container with yeast and found a very small amount. "It don't seem like quite enough. Guess I'll have to see if the general store has any."

The bread making process became more of an undertaking than she'd realized. After returning with the right amount of yeast Jules read on the recipe she needed milk to wet the dough. She shot a glance up and down the street, but no cows wandered nearby, and she didn't have time to run to Sarah's house and back before Drew returned.

"I reckon creek water will have to do." She poured some in each of the containers and tried to equally add the yeast. "It don't hardly seem like enough yeast for all the flour. Maybe I'd better add another cup or two."

She had worked up a sweat by the time she'd mixed and kneaded the bread. It took all of her arm strength to wrestle the dough into as many pans as she could find.

"I reckon it's enough to feed an army instead of a family." She slammed the stove door closed. Ten more pans stood ready and waiting on the table filled with dough. "Hmm. It don't say how long it needs to bake. I guess it'll take a while."

She dusted off her hands. "Might as well muck the stalls while I'm waiting." Jules smiled when she imagined Drew's expression when he returned home to a clean barn and the smell of fresh baked bread. *Won't he be surprised?*

"Becoming a first-rate homemaker may not be so hard after all." She chuckled. "I'll be the wife he wants in no time. Just see if I don't."

The stall took longer than Jules anticipated. It hadn't helped she'd lost her balance and fallen into a fresh pile of manure in the process. She reeked to high heaven, but the barn practically sparkled.

Yesiree, the barn had become one mighty clean place. Champ wouldn't know his stall when he returned with his owner. She dusted her hands off, careful not to wipe her backside. It would take some scraping to clear the mess from her britches. She'd get rid of the soiled clothes in the barn if she knew it'd be a while before Drew got home. Should she risk dropping her drawers? No siree, she'd better wait. Could she traipse through the house without tracking the mess inside though?

The sound of a throat clearing caused her to snap her head around. She stifled a groan when her mother-in-law whipped out her ever present scrap of fabric.

"Good heavens. What is the terrible stench emanating from here?" The woman took a step closer. "Eww. How do you stand the smell? What on earth have you been doing?"

"Cleaning Champ's stall, what's it look like?" Jules chomped her lips tight to keep from saying another answer which came to mind. Did the woman think barns cleaned themselves?

Mrs. Montgomery gagged. "You are the one who smells so disgusting. I knew Drew should have never married you. You are totally unsuitable for the likes of *my* son."

"Like it or not, ma'am, he married *me*." Jules stopped herself from tossing a shovelful of manure on the woman. "If there's nothing you need I've got things to do." *Like kicking yer sorry hide out of here.*

Drew's mother took a step backward, and her eyes grew wide. "Is my son here?"

Jules ground her teeth, shaking her head. The less she said to the woman, the better.

"Can I trust you to pass a message on to him, or are you dimwitted and will forget it?"

Jules's fingers tightened into a fist.

The woman's eyes flew open. "You would not hit me, would you? Were you ever instructed not to hit a lady?"

What does she think I am? She uncurled her fingers and grinned at the woman. "I never heard no rules about sluggin' a woman. Seems like those orders were intended for men."

"If the shoe fits…"

What did she mean by that? Was she calling her a man? What were the words Drew used in his description? *Oh yeah—genteel, honest, and first-rate homemaker.* She'd learn to be genteel, one way or another.

"I'll give the message to Drew provided you tell me what it is." Jules forced a smile.

Her mother-in-law studied her, and Jules refused to flinch. No dragon would get the best of her.

"I am having a formal dinner tomorrow. I expect you both to be in attendance." Mrs. Montgomery edged toward the door. "You will remember something so simple I hope, or do I need to write it down?"

Jules bit hard on the inside of her cheek, drawing blood in the process.

"I am assuming you have enough understanding to read words on a page. Perhaps you *are* a complete barbarian." Icy daggers shot from the woman's eyes.

Genteel. Genteel. Genteel. Even if it kills me. Don't forget the goal—become the wife Drew desires. Look at this creature as a scrawny outlaw throwing her weight around thinking she has something to prove. More than likely she's more bluster than anything else.

"I reckon I can remember anything you have to say. Don't worry none. I'll be sure to tell Drew once he gets home. If there's nothin' else, don't let me stop you from leaving." Jules shot a glance toward the door hoping the woman would take the hint.

"Yes, I uh..."

She stared as her mother-in-law backed toward the door as if afraid to turn away from Jules. The woman's foot hovered above a horse apple Jules had forgotten to shovel into the pile. She opened her mouth to warn the woman, but the deed had already been done. The mess oozed over Mrs. Montgomery's fancy shoes and the hem of her frilly blue dress.

The older woman's face blotched with color, and Jules couldn't keep laughter from gurgling to the surface. She held her side as Mrs. Montgomery shook her skirt, glared at Jules, and stalked out of the building.

The tears streamed on Jules's cheeks as she made her way to the entrance. The woman practically ran down the street. Jules's chortles subsided to a chuckle. It had served the woman right thinking she could come in here and treat her like she had no know-how of anything. Justice had been served, even if Jules hadn't had a hand in it, at least not on purpose.

She hefted the wheelbarrow of manure and dumped the mess in a field behind the church before heading back to the barn. Things were definitely looking up. She'd bested the dragon. As she got closer to the house she caught a whiff of something. She could not identify the smell at first.

Her bread.

Jules dropped the wheelbarrow handles and jogged toward the house. She thrust open the door only to be engulfed with the strong scent of something burning, and fumes pouring from the beast of a cook stove. She couldn't understand why folks liked such contraptions. They were nothing but trouble. An open campfire would suit her fine any old day… instead of the beast her husband insisted she cook on.

~*~

Drew shifted in the saddle at the outskirts of town. A woman ran down the street. He squinted. *Mother?* Should he go and check on her? He jammed his fingers through his hair before clapping his hat in place. Could the day get any worse? He'd already dealt all afternoon with some cantankerous women from his congregation who'd been gossiping. The good Lord never said being a pastor made for an easy task.

He reined Champ toward Mother's home but stopped when one of her servants met her along the way. Let them take care of the situation. *I've dealt with one too many troubles today.* He desired a good hot meal and time to rest his weary bones.

It took a few minutes to unsaddle Champ and brush him down. Drew smiled when he saw the tidy barn. His wife had been busy while he'd been away. Perhaps there was hope for making her into a good helpmeet yet. His pulse quickened when he stepped outside the barn and crossed to the house.

Vapor wisped from the windows.

"Jules." He yelled, ripping the door open. Smoke filled the kitchen and billowed toward him, burning his eyes. He thrust the window outward, squinting and calling for his wife. *Dear Lord, let her be unharmed.*

"I'm here." Her voice broke through the fog. She waved a towel in front of the smoke-belching stove.

He took in the table strewn with overflowing pans of something. He couldn't identify it. Whatever it contained grew faster by the moment.

She yanked pan after pan from the belly of the stove, each bubbling over in a mess of gooey substance. His nostrils burned with the acrid stench.

"W-what is it?" He bent and peered into the cook stove. A black mound smoldered in the bottom.

Moisture glistened at the corner of her flashing eyes. "B-bread." Her chin quivered before she clamped her jaw so tight a muscle twitched in her face.

I can't deal with another emotional female today. Are You listening, Lord? God didn't seem to be paying him much mind.

"What happened?"

She jerked the last of the offending bakeware from the oven. It clattered upon the surface. He cringed, fearing something would break.

Jules poked her finger at his chest. "It's yer fault. I'm tryin' to please you, and I fail every time."

Not exactly what he'd expected. Maybe he needed to treat her like an enraged bull. Give her lots of distance. He took a huge step backward. *There.* Maybe she wouldn't feel so threatened now.

She sank to a chair and held her head in her hands. Several minutes ticked on the clock but finally she answered him. "I came across a receipt in the book of yer ma's for excellent family bread."

Drew studied the small kitchen deluged with flour, dough, half-baked loaves, and burnt remains. He chewed the inside of his cheek to keep from laughing. "D-did you follow the instructions?"

"I think so. At least mostly. It called for a half pint of yeast." Her gaze slanted toward his then flitted away. "I couldn't mix it all in one bowl. There were way too much, so I added a bit more yeast. Do you think it's what caused this?" Her hand swept across the mess of the kitchen.

He chuckled. "I would guess so. Have you worked with yeast much?"

She shook her head. "No. I'm guessing it's not somethin' you add extra of?"

He couldn't stop a roar of mirth from gurgling out. "No. It's one thing you want to be very specific when measuring."

"I'll remember for next time." She ducked her head but not before he saw a lone tear trickle down her cheek. "I'm sorry, Drew."

The words were spoken so softly he had to lean forward to catch them. He crossed the room and tapped her chin.

She lifted her head a smidgen and stood, shifting toward the side. A waft of something foul rolled over him and nearly knocked him backward. What had she stepped in? He gaped at her clothes. What *had* she sat in?

~*~

Drew wrinkled his nose and took a small step backward. Jules had forgotten about her mishap in the barn until she saw his face. What a fine mess she'd made trying to become a better homemaker. She heaved a sigh.

"T-thank you for cleaning the barn." A smile flitted across his face.

He *had* noticed.

She nodded and started gathering the mess.

"What're you going to do with it?"

She shrugged. "I don't rightly know. Any ideas?"

"Dig a hole and bury it?" His eyebrows rose.

"I reckon there's no savin' it no how?"

He shook his head. "I don't think so. Maybe Sarah can share her bread recipe with you. She makes the best bread."

Yet another thing she couldn't do, which every other able-bodied female seemed to be able to. Except her mother-in-law. Jules doubted the woman could do anything useful. "I forgot to tell you, yer ma stopped by while I mucked out the barn."

His hands stilled, and his face paled. "W-what did she want?"

"She said something about invitin' us to a formal dinner tomorrow. Not sure what she meant by it." Jules scraped the goo from the table. It stuck to her hands and refused to budge.

"D-did anything else happen while she visited?" He swallowed and tugged at the neck of his shirt.

"She, uh, stepped into a horse clump I'd missed pickin' up while I cleaned the barn." She couldn't stop the smile from spreading across her face.

~*~

Drew groaned. It must be what had his mother scurrying through town earlier. It's a good thing she scheduled the dinner for tomorrow instead of today. She'll likely spend the rest of the day fuming over the incident. He prayed her temper cooled by the time they next saw her. If not, it would make for one uncomfortable meal. "How about we clean up the mess? I'll grab the shovel and start digging a hole."

His wife nodded and wiped the globs covering her hands on a towel.

Drew had the distinct feeling many more cooking fiascos headed his way in the near future. Maybe he should take over preparing sustenance if he ever wanted to have another decent meal.

9

Jules refused to let yesterday's mess scare her off trying again. She'd attempt something easier, like ginger cookies. Her tongue could taste them already. Wouldn't Drew's ma's mouth drop open at her formal supper when Jules carried in a plate of the sweet treat? She snickered and gathered what she needed.

"Jules, are you busy?" Drew poked his head into the kitchen. He held a shirt in his hands. "I hoped you'd be able to iron a shirt for me for tonight. I guess you forgot to do so after the washing."

"Why sure as long as you tell me what an iron thing is. Is it for brandin'?" Why would the man want a brand on his shirt?

He handed her an odd-shaped object and waved his hand across the top of the cook stove. "Good, it's still warm. Heat it on here." Drew snagged a piece of bacon leftover from breakfast. "I'll be gone for a while but will be back in time to prepare to go to Mother's. Thank you. See you later."

Jules snapped her mouth shut. He hadn't given her a chance to have him tell her how to use the heavy thing. She plunked the iron on the stove top and the shirt on the table. It probably took a long time to heat. Her first order of the day involved cookie making.

She read through the receipt. "'Take one teacup of sugar.' Wonder if a coffee cup is the same as a teacup? I reckon it'll do as long as I have all the right things to mix together. At least there isn't any yeast on the list."

In no time Jules dropped spoonful after spoonful of the batter onto a flat pan. The mounds were perfect. She knew now to keep an eye on them so they wouldn't burn. After cleaning up yesterday's mess she had no desire to make another one.

She closed the door to the stove and spread Drew's shirt wide across the table. "I reckon his branding iron should be hot by now." She cried out when the heat scorched her fingers. Grabbing a towel, she wrapped it around her hand and tried again. Much better.

The heat instantly took the row of wrinkles from the sleeve of the shirt. She worked through one side of the garment and flipped it to the front side. The scent of ginger teased her nostrils.

"Mmm. Them cookies are smellin' right good. I reckon I'd better check to see how they're doin'." She set the iron to work on a particularly stubborn wrinkle while she bustled over to the stove. The cookies were perfect.

She removed them from the tray, set them on the dry sink, and spooned the remaining mixture out for the last batch. "The receipt…uh…re-ci-pee sure didn't make a whole lot. I reckon there might be enough for two cookies each if Drew's ma don't have too many folks for supper."

Jules smiled and hummed. Finally a chance to prove her skills as a good housewife. She closed the door, returning to her ironing. A funny smell she couldn't identify made her nose twitch. "Now what?"

She yanked the iron from the shirt. A gaping hole and a scorched mark on the table mocked her housewifery.

The door flew open. "I forgot my—" Color drained from Drew's face. "W-what have you done to my best shirt?"

He crossed the room and picked up what remained of the garment. "How did this happen? It looks like you set the iron on it and forgot about it. Don't you realize you have to keep it moving while you're pressing so it doesn't burn?"

"You do?" Her words released in a squeak.

Drew shoved his hand through his hair. His fingers tightened around the fabric. "What am I going to wear?"

"There's yer other shirt..." Jules dropped her gaze.

"The cuffs and collar are getting frayed. This will never do." He balled the shirt into a wad and tossed it at the wall. The balled garment bounced and came to a stop beside the water bucket.

She swallowed. "I-I'm sorry."

The door slammed so hard she feared the panes in the window would break. She sank to a chair and buried her head in her hands. Why didn't being a housewife come with some sort of directions?

~*~

Drew smashed his bowler hat on his head and swung onto Champ. The woman would be the death of him yet. What were the church leaders thinking to require a wife in order for him to be a proper pastor? Obviously his choice of a wife hadn't made a lick of a difference. If anything, he struggled more with his temper now than he had his entire life.

He slapped the reins and urged Champ to a gallop. Distance and time away to think. He prayed it would be what he needed. His visitations would have to wait another day. He felt in no mood to talk with his parishioners or anyone else.

His horse had worked to a lather by the time Drew finally slowed the steed to a lazy pace. Reining to a stop, he dismounted and flopped by a stream. Champ flicked a fly with his long tail. Drew heaved a sigh and focused on the bright blue sky. The wind whipped the leaves of a nearby pin oak.

Lord, what were You thinking? She has no idea how to be a proper wife and can't seem to do anything right. Jesus' words taunted him. 'Come unto me, all ye that labour and are heavy laden, and I will give you rest.'

"Lord I don't need rest. I need wisdom to know how to deal with my wife." He rubbed a hand across his forehead.

No answer came.

He stood and crossed to his horse. Gathering his Bible and paper from the saddlebag he settled on the ground to work on his upcoming sermon.

The words and inspiration never came. Restlessness continued to hound him.

~*~

Hours passed and Drew had yet to make an appearance. Jules had nearly forgotten the second batch of cookies. Their blackened edges taunted her. She arranged them on the bottom of the plate and placed the nice looking ones on top. She wanted to leave the burnt ones at home but figured having one cookie each wouldn't be a proper peace offering.

Her head snapped up when she heard the sound of horses' hooves approaching. *Drew.* What would he say? She scurried to the bedroom and ran the brush through her hair, smoothing a crease from her britches. Jules squared her shoulders and headed toward the kitchen. Might as well face down the lion and get it over with.

Drew studied her attire but didn't say a word. Instead he brushed past her and closed the door to his study behind him. He exited a few minutes later dressed in his Sunday morning clothes.

"You ready?"

She nodded and picked up the plate of cookies. Neither of them spoke a word as they walked the short distance to his ma's home. Jules had the feeling they were in for a long evening. She pasted what she hoped resembled a smile on her face while Drew knocked on the door. Surely she could last through a couple hours of the dragon's ranting.

"Come in." A man dressed in fancy clothes bowed at his waist and motioned them inside.

Jules held her breath as they brushed past rows of shiny spoons on shelves and other things she didn't recognize. She hesitated for a moment to take a closer look at one such item but startled when the guy in the gaudy duds cleared his throat.

Drew had disappeared into one of the doorways. She wandered around hoping for some sort of sign of what she should do. The man touched her arm and tipped his head to the room on the left. She hurried forward, nearly stumbling over some sort of cloth thing on the floor.

The fancy-pants man steadied the plate of cookies before they slid to the floor. Jules peered up to see six pairs of eyes noticing her entry. She gulped and slipped her Stetson from her head. "Howdy, folks." Not one single smile welcomed her.

Mrs. Montgomery stepped forward; the shimmering fabric of her dress swooped and bounced with each step. Some sort of stone shone and sparkled around her neck. Matching rocks twinkled on one finger, at her wrist, and in her earlobes.

"Julia, I would like you to meet some of my dear friends." She motioned toward a couple on her right. "This is Michael and Martha Browning. Mr. Browning is the president of our local bank. Next to them are Charles and Ellie Lou Williams. Mr. Williams has a successful ranch located five miles from town."

Jules nodded to them and gripped each of their hands with a, "Pleased to meet you."

Drew looked as if he wanted to crawl under the table and hide. She narrowed her eyes at him. Was he ashamed of her? Was he angry because of his shirt?

"As you can see, Drew's wife is a bit... eccentric. She obviously does not have the astuteness of comprehending a *formal* dinner invitation." The dragon smiled with her teeth but not her eyes. The woman mocked her with all the fancy words.

Jules sneaked a peek at Drew, but he stood with his head down.

The banker's wife's shrill laugh rubbed on Jules's nerves. The rancher's wife sent a small smile in Jules's direction. Her eyes were kind.

"Uh-hem. Dinner is served." The fancy-pants man motioned toward the table and relieved Jules of her plate of cookies. "Please be seated."

Drew held her chair. The table held a mess of dishes and utensils. Why would a body need so many things? Jules snagged the bit of fabric Drew called a napkin and dropped it into her lap.

"Please pray for us, son."

Jules jumped when Drew gripped her hand. His eyes shimmered with some sort of feelings, but she didn't recognize it. A tiny smile flickered across his face then he bowed his head. His touch sparked a lightning bolt which sizzled through the palm of her hand.

She smiled and dipped her head. Would he assist in slaying the dragon if needed? It looked to be a long night.

~*~

"Dear Lord, we thank You for this gathering and pray for Your hand to be upon us as we strive to do Your will in every area of our lives. Bless the food and the hands who prepared it. May we live each day with a longing to grow more like You. Forgive us when we fail. In Jesus' name, amen." Drew squeezed Jules's hand twice and released it. He leaned toward her ear and whispered. "I'm sorry."

A bright smile spread across her face. He supposed she couldn't help being domestically challenged. He needed a bit more patience as she learned how to do things. *She'll improve with time. Right?*

He picked up a small fork and gestured toward Jules. She took the hint and mimicked his movements. His wife only required a bit of coaching in how to be cultured and refined and… He snapped his attention back to the conversation flowing around him.

"How's the banking business?" Charlie Williams stabbed a piece of greens with his fork.

"Never better." Michael Browning thrust his chest like a rooster trying to impress the hens. The man had always been infernally consumed with his social status. He seemed to forget Drew's father was the one who'd given him his job many years ago.

Mrs. Williams carried on a quiet conversation with Jules. Drew released a pent-up breath. He'd forgotten Jules didn't own a dress, but she didn't seem to notice the extravagant apparel of those around her. No doubt Mother had intended the soirée to put his wife completely off her element. He smiled. She didn't look uncomfortable. If anything she appeared to be having a grand old time conversing with the rancher's wife. Jules seemed to have a knack of making friends—only not with Mother.

Drew preferred the simpler meals he experienced in Sarah and David's home. He wondered why they hadn't been invited. Probably because Mother liked to be in control of situations, which wouldn't have happened if Sarah was present.

His thoughts raced while he ate his food. Not one morsel arrested his attention. He knew once they left for the evening he needed to find a way to apologize to Jules. More than likely she'd never used an iron. He should've demonstrated the process before he'd left. He wouldn't make the mistake a second time.

The courses of food seemed to go on and on. Drew relaxed his stiff muscles when James, Mother's butler, brought the dessert into the room. Soon the evening would be over, and he could unwind. So far Jules hadn't said anything to embarrass him or his mother.

"I hope you like raspberry torte. My cook has spent most of the afternoon whipping up the delicacy. I am sure it will melt in your mouths." Mother beamed from her chair at the head of the table.

Jules jumped up and retrieved something from the sideboard. "Don't forget my ginger cookies. I made them special for tonight although the ones on the bottom may not be quite as tasty. They got a bit burnt around the edges." She handed the plate to Mother. "If you all ain't greedy, there should be two each." She smiled and plunked herself back in her chair.

Mother curled her lip but took a small cookie from the plate as it was passed. She set it on the edge of her plate as if afraid it would taint her precious dessert.

"Mmm. This is delicious." Jules smacked her lips and licked raspberry sauce from her fork.

Drew cringed not wanting to see what would happen next.

Mother paled.

He'd better do something quick. He snagged a cookie and bit into it.

Others followed suit.

He tried not to grimace, but he wanted to spit the offending baked good into his napkin. How could she have ruined cookies?

Mother's face mottled with color as she nibbled the small cookie.

Jules peered at their faces. "What is it? What's the matter? Don't the cookies taste good? I'm sure I done it right this time." She plunked the whole cookie in her mouth and chewed. Her eyes watered, and she grabbed for her glass of water. She drank it dry and tugged the water pitcher closer. Another glass of moisture disappeared down her throat. "I don't reckon I know what I did wrong. I followed the re-ci-pee in that book from you, Mrs. Montgomery."

Mother looked as though she wanted to slink away from the conversation.

"The receipt called for sugar, molasses, butter, an egg, ginger, vinegar and flour." She ticked the items off on her fingers. "It also said salaer-atus which is the same as salt. I put one good heaping spoonful in the batter."

Drew coughed and gulped some water. "Salaeratus isn't salt, Jules."

"It isn't?"

He shook his head.

"Some folks call it sodium bicarbonate or baking soda." Mrs. Williams smiled. "Anyone could've made the mistake."

Jules groaned, shoved her chair back, and ran from the room.

10

Taming the wild out of Jules is going to take longer than I'd anticipated. Drew seized his glass and guzzled the water, ignoring the dribbles down his chin. Tears streaked his cheeks.

"It's terrible!" Jules wouldn't look him in the eye.

What had she put into the stew to make it burn his mouth and throat all the way to his stomach? He couldn't lie and tell her he liked the atrocious meal she'd prepared. After three weeks of cooking inside the house, she'd shown no improvement. If anything, she'd gotten worse. The townspeople had finally stopped talking about his wife preparing meals outdoors. It marked one area of improvement. If only her indoor food was palatable.

"I'm a lousy cook." Jules's eyes blinked rapidly.

Oh, no. Not tears. "I didn't—" Drew wiped his sweating forehead.

"You would've been better off…" Jules turned her head away.

"If what?"

The unfinished sentence hung between them.

Jules shoved her chair from the table and made a dash for the outhouse. When she returned, her pale face concerned him. He pulled her into his arms and held her while she sobbed.

"I don't understand." Her body shook.

In one swooping motion Drew lifted and carried her to the sofa. He sat with her snuggled on his lap, rubbing his fingers along her backbone. A waft of the outdoors tinged her clothes, tickling his nostrils.

"What ingredients did you add?"

Her lip quivered. "It was 'sposed to be beef soup. The recipe in the book from yer ma said to add pepper, salt, cloves, and mace. I weren't sure what mace was, and we didn't have no cloves."

"So what did you add instead?" He put his finger under her chin and tilted her head so he could see her beautiful, tear-filled eyes.

"I figured since we didn't have the cloves and mace I'd use

somethin' called cayenne instead. I can't rightly recall the rest of its name."

"Cayenne pepper?"

"Yes, that's it. I put in two heapin' spoonfuls. Do you think it's how I ruined it?"

Drew coughed. No wonder his eyes hadn't stopped watering since the first bite. "Haven't you ever had cayenne pepper? I hear they use it often in Texas dishes. It's very spicy."

"No, we didn't usually have spices along the trail. Salt, if anything. Is that why it tastes so awful?"

"It probably has a lot to do with it." He smiled and tucked a tendril of hair behind her ear, surprised by its softness. When he encircled his arms about her waist, something hard poked him in the ribs. His ran his fingers over the outline of the object.

"Jules Montgomery!" He shoved her from his lap. "How many times have I talked to you about wearing a gun belt? When are you going to listen to me and realize you don't need it anymore?"

She rose to full height. Her eyes snapped fire. She jabbed him in the chest with her finger. "When're *you* going to learn? One day you'll thank me for wanting to protect you and yer family. If I stop wearin' it, you'll be sorry I didn't have it on, and I don't aim to let it happen."

"Fool woman, why must you be as cantankerous and stubborn as a weed?" Drew stomped to the study and snatched his Bible off the desk, then returned to Jules. He flipped the pages and started reading aloud.

"'Wives, submit yourselves unto your own husbands, as unto the Lord. For the husband is the head of the wife, even as Christ is the head of the church: and he is the saviour of the body. Therefore as the church is subject unto Christ, so let the wives be to their own husbands in everything.'" He thumped the Bible for emphasis. Drew stared at her, wanting to shake those slim shoulders. He stretched his hands toward her, but she turned, and fled.

"Lord, I don't understand why You gave me a wife who tries my patience so." He released a long breath of air. "I've been doing what I can to train her, but nothing seems to be working. She won't wear dresses and refuses to give up her weapons. How can I get through to the woman? What else do You want me to do?" Drew paced the room, but no answer came. He sighed, raking his hands through his hair. "What am I'm going to do with her?"

He cringed when he recalled a recent visit to a parishioner home.

One of the Bailey boys had coaxed Jules into teaching them how to shoot her rifle. Their mother had almost fainted when a stray bullet had whizzed past her head. Nobody had been hurt, thank God. So far the church elders weren't aware of the incident. *At least, I hope not.* Never in all of his life had he struggled so much with his anger than he had in the past month of marriage.

"She stirs up the worst in me. What am I to do, Lord?"

~*~

Jules couldn't get away fast enough. She threw the barn door open, ripped a bridle from the hook and shoved it on Champ. She didn't take time for her saddle but jumped on his bare back, kicked his side, and held on tight.

Tears streamed her cheeks. The hiccupping sighs returned. Moisture blurred her vision as scenery raced past on her way to her in-laws. A few seconds later, Jules flew over Champ's shoulders landing with a hard thud. A whoosh of air shoved from her lungs while darkness clouded her vision.

A rustle sounded nearby.

The fog skimming her eyes took its time to clear. She blinked once. Twice.

"Jules? Jules! Are you hurt? Speak to me." Sarah bent beside her, the color draining from her face. "Oh, dear Lord, let her be unharmed."

"I'm fine."

"Thank God." Sarah hugged her tight then shifted backward. "I didn't hurt you, did I?"

Jules started to shake her head, but a throbbing pain demanded she stop. "My head hurts." Actually her whole body hurt.

"Turn your head a bit, and let me look." Sarah's soft hands gently moved Jules's hair out of the way. "There's a nasty gash back here."

Sarah lifted the edge of her skirt and ripped off a strip of petticoat.

"Here, let's sit you up." Sarah put slight pressure on the back of Jules's head with the cloth as she helped her to a sitting position.

The world tilted a bit then righted itself. Jules let Sarah help her to her feet. "I'm fine." She took the cloth from her sister-in-law, making a face when she pushed harder on the cut to stop the flow of blood trickling down her neck and soaking her hair.

Sarah's arm came around her waist, guiding her steps. "I can't believe that horse threw you. It's so unlike him."

"It weren't his fault. I should've been keepin' an eye on the path better. I think he tripped in a hole. I need to make sure he's not hurt." Jules switched routes.

"Oh, no you don't. I'll have David check on him once I get you to the house."

"Yes, ma'am."

"Don't give me any sass." Sarah puffed. "It's about time you let someone take care of you. Tell me, why were you riding Champ so hard?"

Jules watched the ground as they walked.

"Wait." Sarah tugged her to a stop. "Were you crying before your fall?"

A tear escaped. "Buffalo bosh." Jules swiped her cheeks with one hand, holding the bit of cloth with the other. "I don't reckon I know what's the matter with me the past few weeks. I'm not usually weepy." It probably didn't help she hadn't been sleeping much. Her body couldn't seem to let go at night. Somehow it hadn't felt right taking Drew's bed from him. She didn't think she could go much longer without a decent night's rest. *No wonder I'm a teary-eyed female.*

At the house, Sarah ushered her into the kitchen, easing Jules into a chair. "Stay right here, and don't move. I'll find David and return as quick as I can."

She couldn't help but smile when she heard Sarah hollering to her husband to collect Champ and check him over. Her sister-in-law bustled back into the kitchen a few minutes later with a handful of supplies.

"Let me see how bad that cut is."

Jules gasped when a small piece of material stuck to the open wound. She sucked air through clenched teeth while Sarah washed the tender skin and rinsed her hair.

"I don't think you'll need the doctor, but I'm afraid this is going to hurt." She uncorked an amber bottle of liquid and doused a cloth, rubbing it along Jules's hairline.

Spots danced across her vision. She gripped her hands so tight her knuckles were bright white.

Sarah waved something strong under her nose, bringing her back to full attention.

"I thought I almost lost you there for a moment." Sarah dropped the bloody cloth into a bucket. "How're you feeling? Jules? You don't look so good."

Her stomach churned and heaved. She clamped a hand over her mouth and sprinted toward the door.

Sarah helped to hold her hair while she emptied her stomach onto some flowers.

Jules swiped a hand across her mouth, she felt some better. "Sorry, I don't get what's come over me today."

Sarah led her inside, had her sit, and poured her a glass of water. "Here, sip slowly, and I'll bet you'll soon start feeling better."

Jules's hand shook as she brought the drink to her lips. What was wrong with her? One month of living in town and she'd became as slow as molasses. Couldn't seem to do anything to please Drew either. Being a wife was harder than anything else she'd ever done. Except for seven months ago. She shuddered as that day replayed in her mind.

"Tell me what's going on, Jules." Sarah's words pulled her from her bad thoughts.

"I messed up our supper... *again.*" She let her breath go, staring out the window.

"What happened?"

"I made a beef soup like the book said, except I put in cayenne pepper instead of cloves."

"Oh, dear. I can guess what happened. Bad?"

"Awful's more like it. You should've seen Drew's face."

"Did it upset him?"

"No more than any other meal I've failed. It's that beast. It doesn't like me."

"Beast?"

"Yeah, that nasty cook stove Drew has. I'm fine with cookin' over an open fire, but when I have to use that beast, it always acts up on me. He's been making me fix our meals on it. Either our food is undercooked or burnt to such a crisp you can't recognize it. Although I reckon I'm to blame for the mistake today. I figured an extra spoonful or two of the cayenne stuff would take the place of not having cloves and mace."

"Did you say two spoonfuls?" Sarah's eyes grew wide. "Were they the small spoons?"

"No, I used the big one we use for servin' the food and heaped them up real good."

"Oh, my goodness." Sarah doubled over in laughter. "I wish I could've seen Drew's face when he took a bite."

"He weren't too happy."

Sarah struggled to control her giggles. "I can see why he would've been a bit upset. What caused you to cry and run away?"

"What makes you think I ran away?"

"I would guess that you're an experienced horsewoman, and something must've happened to cause you to not to notice where Champ was heading."

Jules chewed her lip, debating how much she should tell. "I... I can't seem to do anything right. Drew got real angry with me for wearin' my six-shooter under my shirt." She hitched the cloth up to show Sarah. "Then he started spoutin' some scripture about being a submissive wife. I couldn't take it no more. I'm trying to be a good wife, but I keep failin'. Today, of all days, I had hoped…"

"Yes?"

Jules fiddled with the strip of cloth wound around her head.

"Don't mess with it." Sarah nudged Jules's fingers away from the injury.

She sighed, and her gaze dropped to her lap. "It's just—"

"It's your birthday, and you were hoping Drew would remember?"

"How'd you know?"

"We discussed it the first day we met."

Tears welled up in her eyes once more. "What's wrong with me?" She sprang to her feet, steadying herself when the room momentarily tipped.

"I'll be right back." Sarah disappeared.

When she returned, she carried a brown-wrapped package, tied with a piece of yarn. "I had planned to give it to you…I thought maybe you could use this now. Happy Birthday, Jules."

"For me?" Jules gathered the bundle into her arms, hugging it tight. "I didn't get many birthday gifts. I only remember a few times Josh got me somethin'"

"Didn't your brother do anything special?"

"I reckon he tried the best he could, when we had money, I guess. He did give me Blue, my horse. We often gave each other a gift for Christmas. Sometimes he'd give me a new pair of boots and once he gave me my rifle. Other things he picked up when he'd go to town, and they had something on what he called a sale. I never got to go to town, so I'd make him somethin' special to eat instead. Josh has always been partial to food. I told him many times he thinks with his stomach."

"You must be especially missing him today." Sarah rubbed her hand. "Perhaps it's why you've struggled with Drew so much."

"I reckon you're right, but I wish he liked me for who I am instead of always wantin' to change me. It's those crazy letters keepin' us apart."

"Letters? What letters?"

"My brother wrote them after he saw some ad Drew had posted in a newspaper. I never knew it until a few weeks ago. I... I think Drew started lovin' me after readin' them, but now he believes I tricked him." Jules gripped the package tighter causing the paper to crinkle.

"Oh, no. Surely you're wrong, Jules."

She shook her head, upsetting her stomach again. "The crazy thing is every word Josh wrote in them said how I feel. They would've been my own words if he'd given me a chance to write them. I don't understand how Josh did it, but it's like he saw in my head or heart."

"So, your brother wrote to Drew, signed your name to them, and never said anything about it?"

"Yes, but I don't think your brother will ever forgive me or believe I feel that way." Jules slumped into a chair. "It's hopeless."

"In the Bible it says, 'And we know all things work together for good to them that love God, to them who are called according to his purpose.' God's going to somehow work it for good in your life too. Trust Him." Sarah smiled.

"That's the problem, you said things work together for them who love God, and I don't."

"You mean you don't love God?"

"I don't rightly know how I can love somebody I never met."

"If I'm not mistaken, you care for my brother, right?"

"Yes, but it's different. I've learned to care for him." When had she started regarding him highly?

"It's not so different. Did you have feelings for him when you first arrived here?"

"No. I didn't know nothin' about him when I arrived. It took some time to get used to him." She liked him, *but love*?

As she said the words, she couldn't help but recall the many acts of kindness he'd showed her each day. Holding her chair, helping her into the buggy, thanking her for the work she did. His sweet smile made her stomach do funny things... and his beautiful eyes. How she longed to taste his lips. If only he would do that kissing thing. *Where had that thought come from?* She *must* be overtired—

"God's the same way, Jules." Sarah's eyes sparkled. "Once you get acquainted with God better, you'll fall in love with Him and desire to serve Him."

"I didn't reckon I could fall in love with God. Is it allowed?"

Sarah laughed. "Yes."

Jules scrunched her face. She couldn't figure it out. She opened her mouth to ask another question.

Someone knocked on the door.

11

Drew stared after his wife when she galloped from the barn on Champ as if ferocious dogs were pursuing her. No point in running after her. They probably could use some time apart to cool their tempers.

The open Bible beckoned him. He smoothed the page under his fingertips, the remainder of the verses from the passage he'd read aloud to Jules rose to taunt him.

"'Husbands, love your wives, even as Christ also loved the church, and gave himself for it; that he might sanctify and cleanse it with the washing of water by the word, that he might present it to himself a glorious church, not having a spot, or wrinkle, or any such thing; but that it should be holy and without blemish. So ought men to love their wives as their own bodies. He that loveth his wife loveth himself. For no man ever yet hated his own flesh; but nourisheth and cherisheth it, even as the Lord the church: For we are members of his body, of his flesh, and of his bones. For this cause shall a man leave his father and mother, and shall be joined unto his wife, and they shall be one flesh.'"

He set the Bible down, headed to the kitchen, and cleared the table of their dishes, dumping the uneaten food in the slop bucket. Jules would be pleased when she arrived home to find the kitchen clean. As Drew scrubbed the food particles from each dish, his thoughts shifted to their argument. He cringed, remembering his harsh words and tone.

"Forgive me, Lord. How is she going to learn to accept Your love when she has me for an example to follow? She's so frustrating though. I can't resolve what to do with her." He snapped the towel in frustration, and then dried the plates and utensils. "What're You trying to teach me, Lord?"

A Bible verse he'd memorized before Jules arrived on the

stagecoach floated into his mind. 'Likewise, ye husbands, dwell with them according to knowledge, giving honour unto the wife, as unto the weaker vessel, and as being heirs together of the grace of life; that your prayers be not hindered.'

"Why are my prayers not getting anywhere, Lord? Is it because of that verse?" He sighed and sank to a chair with his face between his hands. "Lord, I don't have any idea how to get through to her, and You don't seem to be helping any. What am I going to do with Jules? Every time I see her, I remember her betrayal. How could she *not* have knowledge of her brother writing the letters? Why can't she desire the things he recorded in them? How do I make her care for me when she doesn't even love You?"

A groan caught in his throat. Visions of his childhood and the many times he'd sought his mother's attention haunted him. He'd never measured up to the standard she'd set for him.

"How do I convince Jules to have any fondness for me when I'm not good enough for my own mother?" Why should he be concerned with what his wife thought of him? They certainly didn't have a traditional marriage. Drew pounded the table with his fist. "Enough." He forced the insufferable memories into the recesses of his mind again.

"What should I do concerning my missing wife?" He withdrew his pocket watch. 3:30 PM. He should start preparing for tonight. He washed, and then donned his Sunday suit all the while praying for Jules to make an appearance. An hour ticked by and still she hadn't arrived. Unable to wait any longer he scratched a quick note and left it on the table, propping it in front of the sugar bowl. He prayed he'd somehow meet up with her on the way. Before closing the door, he tucked a strip of ribbon into his pocket.

~*~

A sharp knock hammered the door a second time, increasing the throbbing in Jules's head.

"Jules, would you mind getting that for me? I need to check on our supper."

"Sure." She dropped the package on the table and eased herself from the chair, afraid to move too fast. Every muscle in her body ached. It had been too long since she'd been in the saddle. She'd gotten too soft. She flung the door open to halt the persistent thumping.

Drew stood there holding a wriggling mass of fur with a ribbon tied around its neck.

She breathed in the musky scent of her husband's freshly shaved face. His eyes glimmered, making her heart pound while her gaze traveled his length. My, he was handsome.

Drew stepped forward and placed the pup into her arms. "Happy Birthday, Jules." He glanced down at his feet and back up again. "Forgive me?" He whispered the last two words and wrapped his arms around her.

She basked in his presence and didn't want the moment to end.

A pink tongue curled to lick both of their faces, squirming between them.

Laughter burst from her lips. "Yes, I forgive you." She nodded, stopping when the pounding returned.

A frown flitted across Drew's face. His fingers grazed the strip of cloth wound around her head. "What happened?"

"Champ decided to let loose of his rider." Jules shrugged.

"Are you hurt anywhere else?" He guided her to a chair. "Here, let me take the pup."

"No, he's fine." She buried her nose into the mutt's fur, hugging him close. "Is he really for me?"

"Yes, I planned to give him as a gift since you first held him but wanted to wait until he could be away from his mama. I hoped your birthday was a fine time to present him to you." He lifted her hair and examined the bandage, shaking his head. "Oh, my."

Had it been something she thought up, or had his lips touched her neck? She trembled. "It's nothin'." Jules tried to steady her voice. "I'll be fine."

"Don't believe her," Sarah said, walking over to give her brother a hug. "She got thrown from Champ. We're guessing he stepped in a hole or something. David said he wasn't injured, praise God, but Jules hit the ground hard. I witnessed it myself. It took my breath away seeing her fly over Champ's head like she did." She shivered. "She's had a couple times where she almost lost consciousness. I used the smelling salts on her once, and she's lost her lunch, or maybe it was breakfast." She sent a quick smile in Jules's direction. "She hasn't mentioned it, but I believe she's been dizzy a couple times, and I'm sure her body's aching after the slam she took. She had the wind knocked from her. Her head bled but not too bad. I cleaned it up and bandaged her."

Jules glared at Sarah then turned to her husband. "There's no call for concern, Drew. I'm fine, *really*."

"I can't believe Champ would've done such a thing. It isn't like him. Tell me precisely what transpired. Was he acting funny before that? He's trained to be saddle rode and pull my buggy, but maybe he's gotten too familiar with pulling instead of having a rider on his back." Drew caressed her cheek.

She couldn't think with him so close. Couldn't suck in any air either.

"I'm guessing it had nothing to do with Champ, but the fact that Jules was distracted and not watching the terrain. She probably won't tell you, but she cried, Andrew Montgomery." Sarah stamped her foot. "You're to blame."

Drew blushed to the roots of his wavy, blond hair. "W-What do you mean?" His gaze shifted between his sister and Jules. "Don't act surprised." Sarah stabbed her finger into his chest. "You should be ashamed of yourself treating Jules like that, especially on her birthday. What you need to do is get her home after supper and draw a hot bath for her aching body."

Drew opened his mouth, his cheeks flaming with color.

"Don't you argue with me." She punched his arm with her fist, then spun on her heel, and left the room.

"I guess the mama-bear instinct has already taken hold, even though Sarah's babe hasn't arrived yet." Drew smiled. "I *am* sorry, Jules, and pray you can forgive me. I hadn't intended to start your birthday celebration like this."

"Celebration? What do you mean?" The squirming pup refused to be held any longer. Jules placed him on the floor with careful movements. He settled by her boots. The mutt tilted its head, watching her face.

"It's a surprise, at least I'd hoped for it to be one." Drew pulled a chair over and slipped a tendril of her hair behind her left ear.

"You already gave me the puppy. What more could there be?" Her eyes caught sight of the package on the table. "I forgot. Sarah gave me something too. Maybe I oughta wait 'til she comes in again afore I open it."

"Sarah made a special dinner for you to celebrate your birthday."

"I don't reckon I have any idea what to say, Drew. I've never had nothin' done like this in all my life." A blasted tear escaped her eye. She flicked it away with a finger. "It excited me to have one thing." She motioned toward the tied bundle. "It's one of the few times I got a birthday gift but to have this little guy too..." She patted her lap. The pup whimpered then jumped up against her leg, his little paws digging. Jules scooped the dog tight against her chest, kissing his head.

~*~

Drew's heart constricted. She'd hardly ever been given a birthday present? What kind of insensitive brother did Jules have? *Why does it bother me to see the puppy receiving her attention?* He cleared his throat. "What're you going to call the pup?" He patted the dog, hoping she'd not see the moisture his eyes produced.

"Haven't figured one yet, but I'm sure the right name will come to me. Reckon I need to learn his ways first afore I can find one to fit him proper like." Jules ran her hand along the length of the dog's body.

"I see you two finally made amends." Sarah bustled into the kitchen. "Drew, why don't you round up David while Jules and I set the table?"

He opened his mouth to refuse his sister's request. Drew wanted nothing more than to take his wife into his arms and hold her tight. How could her brother be so callous that he'd rarely provided for her other than basic needs? He knew from having a sister that women tended to like the latest contrivances. What would Jules like? Why hadn't he considered it until he might have lost her?

"Drew?" A pucker formed on Sarah's brow.

"I'm going, I'm going." *I'd better get out of here, or she'll be asking questions I've no answer for.* He suddenly longed for the security of the barn. Drew scurried there hoping he'd find his brother-in-law. If anything, he'd get a reprieve from his swirling thoughts.

~*~

Jules couldn't help peeping at Drew.

He smiled, waving as he high-tailed it from the house.

Sarah took the pup from Jules's lap, setting him on the floor. Her sister-in-law placed the wrapped package in his place. "Open it, I can't wait any longer."

Laughter gurgled from Jules. "Shouldn't I wait until after supper when the men-folk are here?"

"No, please hurry." Sarah ran a hand over her slightly swelled stomach.

Jules untied the string and peeled back the wrappings. Inside lay a pretty, bluebell colored dress. She ran her finger along the fancy lace collar. Maybe it was time to give in and start wearing one.

"I hope you don't mind a dress. I thought the color suited you. It took me a while longer than I'd hoped to finish it. Unfortunately, I tire more easily these days."

"You made it for me?" Jules held the cloth to her chest. "You... I..."

"Do you like it?"

"Like it? It's the most purtiest thing I've ever been given, except for Blue and this fella." She nodded toward the sleeping pup at her feet.

"Would you like to try it on to see how it fits? I had to guess with some of the measurements."

"Are you sure we should? I thought you told Drew to fetch David."

"Oh, they'll be conversing awhile before they head inside to wash up. We have plenty of time." Sarah jerked Jules toward the bedroom, closing the door behind them.

"Here, let me help." Sarah held the dress over Jules's head, never bumping the bandage. The cloth rustled as it settled around her slim hips. "Uh, this will work best if you remove the gun belt."

"I forgot I had it on. I reckon I could wear it on top of the dress."

"Why don't you go without it for now, at least until after the birthday meal?"

"I'm not so sure..."

"Stand still, so I can fasten the buttons. There, you look wonderful, Jules." Sarah snagged a hairbrush. "I'll brush the snarls from your hair where I rinsed out the blood. Let's fix you up with a different hairstyle for tonight too."

Jules stared at her reflection as Sarah brushed through her hair. Her sister-in-law's fingers wove a fancy braid at the back of her head. Sarah fastened it with a strip of cloth the same color as the dress.

"How can I ever thank you?" Jules barely knew herself in the mirror. Maybe wearing the dress would make her husband happy. "Do you think Drew'll like it?"

A huge smile wreathed Sarah's face. "He'll love it. Come on, we'd better see to getting food on the table."

Five minutes later, Jules's fingers trembled as she arranged the cutlery at each place setting. The kitchen door opened, and both men stepped inside, laughing together. Her hand stilled when the room grew quiet. She risked a peek at Drew.

He stood with his mouth gaped wide, staring at her.

Her heart fluttered and pounded when he strolled toward her. She lowered her head, afraid to see his reaction up close.

He lifted her chin, and smiled.

She held her breath. His face was only a couple inches away. She licked her lips, waiting for his next movement.

"Save the kissing for your own home." David clapped Drew on the back and chuckled. "I'm not sure about you two, but I'm starved. By the way, Jules, you look great." He sent a smile in her direction.

Jules's gaze sought Drew's again. Her heart pounded. He studied her lips. Had he really almost kissed her?

"You *are* beautiful." He whispered the words in her ear. "The dress is nice too."

Her cheeks flamed. The day shifted toward being almost perfect. It would've been pure bliss if Drew had actually done that kissing thing.

An impatient tapping sounded on the front door.

David excused himself and went to open it.

Nothing could spoil her evening.

"It is about time. I have been standing here for a good five minutes." Mrs. Montgomery's voice echoed down the hallway.

Or maybe not. Jules sighed and braced herself before going to greet her mother-in-law.

"Sorry, Sarah insisted, and she *is* family." Drew spoke quietly for her ears alone.

The temperature of the room changed as soon as the dragon stepped into it. Funny. Despite her fire breathing it felt a good ten degrees cooler. Perhaps she wouldn't spill meanness this time.

"Happy Birthday, Julia." The woman pecked her cheek. "Nice to see you are finally dressed like a woman."

"Mother, *please*. Be nice. After all, it's Jules's birthday." Sarah stepped between them.

The rest of the evening progressed without too many sparks from the dragon.

The cake Sarah baked had been delicious, a special treat Jules had never experienced. As the evening wore on, the pounding in her head returned.

~*~

Drew couldn't help but notice the tightness around Jules's lips. He didn't have to ask to conclude her head bothered her. He could see it in her eyes. "I believe it's time for us to be heading home."

"So soon? Julia has not opened my gift yet." Mother offered a ribbon-wrapped box.

"That's right nice of you." Jules accepted the package.

Drew shifted his gaze, his cheeks burning, when he glimpsed his wife withdrawing a corset. Leave it to Mother to pick such a thing as a gift.

"What is it?" His wife flipped it over, scanning both sides with a puzzled expression on her face.

He had a hard time controlling the snort of laughter broiling beneath the surface.

"Why, it is a corset, you ninny." His mother waved her handkerchief. "Lord knows you are in need of one."

"Thank you." Jules placed the contraption back into the box. He wagered a guess she had no idea of its intended use.

"We need to be going. Jules is tired." He ran a hand along her back.

"Give me a bit of a minute." She disappeared in the direction of Sarah's bedroom. When she reappeared, her gun belt was firmly strapped to her waist, and a bundle of clothes hung at her side.

Sarah stepped forward. "Why don't you leave your clothes and the gift from Mother here for tonight, and I'll bring them to you in the morning. Your hands will be full holding onto this guy." She lifted the puppy into Jules's waiting arms.

Five minutes later, Drew helped her onto Champ. Jules hiked her skirt up to her knee and settled the pup in front of her. He swung up behind her, reaching around to grab the reins.

"Scandalous," Mother said as he kicked his horse's side. He

couldn't help but disagree. He found the shape of his wife's leg quite fetching.

12

Drew didn't understand it. Another month had gone by, and Jules still hadn't improved her indoor cooking skills. With each passing day the circles darkened beneath her deep, brown eyes. He didn't think the two were connected, but he couldn't be sure. Something troubled her, and he determined it time to find out what it was. He stepped from his study to see Jules lifting a glass of sludge to her lips.

"What *are* you drinking?" Drew snatched the glass away before the liquid touched her mouth. He studied the concoction, the mixture causing his gut to twist and roil in response. No wonder she'd appeared ill the past day or so if she'd been guzzling the slime.

"I believe I'm going to die." She held her stomach and groaned.

"No doubt, if you've been drinking this stuff. What is it and what possessed you to drink it?"

"It's egg whites and water and a few spices to make it taste better."

"No wonder you're feeling poorly with this swill filling your belly." Drew shook his head. "Why would you do something like that?" They'd been married two months, and he still couldn't comprehend his wife.

"I've been poisoned." Jules's lips were ashen.

"What? How?" His mind raced with her declaration, his gaze flitting over each object in the room, as if they somehow held an explanation for her odd behavior of late.

"I haven't figured how yet, but someone's been slippin' lead into my food. What I can't understand though, is why you ain't gotten sick too." Her eyebrows lifted in question, her gaze piercing his.

Drew refused to squirm under her perusal but instead held his hands up to defend himself, unsure how the wildcat would respond to him. "Surely you don't believe *I've* been doing it." He could feel his cheeks flame to life when she didn't respond. What was wrong her?

She chewed on her lip, almost as if she'd considered the possibility of his poisoning her food. Jules shook her head. Had she just now ruled out the idea? "I reckon you've shown me nothing but kindness. Can't be you."

Drew breathed a sigh of relief he hadn't realized he'd been holding. He rubbed his temple. "How'd you get the idea you've been poisoned?"

"I've been lookin' in the medical book you bought for me." Jules picked up the *Family Medical Guide* and started reading. "Says here, 'this is a sedative metallic poison, which taken into the stomach, causes violent colicky pains, constant nausea, vomiting, cos-tive-ness.' I'm not sure what that big word is, but you get the idea."

"Let me guess, the treatment is egg whites and water?"

Jules nodded, handed him the book, indicating where she'd been reading. Her chocolate brown eyes implored him for an answer.

"You haven't been vomiting or nauseated have you?" He scratched his head. She *had* made numerous trips to the outhouse today. His fingers grazed across her forehead. Was it his imagination, or did it feel warm? He couldn't tell. "When's the last time you had something decent to eat?" Drew chewed the inside of his cheek. Probably as long as it had been since he'd had a good meal too, but he didn't feel poorly. Famished, but not sick.

"I can't 'xactly remember. I haven't been very hungry." She clenched her stomach, her face paling. Jules swayed on her feet, while tears pooled in her eyes, splashing down each cheek.

Not quite the response he'd expected. He rushed to catch her when her knees buckled.

~*~

"What happened?" Jules rose to a sitting position on the bed.

"You fainted." Drew stood beside her. "Feeling any better? You still don't look so good."

"I'm not sure." Her hand shook as she readjusted her pillow. A soft whimper brought a flicker of a smile to her face. Her pup stood on his hind legs and shoved his head close to her hand.

Drew lifted the pup to the bed. "I still don't understand why you gave him the name Pepper."

Jules snuggled her face into the dog's fur. "He reminds me of my birthday when you gave him to me and also of one of yer sermons. I may have used the wrong ingredient that day, but this guy helps me to remember to be careful with my speech."

"I don't recall what sermon you're talking about."

"The one when you said somethin' about being seasoned with salt. Except I didn't reckon Salt would make a good name for a dog, so I chose Pepper. Besides, his coat is a mix of brown and a bit of white and black."

Drew's eyebrows scrunched together and wrinkles formed on his forehead. "Do you mean the verse in Colossians which says, to 'let your speech be always with grace, seasoned with salt, that ye may know how ye ought to answer every man'?"

"That's the one. I'm tryin' to not respond with cayenne pepper but instead with salt."

Drew chuckled. "You've found an interesting way of looking at it. I guess you've been paying attention to my sermons after all."

"Why wouldn't I? You're my husband. I support you in yer preachin' speeches you give each week. Besides there's always something fun to watch at church." Like how Erma Miller insisted on pushin' her daughter, Gertrude, in the direction of every eligible bachelor in the congregation each Sunday. Jules's grip on Drew's arm tightened when a sudden wave of nausea flooded over her.

~*~

His wife's skin grew clammy under his touch. Pepper must've sensed her distress, because he snuggled close to her side, whining. Jules sat up and clamped a hand over her mouth. Drew stood aside when she darted toward the kitchen door. She made it as far as the back step, doubling over and losing what small amount of food she'd consumed.

His heart clenched, and he snaked an arm around her waist, supporting her while she threw up. Her whole body trembled. He pulled her hair back from her face and handed her a small towel he'd grabbed.

"I'm sorry." Her words were barely discernible. She wiped moisture from her forehead.

"Don't be." He studied her for a moment. "Let's get you back to bed."

"I reckon I'll be fine in a few minutes. Besides, I need to fix yer lunch." At the mention of the word, a green color tinged her face once more. She swayed.

He swept her up in his arms, preventing her from arguing.

Jules sighed and rested her head against his shoulder.

He tightened his grip. Drew couldn't help but like the way she felt in his arms. He struggled to control his thudding heart as he carried her the short distance to the bedroom, wishing for a longer path. With a quick flick of his wrist, he flipped the covers. He experienced a sudden loss when his arms emptied of the burden.

His wife moaned. "I'm not feelin' so good." Her eyelids fluttered shut.

"I kind of got that impression." He chuckled. "Rest for a while." He snugged the quilt under her chin, leaned forward, and kissed her forehead.

As he closed the bedroom door, he bit his lip to keep from groaning aloud. What had he been thinking, to kiss her in such a way? With any luck, she wouldn't remember it just as she hadn't known of the other one. Why did part of him wish she would?

~*~

Jules's fingertips traced where Drew's mouth had been. If only he would've kissed her lips instead. Why would he want to when she'd just spewed her guts? No person in their right mind would kiss somebody who was sick.

Had she really gotten some sickness, or could she be heartsick? Was there such a thing? The only thing she could figure was the unknown feelings only happened whenever Drew was around. She couldn't sleep for hours on end every night as she listened to his even breathing coming from the study. Her stomach seemed to be in protest too, jumping and squirming whenever Drew talked…or gripped her hand at mealtimes. The times his fingers brushed her back when helping her into the buggy. Each touch or word set her body on edge, and Jules couldn't figure out why. She'd never felt like that around anyone else. But then her life up to then had held only Josh and the few people they'd met along the trail. She groaned and punched her pillow. Only one man mattered to her.

Another gush of queasiness swept over her.

The door flew open. "I thought I heard you." Drew rushed forward and shoved a bucket under her mouth just in time.

She wanted to die. It was bad enough to get sick in front of him once, but the second time made her feel downright foolish. Her whole body shook and her stomach heaved. When the bout had stopped, she grew as limp as a fresh-hatched bird. Tears pricked the corners of her eyes. Jules shuddered.

Drew shifted the bucket, and she couldn't see the contents. His fingers rubbed the side of her face.

~*~

His wife's hair felt as soft as the down on a duckling. He thrilled to have it at his fingertips. How could her hair be so different from his? Moisture beaded on her lip. Drew started to wipe it away but stopped himself. Somehow the action seemed too intimate. A step in the direction he wasn't ready to take. It took an incredible amount of energy to force his hand away. Instead he touched the back of his hand to her forehead. The fiery hot skin blazed.

Her liquid coffee eyes stared at him. Had she read his thoughts?

He cleared his throat. "I'll take care of this and be back in a minute." He ran for the door as if a pack of wild wolves chased him. Outside, he forced his breathing to slow. He dumped the bucket, walked to the stream to rinse it, sucking in deep breaths. He stooped beside the slow moving water.

Dear Lord, I don't understand what's going on here, but I could use Your assistance so I don't do something stupid. He swallowed. Back inside, Drew stiffened his resolve. His wife needed his care, not his emotions. He yanked a fresh cloth from a drawer, dipped it into a pot of water, and wrung it. He returned to the bedroom to find Jules in a fitful sleep. Her eyelashes contrasted sharply with her pale face. He draped the cloth across her forehead and prayed her fever would break. Not sure what else to do, he set the bucket beside the bed in case she needed it.

Hours passed, yet her fever raged. Drew carried his desk chair into the bedroom and kept vigil. He flipped through the pages of his Bible, stopping at a passage he'd marked. Its familiar words reverberated in his head, the *very* ones he'd read on the day of Jules's birthday, except this time the admonition for husbands to love their wives beat a steady cadence in his brain. One he couldn't deny.

I don't know how to love her, Lord.

13

Drew hadn't had a decent night's sleep since Jules's sickness. He couldn't get away from the fact God's Word commanded he love his wife. Reading the words hadn't made his sentiments change. If only it were that easy. He sighed. How *did* one go about loving a wife?

The blank pages which should've been filled with notes for his upcoming sermon mocked him. He shoved them aside. *Might as well take care of my errands, since I've made no headway with my preparations for Sunday.*

Jules poked her head into the study. "Are you sure I have to go along? I could stay here and get some work done." She cleared her throat. "I'm feelin' much better."

He welcomed the interruption of his thoughts. "I'm thankful your health has improved, but I'm not comfortable with leaving you alone while I make my calls. Besides, you like visiting with Sarah."

Her face paled far too much for his liking. It'd been two days since she'd last been ill and dark circles still smudged beneath her eyes. Had she not been sleeping enough or could something else be wrong? Drew's heart constricted in his chest. Witnessing her feeling so poorly had almost been his undoing and being helpless to make her better wasn't something he cared to experience again. Not if he could help it.

He shoved back his chair and stood beside her. "Let's get ready, shall we? No more concoctions, all right?" His hand held fast under her chin when she tried to avoid his eyes. "Promise me."

~*~

"No need to worry about the concoctions." Jules shivered. Her hands smoothed the folds of her skirt.

"I appreciate you wearing a dress today." Drew's eyes twinkled.

Jules bit her lip. She wanted to tell him she wore it because it brought him pleasure, but the thing sure was a nuisance. Instead of answering, she nodded her head. Maybe sometimes being a good wife meant *not* sharing one's thoughts, but that made it mighty hard not to say what came to mind.

"We going to ride Champ?" It'd been a month since they'd last ridden together, but she still remembered how it felt having Drew's arms wrapped around her middle. Her husband had been so caring watching out for her. She'd never argue how safe he'd made her feel. Jules rubbed her chin. She'd better get her mind on something else.

"No, with you recently recovered, I think it's best if we take the buggy. Promise me not to overdo, I'll let you lead Champ from his stall while I get the conveyance ready."

"All right." Jules's shoulders slumped as they walked the short distance to the barn, Pepper shadowing her side. "Stay." The pup sat on his haunches keeping an eye on her, his tail wagging.

Drew handed her into the vehicle a few minutes later.

Pepper wiggled, overcome with excitement.

"We probably should leave him here," Drew said.

"He needs the chance to visit with his mama."

"I don't know…"

"Please, Drew?" She placed her hand on his arm. Fire crackled through her fingertips.

"I suppose it can't hurt." He handed her the pup.

Silence bristled between them on the brief ride to Sarah's house. Why couldn't he share what he thought? He hadn't been himself since she'd spewed everywhere.

"Here we are." Drew quickly took his hands off her hips, setting her on the ground and stepping backward. "Feeling dizzy at all? I can assist you inside before I get on my way."

"Don't talk so foolish-like. I'm as fit as a turkey and don't need no help walkin'. No need to worry none about me." Jules snagged her pup from the buggy.

Drew hopped onto the seat. "I won't be long. I'll see you later." He flicked the reins and didn't glance back.

~*~

Drew's heart clenched. Should he have left her? What if she

started feeling queasy? Jules hadn't eaten much the past few days. His heart raced, and he urged Champ to trot. His breathing became rapid and shallow. He needed to make haste. The visits to his parishioners and errands had been delayed as long as he'd possibly dared. *Lord, keep her in Your care.*

The wind whipped his hat. He gripped it with his left hand while maintaining hold of the reins with the other. Dark clouds bunched on the horizon. They hadn't had rain in quite some time. He couldn't remember when there'd last been moisture. Even so, he hoped it'd hold off until after he and Jules were home.

In town, he made a brief stop at the general store. He purchased a few items and was heading out of the building when Hiram Martin called to him.

"Hold up there, Drew. Have a letter that came. Actually, it's got your wife's name on it." The clerk handed over a rumpled envelope.

"Thank you." Drew glimpsed the familiar handwriting, and his gut clenched. It had to be from her brother, which meant she hadn't lied to him about *not* writing those letters. He swallowed. What could her brother want? He gripped the missive tight in his fist.

"Drew? Something wrong?"

"What? No. I'm fine, thank you, Hiram. Good day." He tipped his hat, shoving the envelope into his coat pocket, dissuading any further conversation.

The bell above the door chimed as he stepped outside, striding to the buggy and tucking away the paper-wrapped packages. He vaulted onto the seat, releasing the brake. "Let's go, Champ." Next on the list involved a brief call to Mother. She'd requested…more like ordered him… to stop by over a week ago, but he'd been too busy caring for Jules. Today seemed like the best time to visit especially with his wife preoccupied with Sarah. He didn't have to worry about trying to appease Jules and Mother at the same time or play arbitrator between the two.

A minute later, he tied Champ to the hitching post. "I'll be back soon, fellow, at least if I have any say in the matter, but one never can tell with my mother." He patted the horse and made his way up the path to the house.

He knocked and waited. The door whisked open. "There you are, son. I wondered when you would finally make an appearance. Unfortunately, I had to answer the door myself, since today is the servants day off."

"I'm sorry it's taken me a while, but Jules hasn't been feeling well."

"Humph. Sick, you say? What kind of sickness?"

"Sick to her stomach and not able to keep anything down." Drew removed his hat and ran his fingers through his hair.

"Humph. I wanted to make you aware I have been in contact with a Pinkerton detective." She motioned to a chair.

"A detective? Why would you need a detective?"

"Why to check into your wife's background, what else? I knew you were too lily-livered to do anything, so I have taken matters into my own hands."

He bit back a retort. "What have you discovered?" Drew held his breath, not sure he wanted to hear the answer.

"Nothing definite yet. He is having trouble getting information from his contact in Texas and may need to travel there himself to ferret out the truth. I will inform you as soon as I learn anything new."

He released the air from his lungs.

"Stop fiddling, son. Sometimes I wonder how you have made it to the position you are in. Honestly, I do not understand why you did not go into the railroad business like your father. It would have made you a better man."

"I believe I'm following the path God has for me, Mother."

"Certainly not with that wife of yours. At least there is no child involved in the mix." Her face paled. "Unless…"

"Unless what, Mother? I don't have time for word games today. I have a few more calls I need to make, and I don't want to be gone long from Jules."

"Perhaps it is more evident now why she required a husband so quickly." Her eyes narrowed.

"You're not making any sense, Mother."

"How blind are you, Drew? Add the facts together. Your wife is getting sick. It is obvious she was with child when she married you."

Clearly Mother had become delusional. After all, Jules had a raging fever for an entire day and a half. Women didn't have fevers when they were increasing, did they? He gulped, not sure if he wanted to discover the answer.

~*~

Jules knocked on the door as Drew rode away.

"I'm so happy you're here." Sarah hugged her. "How wonderful to see you up and around. Come in. Couldn't Drew stay?"

"He had some errands he insisted on taking care of, and he didn't want me to be home alone since I've been feelin' poorly."

"How romantic. He's such a sweet, thoughtful husband." Her sister-in-law smiled. "Are you any better? Perhaps you should sit. You *do* look a bit peaked."

"I'm fine, really. It's just..."

Sarah's hug didn't help to stop the tears.

"Sit down, Jules, and tell me what's troubling you. I'm guessing it's more than getting over an upset stomach, although you look like you haven't slept in weeks."

"I haven't much."

Sarah wrapped her warm hands around Jules's cold ones. "Are you still sick?"

She shrugged. "I don't think so. The spewin' and fever are past, but I keep getting this funny feelin' in my gut whenever I'm with Drew. It won't go away neither. I can't hardly sleep at night." Jules blinked back tears.

Drew's sister grinned. "Go on."

"I think he's not sleepin' much either. Maybe I passed some sort of sickness thing on to him. I reckon he hasn't been eatin' much. I hate to see him like this… 'specially if I'm the reason for it. Something's up with him, and I can't figure what it is." She shoved a piece of hair behind her ear.

Sarah chuckled. "I have an idea what's wrong with the two of you."

"Really? What is it?" Jules leaned forward in her chair.

"I believe you're falling in love with each other." Sarah crossed her arms, looking mighty pleased with herself.

Could it be? Her stomach tossed just considering it. *No.* She shook her head. There had to be another reason. He'd been distant ever since she took sick. Besides, the problem not only affected her stomach but also her head and heart. She probably should check the medical guide to see what ailed her. Best to keep her worries to herself though. No need for anyone else to know until she'd figured what was wrong.

Pepper stood up and placed his paw on Jules's leg. She welcomed the distraction. "I suppose he needs to head outdoors."

Sarah stooped to pet him. "He sure is growing."

"I brought him so he could visit his mama. Maybe we could go for a walk so they can play awhile? He must get lonesome for her. I sure would if I was him."

"Our coffee can wait until later." Sarah shifted the pot to the back of the stove. "While we're outside, I'll show you our garden. Things are coming along nicely."

"Drew started one a couple weeks back, but not much is growin' yet."

"He usually gets one in much earlier. I guess he's been a bit preoccupied this spring." Sarah sent a smile her way. "He used to go to the garden whenever something upset him when we were children. I believe it's beneficial for him. He was ten when our father died, and it hit him pretty hard. With me being only five at the time I don't recall as much. Papa enjoyed the garden too. Even though we had servants to take care of almost everything, he tended the vegetable patch. He and Drew would work it together. I recollect many times hearing them talk and laugh."

"Must've been nice. I wish I had some memories of my folks and sister. I've wanted a home and family as long as I can remember, and I can't believe it's finally happened... at least the husband part." Warmth flooded her cheeks. "I miss Josh though."

"Why don't you write him a letter?" Sarah turned toward the house. The two dogs barked and played at their side.

Tears filled Jules's eyes. "I don't reckon I should." She bit her lip. "I wouldn't know the first thing about doing somethin' like that anyway."

"Maybe Drew has the address from when Josh replied to the advertisement. I'd ask Drew."

"I reckon it isn't such a good idea. He weren't too happy about those letters in the first place. He still hasn't forgiven me or Josh." She bit her lip. There *had* to be some way to contact her brother.

"If I were you, I'd ask Drew for the address. He might surprise you and be in favor of you writing Josh. Besides, he's learned not to hold a grudge."

Clearly Sarah wasn't married to the man and didn't know how he could be. Drew never talked about it. She saw it in his eyes every time he glanced at her when he thought she wasn't watching. The words her brother had written in the letters were like a rock wall in her marriage…keeping her husband from drawing closer.

"How about we get some coffee, and I can teach you how to sew." Sarah held the door open.

"Sounds good to me. I could use somethin' to chase away the tumbleweeds, and I reckon I've worked up an appetite too."

Sarah's laughter rang out. "I'm sure I can round up some food."

An hour later, Jules held a bit of cloth to her finger to staunch the flow of blood. "My fingers look like yer pin cushion, though mine have more holes in them. I don't suppose I'll ever figure how to sew without hurtin' myself."

"Don't be discouraged. It takes time." Sarah peeled back the cloth to check Jules's finger. "I've had lots of practice since I learned as a small girl. You can't expect to become an expert in such a short time."

"I doubt I'll ever make stitches like you do. Mine are either way too long or too short." Jules yanked at the fabric in frustration, only to discover she'd sewn it to the skirt of her dress. "I can't even sew on a button. Josh always did it for me."

Sarah chuckled and came to help her.

"I'm hopeless."

"Nonsense. Be patient. It'll become easier as you work on it. In no time you'll be sewing clothes for you and Drew." Sarah snipped the thread, releasing the fabric. "There. Ready to try once more."

Jules groaned. What she wouldn't do to be riding a horse instead of learning how to make tiny stitches. She wouldn't ever be good wife material. Tears clogged her throat and rolled down her cheeks. She swiped the confounded moisture with the edge of her sleeve.

"Awww. What's going on?" Sarah touched her hand.

"I don't know why yer brother ever married me. I can't seem to do anythin' right."

"That's not true, Jules."

"It *is* true. I can't cook, leastwise, not on the beast. I can't sew, and I make a mess of things when I try to knit. I don't speak right and have a habit of sharin' my mind when I'm not 'sposed to. I reckon the only thing I do considerable at is ridin' a horse, trackin', protectin' and anythin' that means bein' outdoors, but Drew don't care about any of those things. He doesn't want me wearin' my guns and don't get why I need 'em. I can't get my own husband to show interest in me."

"Oh, he's interested, all right." Sarah's eyes sparkled. "He just won't admit it yet. Don't give up, Jules and by the way, I happen to love the way you speak."

"I reckon I often say the wrong things, although most times I have no idea how it happens. I thought I could do things until I came here. Now I can't do nothin'." Droplets formed at the corner of her eyes and blazed a trail down her cheeks. She clenched her hands. "The worst possible thing has happened too. I've changed into a weepy female." Jules's shoulders shook. She could no longer control the sobs welling up inside her.

Drew's sister held her until all the tears were spent and hiccupping sighs remained.

"What's wrong with me? Livin' in town is makin' me soft." She took the handkerchief Sarah offered and blew her nose.

"There's nothing wrong with you, silly." Sarah patted her hand. "You're extremely competent, and I believe Drew cares for you. He maybe hasn't actually told you, but I see it in his eyes."

"No, he wishes he'd never married me, and he's stuck with a wife who doesn't act the way he wants."

"Your body is still worn out from being sick. You'll feel better once you've regained strength. Come on. Wash your face and we'll get something more to eat. It'll help."

A few minutes later a sharp rap thudded against the door. Drew stepped into the house.

Jules shifted her head away from him, so he couldn't see her tears. Her chin wobbled.

"How're you doing, brother?"

"Fine." Drew plodded toward Jules, stopping beside her.

She peeked at him.

His fingers traced a path around the brim of his hat. "I don't mean to cut the visit short, but we probably should be headed back to town. There's a storm coming."

"Why don't you stay for lunch? Jules is pretty worn down and needs some nourishment. You could always wait out the storm here." Sarah touched her brother's sleeve.

"No, we need to go." Drew ran his hand through his hair. "Ready, Jules?"

Something *was* wrong. He wouldn't look her in the eye. What could it be? If she had to wager a guess, the dragon had something to do with it.

"Did you happen to stop and see yer mother?" Jules's gaze flitted towards his.

"Why would you ask that?" Did she imagine it or had his hands shook?

"What did Mother have to say?" Sarah stepped between them. "She wanted you to stop by sometime this week, didn't she?"

"Yes."

"What for?" Sarah prompted.

Jules remained quiet, waiting to see if he'd answer.

"She didn't have much to say." He pursed his lips.

"Are you sure? Something seems to be bothering you, dear brother."

"It wasn't anything important." His gaze traveled to the window. "Come on, Jules, we need to leave right away."

"I'll round up Pepper." She excused herself and stepped outside, in a hurry to get away from the thick air in the house.

The wind had picked up and whipped her dress as she walked around the house, calling for her pup. Dark storm clouds piled on the horizon giving an eerie green glow. She quickened her pace. "Pepper, come." She breathed a sigh when his merry bark sounded, and he came running. She scooped him up in her arms, brushing away the twigs and leaves clinging to his fur. "Where were you, little scamp?" She hugged him tight, walking toward the house.

"There you are." Drew stepped forward when he caught sight of her. "Sorry we can't stay longer."

"I'm ready."

"Here." Sarah handed her a small sack with a smile on her face. "Practice some more."

"Thank you." Jules gave her sister-in-law a quick hug. "For everythin'."

"I'll be praying for you."

Jules tried to smile, but tears clogged her throat. *Again.* She held tight to Pepper while Drew handed them both into the buggy. He surveyed the sky, jumped to his seat, and then flicked the reins.

"Let's go, Champ."

They traveled for a few minutes before he dug into his coat pocket. "I forgot. This letter came for you." He handed the white envelope to her.

"Letter?" Her hand trembled, and her heart raced. Only *one* person in the whole world knew where she lived.

14

Her mouth went dry. Why would Josh be sending her a letter? She tucked it into her pocket to read later, without Drew glimpsing her reaction.

"Aren't you going to read it?"

"Not 'til we get home." Had he recognized the handwriting? Was that why he acted so strange? Her mind raced with possibilities. It *had* to be from her brother, since she didn't have any other living relative.

Large droplets of rain started to pelt them, despite the roof of the carriage. She shivered trying to see toward town. Her heart pounded as she pointed. "W-what's that?"

A funnel cloud formed and spiraled down to the ground.

"A twister!" Drew guided Champ off the road and into a ditch. "Hurry, we don't have much time." He yanked her off the seat. "Get under the buggy, quick."

"Not without Pepper."

"Confounded woman, there isn't time. Get down!" He shoved her to the dusty soil. A few seconds later he thrust a whimpering dog into her arms and spread his body over hers. The wind roared like the train she saw once. She tried to cover her ears but couldn't move with Drew firmly on top of her. Pepper squirmed, but she held fast to him, her whole body trembling.

The next instant it grew deathly quiet. The hair on the back of her neck stood on end. "Is it over?" Jules's had trouble speaking with grit lining her mouth.

"No, we're in the center of the storm." His tight words scared her.

"What about Champ?"

"We have to pray God protects him and us."

Next the wind roared so loud she couldn't tell if Drew spoke or not. *Lord, keep us and Champ safe.* She buried her head in Pepper's fur.

Drew's body completely covered hers, pressing her to the ground.

Moments later, Drew gently shook her.

"You can open your eyes now. I believe it's over." He moaned and rolled to his side.

She released Pepper, but the dog stayed close by. *Champ.* Her heart pounded in her throat, afraid of what she'd find. The seat of the buggy had been torn clear off. It lay twisted and mangled in the field beside the road. She glanced at Drew, who stood by the horse.

"Is he hurt?" She had a hard time swallowing past the lump that clogged her throat.

"No, praise God. He protected all of us. It's a miracle, Jules, especially with the twister right on top of us."

"Are Sarah and David in its path?" Jules hugged herself and stared in the direction of their farm.

"No, it looks like it completely died after it hit us." Drew continued to run a hand along Champ, calming the horse.

"Can we make it back to town?"

"I hope so. The buggy is still intact—most of it." Drew chuckled. "It might be uncomfortable riding without a seat though."

Jules stroked Champ's head. "We could ride him together."

"What about Pepper? He's getting a bit too big to ride on the back of a horse with both of us."

"He can stay in the buggy. He can sit on the floor."

"Maybe." Drew continued to speak in soft tones to the horse.

A bright flash of lightning split the sky, followed by a thunderous boom. Champ shifted to the side, stamping his feet as the sky let loose, soaking them in an instant.

"Whoa, boy." Drew held tight to the bridle. "Go ahead and put Pepper in the vehicle. We need to get on our way. It looks like the rain won't let up anytime soon."

Jules scooped up her beloved pet and placed him under what was left of the seat. "Stay, Pepper." He whimpered but didn't move.

Drew placed his hands on her waist and lifted her onto Champ's back before swinging up behind her. It wasn't how she figured their next ride would be. She shivered as the rain ran down her neck, soaking her.

He wrapped his arms tight around her, nudging the horse to move. Jules's teeth chattered. Drew was busy keeping Champ in hand as the rain continued to pour and lightning flashed. By the time they arrived at the barn, she couldn't feel her toes. Drew dismounted and led the horse into the barn while she still stayed atop the gelding.

Inside, Drew's hands gripped her hips, pulled her down, holding her tight for a bit. "You should go into the house. I'll be there after I take care of Champ." He wiped droplets from her face. "I'll bring Pepper with me."

She shook her head. "No, I can help."

"But you're soaking wet and chilled."

"S-so are you." She tried to control the chills shaking her body something terrible.

"You're such a stubborn woman." He sighed and shifted toward Champ, grabbing a curry brush.

Jules wiggled her toes to get some feeling back in them. Once they started tingling, she lifted the sleeping pup out of the buggy and placed him in a mound of hay. She picked up a brush and helped Drew. With the two of them working together, they finished in a short time. She forced her body to obey as she placed the bridle on its hook and the brush on a shelf.

The room swayed when she swiveled around, spots dancing before her eyes.

Drew swept her into his arms and kicked the barn door shut as they moved past it. Pepper pranced at his side. She wrapped her arms around her husband's neck. If only he showed some sign of enjoying hugging her, but his face didn't change.

When he stepped into the kitchen, she struggled to get down. "I need to remove my boots. They're caked with mud."

"The mud doesn't matter. You need to get into some dry clothes."

"But—"

"No buts, woman. Change your clothes, and I'll be back."

~*~

Drew peeked into the room a few minutes later to find his wife sitting on the edge of the bed. Her pale face and haunted eyes tore at his heart. He cleared his throat and edged toward her. Before she could protest he lifted her, pulled the covers downward, and settled her underneath them. With a quick jerk, he tugged the blanket up to her neck and kissed her on the forehead, not stopping to consider his actions. "Get some sleep, Jules."

Her eyelids drooped, and she slept within minutes after closing her eyes. The sound of her even breathing filled the room. The memory of her slight frame cradled in his arms did funny things to his heart. He'd almost lost her to the storm. Drew's hand shook as he pulled a dry set of clothes from the dresser. He closed the bedroom door and padded to the kitchen after he changed. The cook stove was cold. He stirred the embers, added some logs, and lit them. He filled the kettle with water, eager to drink a strong coffee.

He went to get his Bible from his study and sat at the kitchen table while waiting for the water to heat. He flipped through the pages until he stopped at the gospel of Luke. The Lord had brought the passage to his mind during the twister and on the ride back to town.

"'Then said he unto the disciples, It is impossible but that offences will come: but woe unto him, through whom they come! It were better for him that a millstone were hanged about his neck, and he cast into the sea, than that he should offend one of these little ones. Take heed to yourselves: If thy brother trespass against thee, rebuke him; and if he repent, forgive him.'" Drew closed the Bible and bowed his head.

"Lord, I've been a fool. You gave me a precious gift when You gave me Jules, and I've done everything I can to try to change her to what I thought was best. Forgive me, Lord. I could've lost her today, and she wouldn't have had a relationship with You. I've been so worried about making physical changes in her that I've lost sight of what is most important—that she has a spiritual change of heart and realizes her need for You. She's like a small child, and she doesn't understand much about You and Your ways. Jules has never had the opportunity to learn." Moisture pricked his eyes as he sank to his knees. "Forgive me too, Lord, for harboring bitterness toward my wife and her brother. I-I guess she didn't lie to me about those letters, and I can't hold it against her any longer, since she had no idea Josh wrote them. Help me to learn to forgive. I'm ashamed it's taken me so long. I'm not sure how to love her, but I beg You to show me. I want to be obedient to Your Word and learn to be the husband You desire for me to be. She's not the wife I ordered, but for some reason, You've seen fit to give her to me. I believe You don't make mistakes." Drew sighed and wiped the tears from his cheeks. "She frustrates me, Lord, but I'm open to what You want to do in my life and hers. I won't fight against it anymore." A peace washed over him, and he felt better than he had in weeks.

~*~

Jules's sleep grew restless. Her dreams were filled with tornadoes, letters from her brother, and memories from Texas. She thrashed on the bed, kicked the covers from her feet, shivering uncontrollably. Drew rose up beside her saying he should've let the twister take her. He shouldn't have protected her. The winds sucked her up, and her fingers clawed, trying to hold onto Drew. He let go and turned his face away from her. Next, fire blazed all around her, burning her flesh and scorching her soul. No escape and no relief. She cried out again, pleading for someone to help her, but she remained alone. So utterly alone. No matter how hard she tried, no escape provided itself. She wept, knowing somehow she had lost something precious, and she had no idea how to get it back. Drew and everybody else had left her. Nothing remained. There was no hope.

"Jules, honey, wake up."

Her eyes fluttered open. She shuddered and held tight to Drew.

He stroked her hair and face. "Did you have another bad dream, sweetheart?" His face softened and his eyes studied her.

Sweetheart? Had he been injured by the twister, and she hadn't realized it? Could she still be dreaming? "W-were you hurt during the storm?"

"Why would you think that?"

She swallowed. How could she word it? Her mouth parted, but no sound came. Jules shot him a sideways look. Drew was intently studying her lips. A wave of heat washed over her face.

"Want to tell me about your dream?"

No, not really. How could she distract him? She picked at the cover until his hand swallowed hers.

"Jules?"

Tears glistened in her eyes. "You protected me."

"Why wouldn't I protect you, Jules? You're my wife."

Did he really love her, or did he only take care of her because of duty? She sighed.

"Actually, it was God who protected us. We wouldn't have made it through the storm without Him. What a miracle. There's no logical way we should've survived, especially Champ. I guess God has something special in store for each of us." Drew squeezed her hand.

What could God have in store for a horse? "What could God have special for me to do, and why would He? I don't know Him." Jules's voice cracked.

He stroked her cheek. "You could."

She fidgeted with the buttons on her shirt. How did she know when she'd be ready to take that step? Jules licked her lips, trying to concentrate. She remembered her conversation with Sarah, and how she'd told her the more one got to know God the more they'd love Him. "I reckon I need to learn more about Him afore I can decide whether or not I accept Him." Reminders of her dream flashed through her mind, the flames and torment, and the sense of being totally alone. She argued with herself about asking Drew what he thought of it but decided against it. No, she'd do better to figure things out on her own.

"Perhaps I can help you to learn more about God and His ways." Drew's voice shook. "I don't suppose I've done a very good job the past couple months, but I promise it'll change."

What did he mean?

~*~

Drew wanted to tell Jules so many things, but he didn't want to overwhelm her. He also had the distinct feeling she wasn't being forthright with him. Shadows smudged beneath her eyes, and he couldn't tell if it was from the twister or the dream. Either way, he recognized the need to pray for her. He clasped both of her hands in his. "Lord, thanks for Your protection over us today. I especially thank You for saving us from destruction. I would've been lost without Jules. Thank You for my dear wife and help me to be the husband she needs. Soften her heart towards You, in Jesus' name, amen."

He opened his eyes. She blinked those big eyes he loved to see each morning. Drew sensed a wave of peace had settled upon her. He promised himself to pray with Jules on a daily basis. Perhaps his petitions would be instrumental in leading her to the Lord. He should've started the practice from the beginning of their marriage.

"I always thought I'd be the one to protect you."

He had to lean forward to hear her. "Often the man is the one who tries to provide for the woman God has given him. I'm sure there have been many times your brother sheltered you. Have you ever been in a situation like that?"

Jules nodded, sweat glistened on her forehead, and the haunted look returned to her eyes.

"Want to tell me about it? It might help you to sleep better." He brought her hand to his lips and kissed her knuckles.

Her eyes widened and she picked at the blanket. "It's in the past."

Was it? Something seemed to have a hold on her. Perhaps the subject should be left alone…but first. "You can't keep relying on *yourself* for protection, Jules. One day, you'll find all your weapons won't be enough. The question is what will you do then?"

15

Beads of sweat broke out on Jules's forehead. Had Drew learned about her past somehow? Had she blurted Burt's name when she was dreaming? She licked her lips and un-fisted her hand. Taking a slow breath in, she shoved her concerns away and thrust aside the covers. Time to start working at becoming the wife Drew desired. She'd lived through the tornado, which gave her the chance to become a better wife, and she wouldn't fail. She'd not lose the home and family she'd finally gotten in her grasp. *I'll do whatever it takes to be the wife Drew dreams of. Just wait and see.*

"Why don't you work on yer sermon, Drew, and I'll fix us somethin' to eat."

"Actually, I prepared a meal and have it in the warmer. I presumed you'd be hungry." He smiled. "Ready for lunch?"

"I think my belly is scrapin' against my ribs. I'm hungry enough to eat a whole heap of something, 'specially if it ain't my cookin'." She bit her lip.

Drew chuckled. "Let's get your stomach filled."

"I'll be there in two shakes. Go on ahead."

She bent to retrieve her wet dress from the corner of the room. Her hand searched through the folds of drenched fabric for the letter, coming up empty. "I'm right sure I put it in here afore the twister hit." Had she somehow lost it in the storm? "Drew." She ran to the kitchen, colliding with him at the doorway.

"What's the matter?"

"Did you take that letter outta my dress pocket?"

"No, can't you find it?"

She shook her head, her heart pounding. I finally get something from my brother, and lose it afore I can read it.

"I wonder if it was lost during the twister or on our ride home. I'm pretty sure it was from your brother. I recognized..."

"I figured the same thing." She didn't meet his eyes, knowing it wasn't a topic he liked to discuss.

"I'm sorry, sweetheart."

There was *that* word again. He must've hit his head during the storm somehow. She stretched to nestle her hand in his hair. When she searched his head, feeling for a lump, he gathered her hands and held them to his cheek. He must've been hurt for sure. He'd acted mighty strange since they'd returned home.

She yanked her hands free. "I thought after we ate I'd head to the general store and pick up some cloth, if you don't mind." She pulled flatware from the drawer and set them on the table.

He stopped and stared at her. One eyebrow lifted. "Are you sure?"

"Why sure. Sarah showed me how to sew today, in fact she gave me a needle, thread and a bit of fabric. Oh, no." She threw open the kitchen door and raced toward the barn, hopping over puddles.

Drew followed, waiting while she searched the mangled buggy. "What's the matter?"

"It's gone." She slumped into a mound of hay.

"We can replace whatever it is when we go to the store after lunch. Don't fret, Jules."

"We got enough to buy cloth, needles, and thread? I'd hoped to get enough to make that suit coat you've been wantin' and maybe another dress for me."

His faced beamed like the sun coming up. "Leave the money to me. We'll get whatever you need. Let's go eat so we can get going after lunch."

They made short work of eating and clearing dishes. When they poked their heads outdoors, the rain had slowed to a brief sprinkle. The sun poked through the clouds as they got closer to the store.

Drew pointed to the sky. "A rainbow."

Jules sighed. "It sure is purty. Reckon I'll never get tired of seein' 'em."

"Me, either. It always reminds me of God's covenant."

"What d'ya mean?"

"God told Noah after the flood that whenever there was a rainbow in the sky, it would be a reminder of God's promise to never destroy the earth with another flood."

"Don't think Josh ever told me that story." Jules smiled at Drew when he looped her arm through his.

"I could read it tonight when we study the Bible together."

"I'd like that. Uh, Drew?"

"Yes, sweetheart?"

She fingered the sides of her pants. "I'm sorry to have to wear this to town today. My dress is wet."

"I'm not complaining." He lowered his voice, bending toward her ear. "I happen to find my wife very attractive no matter what she's wearing."

Jules's mouth dropped open. Her face grew hotter than a summer day in Texas as Edna Miller stepped into their path with Gertrude in tow.

"Good day, Pastor." She sniffed and lifted her nose after looking at Jules's clothes. "I see you're dressed for town, Julia."

Jules balled her hand into a fist.

"Actually, my wife dressed quite beautifully this morning, but we were caught in the storm on our way home and were drenched. We're on our way to purchase some material so she can make a new dress."

She squeezed his arm and sent a small smile in his direction.

"Does she know how to sew? My Gertrude is a fine seamstress. Has been since the age of four."

Gertrude looked as if she wished the ground would swallow her. "Mother, please." She whispered the words, but Mrs. Miller didn't appear to have heard them.

"She's an expert cook too. You should taste her pot roast, Pastor. It's close to heaven itself." She patted her daughter's arm.

"Yes, excuse us, ladies; we have some shopping to do." Drew lifted his hat and steered Jules away from the two.

"We are also on our way to the mercantile. Isn't that convenient?" Mrs. Miller bustled close to them.

Not really. So much for having some time alone with Drew. Jules sighed.

Drew smiled at her, shrugging his shoulders.

Guess they were stuck with the woman's presence whether they wanted it or not.

Jules took in a deep breath as they walked into the store, catching a lot of different smells. Clear containers filled with different kinds of candy, lined the counter. She lifted the lid of each one and inhaled deeply.

"Would you like a piece?" Drew leaned close, his eyes sparkling.

"Oh, could we?" She bounced on her toes.

He chuckled. "Hiram, we'd like two peppermint sticks while we shop." He placed a coin on the counter, dug into the candy jar and withdrew the sweet, handing her one.

"Harrumph." Edna Miller snorted like a horse. "Like two children. Come on, Gertrude." She yanked her daughter in the direction of two piles of cloth.

Jules bit her tongue to keep her laughter from bubbling out.

Drew winked, taking a lick of his piece of candy.

"Do we have time to look around or are you in a hurry?"

"Take as long as you need, sweetheart."

"Hello, Mrs. Montgomery. I hope your letter had some good news in it." Hiram Martin stopped sweeping the floor.

Tears filled her eyes, clogging her throat something terrible.

Drew's arm snaked around her waist, pulling her into him. "Unfortunately the letter got lost in the storm before my wife had the opportunity to read it."

"What a shame. Who do you think sent it?" The shopkeeper peered at her over his spectacles.

"I reckon my brother, since he's my only relative." Jules wiped her tears.

"Is that so?"

Two fellas stepped into the store, cutting off their talk.

"Hello, Hiram. Did ya hear a twister set down south of town? Levi Smith said he saw it coming, and the next minute part of a buggy flew into his back yard. He couldn't tell where it came from." The man scratched his head.

Drew chuckled. "It's the top of my conveyance. We were on our way to town when the tornado set upon us."

Hiram Martin crowded closer, probably eager for some new gossip.

"We'd left Sarah and David's house when Jules spotted the funnel cloud a short time after."

"Drew drove us into the ditch, yanked me and Pepper off the buggy, and shoved us underneath it. He crawled on top, protectin' us." Jules smiled up at him. "My Drew's a hero. I wouldn't be here if it weren't for him." She squeezed his arm. Her fingers gripped his corded muscles. She swallowed as her breath hitched.

"That'd have been no great loss." Edna Miller muttered.

"Mother!"

"The Lord definitely provided for us." Drew stroked her fingers.

"What a miracle. The twister passed right over, but God spared our lives."

"What about your horse and buggy?" One of the strangers interjected.

"Champ wasn't hurt, and he didn't bolt either. The top of the buggy got torn completely off and the seat mangled, but nothing else." Drew scraped his hand along his chin. "We were soaked through by the time we made it to town, but uninjured, praise God."

"Except I lost my letter and the sewing supplies from Sarah." A knot formed in Jules's throat.

"That's a right shame." The first man scratched his scraggly beard.

"Who's Pepper?" The second man jostled his way forward.

"He's my puppy." Jules smiled. "A birthday gift from my husband."

"Strange name." The man raised his eyebrows.

Jules bristled. How dare he? She started to lash at him but remembered the decision she'd made earlier to be a better wife. It took some doing, but she clenched and unclenched her hands instead of harming the man.

"Careful there, George. I think she's itching to haul off and slug ya." The first man cackled.

"I'd appreciate it if you'd treat my wife like the lady she is." Drew cleared his throat.

"If she's such a lady, then why is she always wearing britches and dressed like a man?" The second man inched closer to Drew. "Goes to show the kind of man you are. Maybe you should be wearing a skirt, since your wife's wearing the pants."

Jules charged the man, her fists flying as she made contact with his face. Blood spurted everywhere. He held his hand to his gushing nose and took a swing at her eye. Her head snapped back, as his fist connected with her jaw. The room tilted and spun out of control, and she slumped to the floor like a sack of beans.

~*~

Jules awoke.

Drew, sporting a black eye, was picking up things on the floor. Blood dotted his knuckles.

"She's awake, Pastor." Gertrude motioned.

As Jules sat up, she realized the young woman had been cradling her head in her lap. Maybe the girl wasn't so bad after all.

Drew hurried to her side. "I've been worried, sweetheart. Don't try to stand yet."

"I guess you should've been a bit choosier in the selection of a wife, Pastor." Edna Miller stood with her hands on her hips.

"Mother, that's none of our business." Gertrude guided her to the front of the store. When they got to the door, she peered back at Jules with a small smile on her face.

"Thanks," Jules mouthed. Then she smiled, too.

Gertrude waved and walked outside.

Jules glanced around the store, thankful to see the two men were gone.

Drew held onto her arm as she struggled to stand. She wished she could read his thoughts. His look did funny things to her. She dipped her chin, her gaze catching sight of his bloodied hands. Jules lifted one, turning it over, gently rubbing his fingers. "You're hurt. Mr. Miller, you got any salve and bandages?"

"I'll be fine." Drew snatched his hand away. "I'm more concerned for your welfare."

Ashamed would be more like it. Jules's body trembled as the truth of what she'd done washed over her. She had decided to make Drew proud of her, and in the next minute she'd fought in the general store. She hung her head. How could he ever forgive her? News would spread throughout the town like a grassfire. Would it affect his position as the town preacher? She broke into tears. Once they flowed, the flood gates couldn't be held back. Jules clung to Drew, sobbing her heart out. Hot tears soaked her face and his shirt. Next, her nose ran, followed by loud hiccupping sighs.

His arms stiffened. What could he be thinking of her?

Drew patted her back. "Shh, it's going to be all right, sweetheart. Don't fret. There's no reason to cry."

There was *every* reason to cry. She'd never been so ashamed. How could she ever come to town, or show her face in church on Sunday? Drew would've been better off if he'd never married her. The day couldn't possibly get any worse. Jules's gaze traveled to the front of the store as the bell tinkled above the door.

Her mother-in-law walked in.

16

Drew flinched when he spotted Mother. How did she always manage to show up at the most inopportune times? *Lord, give me the words to say...or not say.*

"What is going on here, Andrew? Have *you* been fighting?" Mother's jaw dropped open and her arms went limp at her sides.

"We had a slight altercation. There's no need to concern yourself."

"Fight was more like it," Hiram Martin interjected. "You should've seen them, scrapping like a bunch of alley cats." He waved his hand at the overturned boxes and cans. "I expect you to be paying for the damages, Drew."

"Don't worry, Hiram. We'll settle our accounts. Allow me to help with the cleanup." Drew grabbed a broom and swept up the broken glass.

Jules joined him, holding the dustpan when he had need of it. Thankfully she'd gotten those tears to stop. They worked in quiet, side by side, putting the store back in order.

He chose to ignore the steady stream of conversation between Mother and Hiram, concerning the brawl.

When he swept the last bit of dirt into the dustpan Jules held, he noticed her trembling hands. He examined her pale face. Drew guided her to the back corner of the store. "Jules, sweetheart, are you hurt?" He traced his finger along the curve of her cheek. "You're a bit peaked. Perhaps we shouldn't have come out just yet. Shall we come another time to do our shopping? It appears you could use a good rest."

Her spine stiffened and her chin jutted out. "No, I'm fine."

"That's my girl." He smiled when her gaze darted to meet his. "How about we start collecting the things on your list?"

Drew led her to the dry goods section. A rack on the side caught his attention. "Jules, this is something new. Hiram has ready-made clothes. They weren't here the last time I came in."

Jules's fingers ran along the sleeve of a green dress hanging from a hook. Not allowing her to argue, he draped it in front of her. "It seems like it would fit. Hiram, do you have somewhere my wife could try on a dress?"

The balding man bustled toward them, motioning to a curtained doorway. "Go on through there, missy, and try it on. I'll see to it nobody goes in that room." He headed back to the counter.

"Are you sure?" Her gaze went to Drew. She held the dress to her chest as if it were made of fine china.

"Absolutely. Let me see when you have it on though." He winked at her.

"Only if it fits me." Her cheeks took on a rosy glow before she thrust through the curtain.

"I cannot believe you and your wife would be tussling like common outlaws." Mother murmured behind him.

He pivoted toward her.

"I expected it of Julia, but certainly not my son. This was not how you were raised. This marriage is damaging your reputation. We need to find a way to end it."

~*~

Jules held her breath behind the curtain, listening to her mother-in-law spew words of hatred. Did Drew really wish he hadn't married her? Her body quivered at the thought he might have regrets. Could she go back to life on the trail after getting a family as she'd always wanted? No, she'd fight to keep what she had with him.

"What were you thinking? I guess the problem is that you were not. You never consider things first." Mrs. Montgomery's words grated like a burr in the toe of a boot.

"What was I thinking, Mother?" Drew's voice rose. "I had no thought but to protect my wife's honor, and I defended her when faced with purposeless insults." Drew's voice rose.

He'd gotten a banged-up eye 'cause of her? Jules straightened. Did that mean he cared for her?

"Father taught me to safeguard a women's honor, whether I agree with the woman's actions or not."

Jules's shoulders slumped. He *was* ashamed of her. She didn't need to hear any more. Served her right for secretly listening. A tear rolled down her cheek. She scurried to the shop owner's bedroom and latched the door. Her body shook when she caught a glimpse of herself in the mirror on the wall. Her jaw had a mix of colors, and her cheeks were blotchy. Sobs shook her frame as she unbuttoned her shirt and slid the dress over her head.

The dress was purty, and Jules thought it fit, but she truly wanted to see how Drew would act when he saw her in it. She picked up her shirt and wiped her tears and nose on the sleeve, so he wouldn't notice she'd gone and cried some more. *Again.* Good thing Josh hadn't seen all those tears and her beat-up face.

Her heart pounded when she reached for the curtain. She let out some air, cocking her ear, but heard nothing more between Drew and his mother. Jules walked into the store room searching for her husband. He turned towards her when her boots scraped against the wood floor. Her shoulders relaxed when she noticed her mother-in-law had left.

He closed the distance between them. "Why, you're beautiful." He pushed her Stetson back and lifted her chin.

She glanced down.

"Jules. Please look at me."

She hesitated then dragged her gaze toward his only to drop it.

"Have you been crying?"

He stepped closer…so close, she could barely breathe. She had to move. She'd made enough of a fool of herself with all the bawling. "Do you like it?" She moved backward and twirled, so he'd not be able to touch her face with his gentle hands.

"It's right pretty." The shop owner came up behind her. "Those readymade clothes are a new experiment I'm trying to see if people are interested in them. Gertrude Miller makes them for me. Heard tell she'd like a shop of her own someday, if she can ever get away from her mother's clutches." He cackled. "She offers free alterations if needed, but don't look like that's gonna be necessary."

Al-ter-ations? Should she ask what that was? Sounded mighty painful.

"I don't think we'll need Gertrude's services, Hiram. The dress appears to have been made for Jules. Tabulate it onto my bill, and we'll finish our shopping."

She started to head back to get changed when Drew snagged her hand. "Why not leave it on? That forest green color suits you."

He *did* like it on her. She swallowed. "I'll go fetch my other clothes."

Drew reached for her garments when she returned. "Let me get those." His hands grazed hers when he took them.

Her fingers trembled. What is wrong with me?

"I'm not sure what else we'll need." Jules touched the different goods, hoping he'd not notice her shaking.

"This one would be good for a new suit coat." Drew pulled out a rolled-up piece of cloth from a big stack. He put thread, sewing needles, and a pair of shears into a pile on the counter. Next he added knitting needles and a few different colors of yarn.

"Sure we're not spendin' too much?" Jules watched the growing heap. "We could wait on some of the things."

"Nonsense, nothing but the best for my wife."

~*~

They both were silent on the trip home.

Drew didn't want to bring up the fight, and he surmised Jules didn't either. He couldn't understand what had come over him when bachelor brothers, George and Charlie Williams, started insulting his wife. Those remarks about him didn't rankle like the ones they'd shot at Jules. He would've belted Charlie first if she hadn't beaten him to it. The thought shocked him. He'd always claimed to be a man of peace.

Bible verses floated through his mind. 'A soft answer turneth away wrath: but grievous words stir up anger.' The brothers' words sure had stirred up his anger. Jules had been riled up too. 'A wrathful man stirreth up strife: but he that is slow to anger appeaseth strife.'

Forgive me, Lord, for not being slow to anger. He massaged the tight muscles in his neck. Jules studied him without uttering a word. He wished he knew what she was thinking.

At home, Jules murmured, "I'll be outside if you need me." She slipped from the house.

Perhaps they needed some time apart. He needed time to pray. His knees had barely touched the floor when a hefty knock hit the door. "Who could that be?"

Drew cringed when he saw Edward Miller, Henry Smith, and James Adams standing on his doorstep. Any time they'd shown up at his door, they'd been the bearers of bad tidings. The latest escapade they'd chastised him for involved Jules using her new corset to support the growing tomato plants in his garden. It had been the talk of the town for a whole week.

"Come in, gentleman. What can I do for you?" He ushered them into the sitting room. "Please, have a seat. May I offer some refreshment?"

"We didn't come for pleasantries." Edward Miller chose a chair and sat on the very edge of the cushion.

The other two men glanced at Edward as if waiting for him to be the first to broach the subject.

"I'll get right to the point. My wife told me the two of you tussled with the Williams brothers. Is it true?"

"Yes, but—"

Henry Smith held up his hand. "Hear us out."

"My Edna says you two were fighting for no reason. I have to say I'm flabbergasted, Preacher. I never expected such behavior, especially with the upbringing you had. As soon as I found out, I called a meeting of the elders, and we've made a decision."

Drew's stomach churned. Dear God, give me strength for whatever's coming.

"We decided." Edward cleared his throat. "We, uh, won't allow this type of brash behavior in our congregation, let alone our pastor. Even though your father founded our town, we can't let our pastor set a bad example for the people. Despite several warnings, your wife hasn't been gentled. We're relieving you as pastor, effective immediately."

No, Lord. Anything but that. Drew's heart pounded in his head, thumping with each breath he took. It couldn't be happening. He wanted to rant at the unfairness of the situation. They hadn't allowed him to share what had really happened. They were only aware of the twisted view of a bitter woman.

"After you made the decision to order a wife instead of choosing from one of our fine daughters, and now this…" Edward shook his head. "Well, we conclude it's best you seek a preaching position somewhere other than Burrton Springs."

Now he understood why they'd given him those conditions...in the hopes he would marry one of their eligible daughters. That made perfect sense. Finally. He had a feeling the men's wives were trying to get back at him, not the elders themselves. But what could he to do? His first desire involved serving God, how could he if he wasn't a preacher?

~*~

Jules stood in the kitchen, listening to every word the men spoke, but those last words echoed in her head. Drew had sent for her to keep his job. He didn't really *want* a wife or need one. No wonder Edna Miller kept pushing Gertrude in front of Drew, trying to snag his attention. She likely planned the whole thing to get him to marry her daughter, but her plans didn't get her what she wanted. Jules 'sposed she should be thankful for that much, but did she really want to be a wife who never knew real love? She shuddered at the thought, wrapping her arms around her chilled body. His earlier caring for her must've been a show. It felt like a boulder turned in her gut.

What would Drew do if he no longer preached at the church next door? She squared her shoulders. He maybe didn't want a wife, but she refused to sit back and allow those men to bully her husband into losing his place. There had to be something she could do.

17

Jules snagged her rifle and marched out of the house, stalking toward the barn. Pepper barked, following her. She spotted her saddle in a dim corner, yanked it free, and tossed it onto Champ. She hiked her dress to her knees and swung into the saddle. "We're going for a ride, boy. I reckon you've already had a full day with the twister and all, but we need to help Drew."

In no time they were out the door with the wind blowing on her face. She let Champ run as fast as he wanted. It suited her that he had a desire for speed, because it matched her roiling thoughts. How she missed riding for hours on end with the gentle hills soothing her frayed feelings. There was no time for loafing.

She got to the farm before her riled mind had a chance to settle any. Jules vaulted from Champ and pounded on her sister-in-law's door.

It flew open.

"What is it? What's the matter?" Color drained from Sarah's face.

"I don't have time to jaw, but can you tell me how to get to the Miller home?"

Sarah's mouth gaped open like a baby bird in search of food from its mother. A full ten seconds passed then she snapped it shut. "They live two miles down the road." She pointed past their barn. "It's the next farm after ours. You can't miss it."

Jules left, giving Drew's sister no chance to ask any more questions. She rode Champ hard, covering the miles within minutes. The door opened as she tied the horse to the post, and Gertrude stepped out onto the porch.

Jules struggled to get her seething under control. She clenched her fist when the small, brown-haired girl came within striking distance.

Gertrude's eyes widened.

"Don't come no closer." Jules rested a hand on the butt end of her rifle.

Gertrude's cornflower blue eyes blinked quickly, like butterfly wings. She swallowed, holding her hands up. Her fingers shook.

"Put yer blasted arms down, Gertrude. I don't aim to shoot. It's yer *ma* I plan to have dealin's with." Jules nodded toward the house. "Where is she?"

"S-she's not here." Her chin wobbled, and a single tear slid down her face.

"Where can I find her?" Jules released the tight grip on her gun.

"Ma didn't say. S-she just told me she'd be gone for a couple hours."

"You better not be lyin' to me. How do I know I can trust you? From the sounds of things, yer ma ain't trustworthy one bit."

"N-no, I wouldn't lie to you. Please come inside. Tell me what Mama has done *this* time." Gertrude trekked to the house. She held the door when they stepped onto the porch. "Feel free to leave the gun outside."

"Nope, I'm keepin' it with me." Jules shouldered it and took a step inside the house.

"I'll fix us some tea, and you can tell me what's happened." Gertrude busied herself pulling out fancy cups and plates and a pot with a matching design.

Jules had never seen anything like it, tracing her finger along the blue flowers. They were right purty.

"Please, have a seat while I pour the water into the teapot to steep."

How's it gonna go uphill in a teapot?

The girl's quiet movements made the tight coil in Jules's gut loosen. She hoisted her skirt and swung her leg over a chair, straddling it. The pleasant smell of the tea carried to her nose.

"Your shoulders are knotted tighter than my thread when I first learned to sew." Gertrude shot a glance at Jules. "I see Drew bought the dress I made. I knew it'd fit you perfectly."

"What d'ya mean?"

"I had you in mind when I sewed it and hoped it'd catch your eye at the store." A smile spread across her face. "I'd like to own my own shop someday. I've not told Mama, but I've been saving money towards it."

So the woman had some backbone after all. Jules couldn't help but smile. "I'm not good with needle and thread. Sarah tried to show me a few things earlier, but I'm hopeless."

"Oh, no, I'm sure you could learn." Gertrude's gaze shifted down to the clutched hands in her lap. "I-I'd be happy to help if you'd like."

"Really? Drew's been in need of some things, and I don't know the first thing about cuttin' out cloth, let alone sewin' it." At the mention of her husband, she was reminded of the reason for her visit.

Gertrude thrust a cup of tea into her hand. "Here, try it. I hope you'll like it."

Jules took a sip and nodded. "Thanks. Now, about yer ma."

The girl cleared her throat. "Tell me what's she's done. I'm so sorry for how she treated you in the store earlier. She can be really nasty sometimes, especially when she has her mind set to something." Her cheeks glowed bright red.

"Like tryin' to have Drew marry *you,* instead of me."

Gertrude's ears turned bright pink. "She's the one who came up with the terrible idea to force Pastor Montgomery to pick a wife if he wanted to keep his job. She was sure it would get him to agree to marry me, but I've never been inclined toward him in any way. She wouldn't listen to me though."

"You aren't wantin' Drew?"

"No. T-there's this gentleman in Boston… Oh, but I've said too much." Her cheeks glowed with color.

"Don't that beat all." Jules scratched her head. "It's good to see you've got some spunk."

Gertrude paled. "Please don't say anything to Mama. She doesn't know I've been exchanging letters with a man."

Jules slapped her leg and let out a roar of laughter. "I think I like you, Gertrude Miller."

"I believe I like you too, Julia." Her lips curled upward.

"Please, call me Jules."

"So, tell me, what else has Mama done besides make my life difficult?"

"It's her fault Drew got sacked."

"W-what do you mean?"

"Right afore I left, yer father and two men came to talk to Drew. They relieved him of his duties as preacher."

"She didn't. Oh, dear, I heard her talking to Papa shortly before she departed, but I hadn't realized what they were discussing. What reason did they give for Pastor Montgomery's dismissal?" Gertrude placed her clattering cup and saucer onto the table.

"'Cause of the fight I started in the store." Tears filled Jules's eyes. "I'm the one to blame for it, and Drew has to pay for my foolishness. They wouldn't give him a chance to tell his side. It's not fair." She thumped her fist on the table, making the dishes rattle.

Gertrude sopped up the spilled tea.

"Sorry. It makes me hoppin' mad like a horned toad. I can't ponder what he'll do without his preachin'." She swiped at the tears blurring her eyes. "He just bought all those sewin' and knittin' supplies for me too. Maybe I can take them back to Hiram without Drew findin' out."

"I'm sure he'd want you to keep them." Her new friend gripped Jules's hand.

"What am I gonna do if he can't find another job? There ain't any other church in town is there?" Jules jumped up to pace around the kitchen.

"No," Gertrude said. "We'll have to think of something else."

"I don't want to move now I've finally got me a home." Jules yanked her hat off and twirled it in her hands. "Maybe I won't never be able to get Drew to love me, but I'm not goin' to give up without a fight and let yer ma win this battle. No siree. I don't aim to lose."

Gertrude linked her arms through Jules's. "Don't worry. We'll come up with something together. Let's pray, shall we?"

~*~

Drew sat in stunned silence after the trio left. He'd heard Jules tear out of the stable on Champ earlier but hadn't been free to chase after her. *Wonder what has her riled this time?* He chuckled as he thought about his tumultuous wife. His life certainly hadn't been dull since she'd entered it. When he heard a scratching at the door, he got up to investigate.

As soon as the door opened a crack, Pepper pushed his way inside, his tail wagging. He jumped up and placed his front paws on Drew's pant leg.

"What's the matter, fellow? Did she leave you behind too?"

The dog whined and shoved his head under Drew's hand. He obliged by scratching behind the pup's ear. "I wish my problems could be solved as easily as yours, Pepper. A little food, some time outside, and a little attention, and you're happy. Sure would be nice."

Pepper pressed closer as if he somehow understood Drew's internal struggle. "Lord, how am I to be settled when my only way to serve You and the people of this town has been snatched away? What are You trying to teach me? All I desire is to do Your will, but I don't see how I can when my job is gone. What were You thinking, Lord?" His questions reverberated off the walls of the kitchen. Drew let out a heavy sigh.

Pepper whimpered, placing a tiny paw on his leg.

"Come on, boy. I believe it's time I sought some counsel other than yours."

The dog kept pace with him while he walked the couple miles to David's home. When he arrived at the part of the road where the twister had hit earlier, Drew fell to his knees for a moment to praise God for keeping them all safe. "I have to believe You saved us for a reason, Lord, but things are kind of muddy right now. I sure could use some clarity."

Pepper nosed under his arm as if he wanted Drew to get up and keep walking. "What's the matter, fellow?"

The dog barked, racing down the road a short distance then sprinted back.

He laughed. "I guess that means I need to keep moving forward, right? Or maybe it's just a visit to your mama that's driving you."

The dog yipped and took off.

A few minutes later they reached the farm.

Drew bypassed the house and strolled to the barn, hoping to find his brother-in-law without his sister spotting him. If she saw him first, she'd hammer him with questions.

A clanking drew his attention, and he followed its sound. David stood hammering out a dent from his plow. He glanced up as Drew grew closer.

"That's a sight I never imagined I'd see." David motioned toward Drew's face.

"What do you mean?"

"You sporting what's sure to become a black eye."

Drew winced as he touched the tender skin on his face. "Yeah, it's been an eventful day."

"Do tell. I'm nearly finished with this. We could go inside. It's sure hot today." David whacked the plow blade one more time with the hammer before putting the tool away.

"I'd prefer staying here." He dragged a barrel closer and sat.

"Suits me fine." His brother-in-law pulled over another container. "What's on your mind? I didn't get a chance to say anything earlier, but were you caught in that storm on your way to town?"

Drew nodded. "Yeah, in fact a funnel cloud appeared on the road right in front of us."

"What happened?"

"I drove the buggy into a ditch. There wasn't time to un-harness Champ. I got Jules and Pepper under it and lay on top of them, and the twister bore down us." He shuddered. "We were in the center of the storm, David. It's a miracle we weren't killed. The winds tore off the top of the vehicle, and the seat will never be the same, but we were unharmed."

"Even Champ?"

"Yes, even him. I don't know why he didn't spook and run away, but he didn't."

"Whew-wee, I'd say you *have* had an eventful day."

"And that's just the beginning. After the storm, Jules wanted to go shopping. We had a uh, slight run-in with the Williams brothers." Drew ran his finger between his collar and neck.

"Those two are always spoiling for a fight. Let me guess. They're the reason you got the sore eye?" David gestured toward Drew's face.

"I got this, and Jules got hit in the jaw."

"They hit a woman? I can't believe it. Those two are rowdy, but I never thought they'd strike a lady."

"They made some unkind remarks about Jules... and me. Before I could do anything to defend her honor, Jules threw the first punch."

"You don't say." A smile flitted across his brother-in-law's face. "She *is* a wildcat, isn't she?"

"She sure is. I don't think I'll ever gentle her. The elders have warned me several times concerning Jules's behavior, but I've only been able to do so much." He shook his head, remembering the time she'd insisted on taking him on a hunting trip. "It wouldn't have been too bad, except Edna Miller and her daughter were at the store too."

"That woman is nothing but trouble. Let me guess. She ran home and told Edward?"

Drew let out a sigh. "Yes, and within an hour he and the other two elders were at our door."

"Oh, no."

"Oh, yes, and they proceeded to tell me my services were no longer needed." He clenched his hand so tight his knuckles hurt.

"What am I to do, David? Preaching and serving God is all I've ever been called to do."

His brother-in-law plucked a piece of hay from a pile and chewed on it, not saying a single word.

So much for my hope of counsel. Drew sighed. A good five minutes passed.

"I've been praying, Drew, and I believe God has given me a scripture for the situation. I have to say though; you probably aren't going to like it or maybe even appreciate it." David flicked the hay to the floor and studied him.

Drew's muscles tightened. "Let's hear it."

"I read something in the book of Psalms last evening. It says 'Be still, and know that I am God: I will be exalted among the heathen, I will be exalted in the earth.'"

"That's it? How can you expect me to be still, when the elders wouldn't give me a chance to explain? Any man would defend his wife's honor. It's not like I'm in brawls all the time. In fact, I've never been involved in a fight until today. You don't understand, David. How can I serve God when they've taken away my position?" He vaulted from his seat.

"Simmer down, Drew, and listen to me for a minute. We both know you don't need to be preaching in order to be a servant. There are plenty of ways to help people in our community. I think right now, there's somebody even more important you need to be focusing your attention on." David clapped his hand on Drew's shoulder.

"Yeah, who might that be?" He ground out the words.

"Your wife. If I'm not mistaken, she doesn't have faith in God. I believe you've been given this time, so you can teach her His ways, not necessarily society, or a woman's ways. She needs to experience your love, not rules to change her. Have you told her yet you love her?"

Love? There was that word again. Would God ever stop hounding him? He gulped and licked his lips. Wasn't it enough to share God's love with her? He'd bought her a bunch of things at the store. It had to count for something, right? Hadn't he made more of an effort to be understanding since their experience with the tornado earlier? After all, he'd come to her aid with the Williams brothers.

"God's calling you to be still, and quiet, Drew, so you can see the needs around you." David patted his shoulder. "Jules has been doing everything she can to try to please you, or haven't you bothered to notice?"

The words rocked him to his very core. His brother-in-law had a knack at keeping from mollifying one's actions.

"You may never get the pastorate position back. Are you willing to accept the fact that God's calling may be to center your attention on Jules for now, as well as those around you who're hurting?"

18

Drew released a pent up-breath while running a hand across his sweaty forehead. The hot, late September breeze did little to cool him. It had been two and a half months since his discussion with his brother-in-law, and he had yet to come up with a clear solution to his problems. The church appeared agreeable to the circuit preacher who came every other week. He had a difficult time sitting on the pew each Sunday, rather than facing the congregation from the pulpit. On the off weeks, Edward Miller led the services. It shouldn't have, but the way the elders had handled the entire situation continued to rankle him.

He wasn't doing much better with Jules either. Whenever he tried to do something special for her, it either didn't work, or she took it the wrong way and ended up hurt. "I can't seem to get anything right, Lord." He walked beside a row of corn in his garden fingering the dry, crackly leaves. Normally he would have harvested the crop by now. He chuckled, recalling the day Jules came inside proud of her latest accomplishment.

"I weeded the garden for you, Drew."

"But I just did that this morning."

"There were two whole rows of grass coming up, and I pulled them right out for you."

She'd smiled, expecting his approval. Instead he'd growled at her because she'd yanked up his newly growing stalks of corn. So much for showing her God's love. He'd lost his temper then and many times since. Drew sighed, massaging the tight muscles in his neck.

"I'm having a hard time being still, Lord." He kept waiting for God to restore his job, but it hadn't happened. At this rate, it wouldn't ever occur.

He heard footsteps behind him and turned.

Jules strolled toward him carrying a glass of water. Shadows continued to haunt her face, but at least she hadn't been sick again. If anything, she'd *lost* weight, which had to prove Mother's concerns unwarranted. His cheeks flamed at the thought.

Drew pasted on a smile and prayed she wouldn't question him. At least he hoped it looked like one. "Thank you, sweetheart." The endearment slipped out before he could grab it back.

Her haunted gaze met his. "It's mighty hot, so I reckoned you could use a drink." She shielded her eyes from the bright sun.

"I'm surprised you didn't put on your Stetson." He took a long drink and wiped moisture from his mouth with the back of his hand.

"I plumb forgot it. The heat must've fried my brain." Jules fanned her face with the apron she wore over her green dress. She studied the fields beyond the church. "It sure is mighty dry. Reckon it'll rain anytime soon?"

He peered at the sky. Not a single cloud in sight. "Doesn't appear like it will. It's strange we haven't had any moisture since the tornado came through. I'm afraid we won't have the best season of crops this fall." He pulled an ear of corn from the stalk, peeling it back. "See, there are hardly any kernels."

Jules nodded, not meeting his gaze. He cringed. His words weren't intended to remind her of the day she'd 'weeded' his garden, but he'd hurt her again. Her bottom lip trembled.

"Come here, sweetheart." He gathered her in his arms, resting his chin on the top of her head. She stood rigid for a minute then softened. The scent of roses wafted under his nose. Drew breathed deep as his gut performed crazy flips and turns.

~*~

There they were again. Those words of affection he'd often spoken to her and didn't seem to realize. He never said the three words she longed to hear though. Jules sighed. She knew the toll of the job loss continued to weigh on him. Drew never mentioned their finances, so she didn't know how much longer he could go without seeking another position. The past two months he'd helped people whenever they'd expressed a need—repairing a barn roof, harvesting wheat or clearing a field. Most days he was gone early, getting home at night, sweaty and tired. She wondered how much longer she could handle what their life had become.

The losing struggle to become a good wife ate her alive. Doubts plagued her like the story Drew had read to her about Moses. She couldn't remember how many times she'd walked almost all the way to the Millers' house to demand they give Drew his job, only to stop herself at the edge of their property. Her temper had gotten him in the fix they were in, and she wasn't gonna make things worse. If they could get any worse.

Gertrude had failed to come up with any ideas of how to solve Jules's problems.

Jules sighed. What good was a husband and a home if he didn't love her?

When Drew left her each day, the silence filled the rooms.

She missed him and how things used to be the first few weeks of their marriage. Even though she'd often done things wrong and had shamed him in those early days, Jules had thought he'd cared for her. Everything changed when she'd learned he'd only ordered her to save his job. Ordered her like sending for something in a seed catalog. She bit back the tears.

What had Gertrude called it? A marriage of convenience? There weren't anything convenient about it as far as Jules could see.

"Sweetheart?" His lips nuzzled her ear, causing her breath to come in short bursts. "What're you thinking?"

I want to be a real wife. One who is loved and special. One you want to come home to, instead of always wanting to be away from. She shook her head. He wouldn't want to hear her thoughts. She didn't want to hear them either, because it did no good. Jules forced the images from her mind. Silence stretched between them.

"Surely, something must be bothering you." Drew tilted her chin, forcing her to stare him in the eyes. Her heart pounded. Could he read her mind?

He leaned in closer, claiming her lips. She wrapped her arms around his broad shoulders, and her heart skipped and fluttered when his kiss deepened. Tears pricked her eyes. Drew ran his hand along her back, his touch stirring her very soul. Was she dreaming?

Drew moaned and stepped away, his arms dropping from their embrace. Did he miss her touch as much as she missed his?

"I'm sorry." He mumbled the words. "It won't happen again."

What did he mean? Her head thudded harder. It was then that the ringing school bell registered in her mind.

"Fire!"

Jules spun and saw a spiral of smoke rising from the outskirts of town. Drew dropped his hoe and took off at a run. She struggled to keep up with his long strides.

"You'd best stay here." Drew snatched a bucket from the barn and disappeared.

Pepper barked and followed him to the edge of the yard.

"No, boy."

The dog whined but trotted to Jules's side. His tongue lolled to the side as he sat panting.

She continued to study the glow of the fire, and her heart tightened when she realized it was near where her mother-in-law lived. "Oh, no, I've got to go, boy. I can't sit back and not help. I'm goin', whether he wants me or not." She snapped her fingers, and Pepper followed her to the house.

Jules snagged some towels and soaked them in the pot of water on the beastly stove. She dumped the water into a bucket and placed the wet towels inside. "Be good, Pepper, and I'll be back." She closed the door behind her and ran. Her heart pounded with each step.

The men from town struggled to kill the flames licking their way at the corner of the house. Her heart sank when she realized it *was* Drew's childhood home.

The women had formed a bucket brigade using whatever containers they had at hand in their effort to help.

Jules coughed when the smoke swirled in her direction.

Drew worked alongside David. She hurried over to her husband, pressings the towels into his hands.

"Get back! I told you to stay at home." He panted the words in between striking at the hungry flames.

It wasn't the time to argue. All the other women were working, and she belonged by his side. She shrank away and joined the line of women. *I refuse to be sent home like a child.*

As she worked, her gaze searched the crowd, watching for Drew's mother. She finally saw her standing off to the side with a dazed expression on her face. Tears rolled down her soot-filled cheeks. For the first time in her marriage, Jules actually felt sorry for the woman who stood alone, staring as her home burned. She debated whether she should go and comfort her mother-in-law or continue to aid the battle to save the house.

Her arms soon quivered as she passed heavy buckets down the line. All the time she kept an eye on Mrs. Montgomery. When she thought she couldn't lift one more canister, she noticed Drew's ma tearing at the sleeves of her dress. She yelled something, but Jules couldn't hear over the crackle of the fire or shouts of the workers.

All of a sudden, the woman tore off toward the burning building and entered a doorway despite the flames jumping and swirling around her.

"No!" Jules yelled. "Drew, Drew!" She tried to get his attention, but he couldn't hear her. There was no time to spare.

She soaked her apron in the closest bucket, dropped the tin of water, and ran to the entry of the house. Smoke immediately choked her throat and cut off her breathing. Jules covered her nose and mouth with the wet piece of cloth. She searched the room. "Mrs. Montgomery?" Even if the woman answered her, she wouldn't be able to hear her above the howl of the leaping flames. She'd have to go through each room until she found her.

The heat from the fire singed Jules's skin. She stepped over charred pieces of wood, going from room to room, trying to miss getting touched by flames licking up everything in its path. Jules finished searching the main floor, not finding Drew's ma. She gripped the hot handrail, making her way up the groaning steps. Time was running out. She had to find the woman soon.

When she stepped into a smoke-filled bedroom, she tripped over a huge lump on the floor. She dropped to her hands and knees, touching the lump enough to find it was her mother-in-law. The woman clutched something tight in her fist, but Jules couldn't tell what was in it. Her chest hurt from not getting enough air. Taking hold of the woman's high-top shoes, Jules yanked as hard as she could.

Somehow, she managed to ease the unconscious woman down the steps, but by the time she made it to the landing her energy faded. She argued with her body to move, but it wouldn't obey. Blessed air was thirty feet away. It wouldn't matter if it was only two feet, Jules couldn't take another step. She sank to the ground, slipped the damp apron from her face and covered her mother-in-law's head instead. Jules's breathing became ragged, and her chest burned from the heat and smoke-filled air. Within a minute her eyes fluttered shut.

~*~

They fought a losing battle. Drew's numb fingers continued to beat at the flames, but they weren't making a difference. Flames engulfed over half of the house. He breathed a prayer, thankful Mother remained unharmed. His eyes, nose, and throat stung from the smoke. Drew dipped the fabric in water and glanced at the line of women to check on Jules. His chest tightened. She wasn't there. He dropped the towel and scanned the area where his mother had stood. She too was missing.

"What's wrong?" David gasped for breath.

"Jules. Mother."

David glanced around. "Don't think your mother went back into the house?"

"Drew!" Gertrude Miller ran up to his side, panting. "I can't find Jules or your mama. The blacksmith's wife thinks they went inside." She pointed at the enflamed house.

"No!" A cry wrenched from his throat. He sprinted toward the flame-filled doorway and ran through. Smoke immediately choked off his air supply and blinded him. David plowed into his back, resting a hand on his shoulder.

Together they crept their way forward until Drew stumbled over something on the floor. He dropped and felt two bodies lying on the carpet. *Dear God, don't let them die.* He couldn't tell if they were breathing or not, but he scooped up Jules's body and cradled her in his arms. David grunted as he lifted Drew's mother.

It felt like a hundred years passed before they found their way outdoors. Men huddled around them, beating flames from their clothes. Drew refused to release his grip on his wife but sank to his knees on the ground. Sobs ripped from his chest.

Mother stirred, a ragged cough racking her body. At least *she* would live. She unfurled her fingers, and he saw a handkerchief. It was the last thing his father had given her after he'd returned home from a business trip, just one week before his death.

Drew touched Jules's face, tears filling his eyes and blurring his vision. *Lord, save her.*

19

Drew paced back and forth in the kitchen while he waited for Doctor Adams to make an appearance. His clothes reeked of smoke, but thoughts of Jules filled his mind. When he'd carried her to the house a few minutes ago, she hadn't stirred once.

David placed a hand on his shoulder to stop his movement. "She's strong, Drew. I'm sure she'll pull through this."

"What if she doesn't? She'll never know I'm beginning to care for her."

David studied him, and Drew couldn't help squirming.

"You mean you still haven't told her? What have you been waiting for?"

He shrugged, sighing. "I almost said something right as we heard the fire call." Warmth spread into his neck and face. Their kiss lingered in his mind. He didn't know what'd come over him. What kind of fool kissed his wife then said it wouldn't happen again? Why had he kissed her? It merely complicated matters.

"What's so difficult about letting go and loving your wife? She's good for you." David clapped him on the back. "When are you going to accept it?"

Drew rubbed his neck, hoping to loosen the constriction in his throat. He coughed. It wasn't true, was it? Couldn't he show her God's love without his own feelings getting in the way? He had to admit, though, carrying her unconscious body had done funny things to his heart.

Drew stiffened his shoulders when the doctor entered the room. His mouth went dry, and he couldn't speak.

"How are they, Doc?" David came to his rescue.

"With rest, I think your mother-in-law is going to be fine, but it's best if we don't move her. I suppose normally I'd have Sarah take care of her, but she doesn't need the added stress in her current condition."

Drew coughed and cleared his throat. "A-and Jules?"

"She woke up a few minutes ago and has a horrible cough, much worse than your mother's. I'm quite concerned. She's pale, and her pulse is uneven. I'd feel more comfortable if she stayed in bed for a week or so, depending upon how she progresses. I'll likely let the elder Mrs. Montgomery up sooner, but I won't risk it with your wife. I don't care for her skin tone either." The doctor scratched his head. "In fact, it would make it easier if both patients stayed right here for the time being."

"Certainly." Drew flexed his tense muscles. "Whatever you feel is best for them."

"I'm afraid this will make your own sleeping uncomfortable for a bit." Doc rummaged in his medical bag.

Heat rose in Drew's face. If only Doc knew how little it'd change things for him, regarding their sleeping arrangement. He cleared his throat. "Can I see her now?"

"Yes, but don't be in there long. Rest is the best medicine." Doctor Adams handed him a small packet. "Here's a sedative to mix in a glass of water if either of them are in pain. The instructions are written on it. I'll check back tomorrow to see how they're faring."

"Thanks, Doc."

Drew didn't wait until the man exited the kitchen but sprinted for the bedroom. The door creaked as he opened it. The two women lay side-by-side in the bed. Mother's eyes were closed, but Jules's were open. He knelt beside the bed, taking her hand in his.

"How're you feeling, sweetheart?" He whispered so as not to disturb Mother.

"Fine," she croaked.

He eased onto the edge of the bed, being careful not to jar her as he sat.

Her dark eyes contrasted boldly with her pale face. Drew ran his finger along the side of her cheek.

"I'll get up and fix yer supper right soon, I promise." Her eyelashes fluttered to rest on her cheeks. "Let me rest an hour, and I'll get to it." She yawned, opened, and then closed her eyes.

He stroked her hand. Drew opened his mouth to say something, but she'd already fallen asleep. He studied the steady rise and fall of her chest. Sighing, he tugged the covers to her chin. "Sleep well, Jules."

He praised God she was alive, giving him a second chance with her, but he also wanted to throttle her for risking her life by running into a burning building. If she hadn't though, Mother would've died.

~*~

Jules stirred and stretched. Why did her body ache all over, and why did she reek of smoke? Her haggard cough brought back the memories of the burning house. She shuddered, remembering the dream she'd had after the tornado, seeing the searing flames and feeling so alone. She wasn't alone now, even with it daylight outside, Drew's warm body was beside her. What had made him decide to join her after all those months? She snuggled closer, stretching forward with her toe to touch his leg.

"What do you think you are doing?" A harsh voice startled her.

Jules shifted away, shocked to see her mother-in-law in the bed beside her. When had that happened? The last thing she recalled was trying to get them both out of the burning building, but she'd no longer had any strength left.

"Stop gaping with your mouth open like a fish. Get out of this bed and get me some breakfast. I cannot believe my son allows his wife to stay in bed so long. Stop lollygagging and move. Can you not see I am an invalid?" The dragon spewed her fire.

"I-I'm sorry." Jules flipped back the covers and sat up. Despite her pounding head, she rose to her feet, holding tight to the bedpost when the room started to sway. She gritted her teeth, determined not to further anger Drew's ma.

The house stood empty, and she wondered where Drew could be. Maybe he'd gone to sift through the remains of his childhood home to see if there was anything worth saving. Fortunately he'd already started a fire in the beast. Jules added a log to the stove then headed to the outhouse.

The trip to the necessary drained her energy. By the time she got to the kitchen, she hacked continually. The room tilted, and she collapsed to a chair, trying to catch her breath. Breaking out in a cold sweat, she dropped her head to the table, hoping everything would soon stop spinning.

Enough, Jules. Time to get moving and make breakfast. She forced herself to stand. When the trembling in her legs eased up, she crossed the room to a basket of eggs sitting on the dry sink. *Thanks, Drew. I couldn't handle another trip as wobbly as I've been on my feet.*

The fry pan sizzled when she cracked eggs into it. They were one of the few things she'd managed to cook on the beast and not ruin. Hopefully her mother-in-law didn't expect anything other than eggs, otherwise she'd be disappointed.

While their breakfast cooked, Jules swayed, struggling to stay standing. If she didn't keep a close eye on them eggs, they'd burn, and the dragon would get further riled. Her strength drained with each passing minute. Another bout of that hacking cough returned, and black spots danced in front of her eyes, taking what breath she had away from her. She bumped the table and lost her footing. Her legs gave way beneath her.

~*~

Drew stepped into the kitchen and rushed to catch Jules's body as she fainted. He swept her into his arms and carried her back to the bedroom. Mother sat up in the bed when he nudged the door open with his foot.

"I have been wondering what was keeping that lazy Julia. Do not let her fool you with her theatrics, Drew. Make her get up and fix our breakfast. Honestly, I do not know why you put up with this kind of behavior." She adjusted the covers.

Drew bit back a retort and laid his wife on the bed. Her face was so pale. Her lips had a bluish tint to them.

"Son, something is burning. Go. Leave the girl alone." Mother barked the orders. Her face drained of color, and her fingers clenched the blanket.

Back in the kitchen, Drew pulled the smoldering pan from the stove, dropping it when pain scorched through his hand. Eggs flew everywhere, and Pepper eagerly assisted with the cleaning process. Drew snatched a towel and picked the pan off the floor. What was the matter with him? How could he so easily stand up to the Williams brothers but not his own mother? Why did he let her intimidate him?

"Here, let me help," Sarah said.

Drew jumped. "Where'd you come from?"

"David wouldn't allow me to come until now. I slept through the school bell's ringing yesterday, and it was late in the evening when he returned home and told me what had happened." Sarah eased Drew into a chair and wrapped a cool cloth around his throbbing hand.

"I need to go check on Jules. Mother had her up, fixing breakfast, and she collapsed. They'd been sound asleep when I checked on them earlier, so I decided to clean Champ's stall. Should've stayed inside. I walked in, and she'd been cooking eggs. I caught her as she fainted." He ran his unwounded hand across the back of his neck.

"Wait here and I'll go see how she's doing." Sarah squeezed his wrist. "Promise me you'll keep that towel on your hand and won't move." She whirled around the kitchen, soaking another cloth in the bucket of water he'd brought from the stream earlier. She set the bucket within his reach, dropping another cloth in it. "When the rag on your hand warms up, switch it with the cooler one. I'll call if I need you."

Drew groaned after Sarah left the room. He hadn't slept a wink—unable to forget the kiss he'd exchanged with Jules in a moment of weakness and how his heart had tightened in his chest when he saw her pale face upon waking the day before. "What're You trying to teach me, Lord?" He paced the small room.

Pepper's head raised, and he wagged his tail. *At least someone's happy.*

When the pulsating in his hand worsened, Drew changed the cloths as Sarah had instructed and dropped to his chair. He sighed. How could he to take care of Jules with Mother making demands? "Lord, help or I'm never going to live through this."

Minutes ticked by. Drew squirmed in his seat. It'd been too long. He needed to go check on his wife. He crept toward the doorway, holding his throbbing hand above his shoulder, cupping the elbow with his uninjured hand, but the three women hadn't noticed him.

"Sarah, my dear, would you see what is keeping Drew? I suppose this simpleton ruined my meal. What *is* that wretched smell?"

"Honestly, Mother, what's gotten into you?" Sarah crossed the room and sat beside Jules, patting her cheeks. "Come on, Jules, wake up." She took her friend's hand in hers.

His wife's eyes fluttered open.

"W-what happened?"

"Happened? Spoiling my breakfast is what happened."

"Mother. *Please.* There's no reason for such unkind remarks. Why do you treat Jules so wretchedly? From what David told me, you wouldn't be here if it weren't for her. She saved your life."

Drew decided it was time to make his presence known. "Sweetheart, are you all right?" He knelt by her side.

"You're hurt." Jules's voice croaked in a strained whisper. She rested her hand above his wrapped appendage.

"It's nothing. How are *you* feeling?" His fingers seemed to disobey his brain as they traced the curve of her cheek down to her dry, cracked lips. It was all he could do to keep himself from pulling her into his arms. Why should that cause such an ache in the pit of his stomach?

She licked her lips while studying him with those chocolate orbs of hers. Drew groaned, struggling to keep himself from dipping his head to caress her mouth with his. Beads of sweat covered his forehead. What had come over him? He'd always prided himself with having a tight control on his emotions, but somehow, she'd sneaked past his firm resolve. His heart pounded.

She blinked and shifted her head away from him. Had she remembered their kiss? Ice took up residence in his heart. A sudden sense of loss overwhelmed him, and he didn't understand why.

"Enough of this nonsense. Stop treating her as if she is made of glass. She is not going to break, and it is about time she did something useful." Mother waved her handkerchief.

Drew ripped the slip of fabric from her hands. "If Jules hadn't seen you enter that burning house, we'd be having a funeral. You're the reason she's in bed. From now on, I expect you to give my wife the respect she deserves. Do I make myself clear?"

"Harrumph." She snatched her hankie from his hold, refusing so much as to glance at him.

Jules's fingers grazed his sleeve.

Her touch immediately calmed his seething emotions. "If you need me, I'll be out in the kitchen making breakfast for my wife, and you too, Mother, if you choose to be civil."

"I never." Mother rolled to her side away from them.

"I'll be back in a bit, sweetheart. Get some rest. Don't worry about anything. I'll take care of you." His gaze lingered on her face momentarily before he exited the room. His sister followed after him.

In the kitchen, Drew scraped the singed egg residue from the pan. *Lord, I don't know how I'm going to make it through a week of having Mother here.* His hands shook. It was the first time he'd ever stood up to her. Perhaps he should've done it long ago. He refused to let her words and actions torment him any longer. He prayed one day she'd accept him as he was and Jules as his wife.

"Feeling better, Drew?" Sarah slipped her arm around his waist.

He nodded. His fingers flew, turning slices of bacon in one pan and then cracking the eggs into another. He cut hunks of bread from a loaf Jules had baked the previous day. She'd been so proud of her first successful attempt.

"I don't know why Mother badgers you so, but please know she truly loves you." Sarah stood with her arms resting on top of her bulging stomach.

"I've never measured up to her expectations for me." Drew sighed and flipped the bacon in the pan. "She's disappointed I didn't follow Papa in his profession. While we were growing up I only wanted her to be proud of me."

"She *is*."

He shook his head. "How can she be when I don't have a job anymore? I've been dipping into my inheritance from Father each month, but I can't keep going on like this forever. I'm not sure what I should do. Perhaps it's time I wrote some letters to see if any churches in nearby towns are in need of a preacher. I've avoided it, because I didn't want to leave here. Maybe God's calling me to make a fresh start in a new place, somewhere I'm not haunted by continual failures."

"Surely there's another way, Drew." Tears filled his sister's eyes.

"I don't think so. I'll keep praying, but for now, please don't tell anyone." Drew scooped the eggs and bacon from the pans.

"You need to share this burden with Jules. She's your wife."

"No, not yet. I won't risk anything that will jeopardize her health. This is something I need to work through on my own."

"I'm sure David could help in some way. At least confide in him, so he can pray for you."

"No, not this time." He moved away from Sarah. "Would you mind grabbing the plate of food for Mother?"

When he entered the bedroom, silence greeted him. He cleared his throat and handed the steaming food to Jules.

"I recommend you find a way to get along with my wife, Mother, since you'll both be staying in bed for the next week, like it or not."

20

A whole week. Jules's heart sank. How could she survive seven days with her mother-in-law in such close proximity—sharing her bed no less? Having Drew's mother there would lessen her chance of being alone with him. Perhaps it was for the best. How could she face a man who regretted kissing her? What a kiss that had been. *I'd been wondering what it'd be like. If only—*

"Jules? Are you feeling worse? You haven't eaten anything?" Drew's brow wrinkled.

"What? I'm fine." She took a bite of her eggs. "They're good." Her cheeks got hot. "I reckon this is the best breakfast I've had in a while." Jules wanted to snatch the words back as soon as they'd escaped. His ma didn't need to hear what a poor wife she made. Her gaze skittered to her mother-in-law's. The woman's lips were pressed tight together. It probably riled her something awful not to make a nasty comment. Let the dragon stew. Her husband had finally stood up to his ma. She chuckled.

Drew glanced at her, and she couldn't hold back the laughter any longer. It bubbled from her mouth like the fresh springs that ran along the Blanco River. She laughed so hard she soon doubled over because of the pain in her chest from the ragged cough.

The doctor knocked at the open bedroom door.

"I called but nobody answered, so I let myself in. It sounds like I got here right on time. Young lady, it's important to take it easy, and don't do anything to bring on that cough. I'm concerned about you." He pulled out a funny-looking thing from his black bag.

It took a moment for Jules to catch her breath. "What's that there?"

He put part of the thing in his ears. "It's a stethoscope, now shush."

Her heart pounded as he shifted the thing to different parts of her chest. She tried to hold real still. Each time he asked her to take a deep breath, she fell into a fit of coughing. She could hardly take in any air at all by the time he took the item from his ears.

The man's eyes appeared to pierce her clear through. "I don't like the sound of your lungs. Have you been having difficulty breathing, dizziness, headache or sore throat?"

Jules chewed on her lip.

Drew took her hand and squeezed it.

She snatched it away and shifted her gaze toward the doctor. "Yes."

"She fainted earlier."

The doc's brow wrinkled. "It's extremely important not to overdo, so your body has time to heal. I'm ordering bed rest for two weeks, and your color still concerns me. Maybe in a week you'll be strong enough to get a few minutes of fresh air, providing Drew is there to assist you. Do I make myself clear?" He peered at both of them. "Any questions?"

"I'll make sure she obeys orders," Drew said.

The doc walked to the other side of the bed, getting that listening thing ready again. "Good. Let's see how Mrs. Montgomery is faring, shall we?"

Jules tried to hold back a cough while the man listened to her mother-in-law's chest. The doctor's shaggy brows rose whenever Jules coughed. She held her breath, trying to stop the barking.

"Hmm, it appears you are doing much better, ma'am. Should be up and around, well before Jules, but it's important not to drain precious energy. Stay in bed at least the rest of today and tomorrow, but try short times getting up, taking in some fresh air, and see how it goes." The man put everything away, snapping his bag shut then clapped Drew on the back. "Looks like you'll be sleeping in the sitting room for a while yet."

Her mother-in-law scowled at the doc.

"I'll do whatever it takes to get them better." Her husband acted skittish sudden-like.

As much as she didn't like the dragon, Jules welcomed the company and time away from Drew. She needed time to ponder why it hurt so much for him to be sorry for kissing her. Had she been that bad at it?

"Cheer up, Jules. The time will pass quickly. I can come each day, and if you're up to it, we can work on knitting and sewing." Sarah grasped her hand.

"I 'spose." She'd need something to pass the time. *I'll go plumb loco if I think too long on Drew's firm lips.* Heat flamed in her cheeks.

"We'd better let them rest." Doctor Adams interrupted her wayward thoughts. "I'll be back in a couple days, unless you need me sooner."

"Thanks, Doc. I'll see you to the door."

Drew waggled his eyebrows at Jules and smiled as he got up to follow the doctor. She swallowed. *What's he doing that for?*

"I guess I should go too. Get some rest, and I'll see you tomorrow." Sarah waved to them.

The room grew quiet after Sarah closed the door.

Jules didn't feel sleepy. The plate of unfinished food didn't interest her. She shoved it onto the table and chanced a peek at her mother-in-law. The woman stared straight ahead while she finished her breakfast. Jules heaved a sigh.

"What is the matter?" Drew's mother finished the last bite, stretching to place her plate on a small table near the bed. "Are you afraid you will not be able to keep up the deception much longer with me here?"

Jules squinted. *What is she talking about?* So much for being glad to have Mrs. Montgomery around. She cleared her throat. "What's that?"

"It is very obvious, is it not?" Her mother-in-law's face puckered like she'd eaten a handful of sour apples.

"I don't rightly know what yer yappin' about." Jules shifted higher on the bed.

"Drew may be easily fooled, but *I* see right through your schemes."

"Might as well spit it out, ma'am, 'cause I have no idea what yer tryin' to say."

The woman stared at Jules for a good many minutes then said, "I *know* your marriage to Drew is to cover up the fact that you are with child. I am never duped by one's shenanigans."

Jules's mouth gaped open before she shook her head. "I reckon I don't have any idea what them big word means, Mrs. Montgomery, but I can sure enough promise you, I'm not carryin' any child." She curled her hand into a fist.

"I expected you to deny it, but what other reason is there for those continuous stomach woes and your ill appearance as of late?"

Heat blasted Jules's cheeks and neck. "I don't lie, ma'am. I tell you, there ain't no child." She clamped her jaw shut. Nor would there likely ever be one. How could there be when her husband regretted marrying her?

"Harrumph. It is exactly what I would expect you to say." Drew's mother clutched the covers.

"Don't make me wish I hadn't saved yer sorry hide." Jules growled the words, coughing when she finished.

The woman backed off, and it got awful quiet. Did Drew think the same as his ma? She didn't think she wanted to know the answer.

~*~

A couple days of Jules sharing bits and pieces of her life finally wore the dragon down. A hole flickered in her scaly armor. Three days of lying in the same bed probably had something to do with it. If anything, a truce of sorts had been called.

The room swayed in front of her eyes, her skin grew clammy, and she forced her breathing to slow. Maybe she'd overdone it earlier when Drew allowed her up for a few minutes.

"You look as though you are feeling ill." Mrs. Montgomery helped her to the bed and sat beside her.

"I'm sure I'll be as fit as a coyote in a minute."

"I suppose I spoke too harshly the other day. Maybe you are telling the truth about not carrying a child. If you were, I think there would be some signs, but I have not seen any. I guess time will tell."

Jules scratched her head. How could she convince the stubborn woman? It hurt too much to tell her mother-in-law that her son had married Jules to keep his job, and now that had failed too. He hadn't married her for love, or even friendship. Of that she could be sure. Tears welled up, but she refused to let them fall. She forced herself to concentrate on the woman's steady stream of talking.

"I suppose I should thank you. Most would say I am silly for running back into my house the other day. I did not mean to risk your life for me." Mrs. Montgomery stopped for a moment, swiping at her eyes with her bit of cloth. "This handkerchief means the most to me." She waved it.

"W-why is it so special?" Jules reached a hand toward her. The woman hesitated a moment then squeezed it.

"Most people would say I am a sentimental fool, but this hankie was the last thing my husband purchased for me before he died. He gave it as a gift after a trip to New York. The night before he left on another business excursion, we argued. I was furious because he had to leave me and the children once more. He departed the next morning, and I refused to say goodbye."

"What happened?"

"He was killed in a train accident. I never had the opportunity to ask him to forgive me or to tell him I loved him." Her lip trembled. "I have never forgiven myself."

Jules wrapped her arms around her mother-in-law. "I'm so sorry. It must've been awful. How'd you make it through that?"

"I poured my life into the children. I suppose that is not completely truthful. I doted on Sarah. She became my only joy."

"Where'd that leave Drew? You had him too."

"I had a hard time looking at my son because he reminded me so much of his father and how I failed to be a supportive wife when he needed me the most."

The woman's sobs wrung Jules's heart. As she gathered Mrs. Montgomery close, she ached, not only for the loss Drew's mother had experienced, but also for the young boy who'd lost his pa and his ma's love all in one day. Maybe it explained why his ma had become such a cantankerous woman, one who was so difficult to please.

Jules waited while her mother-in-law cried, patting her back from time to time. When the tears finally ceased, she cleared her throat. "H-have you ever told Drew of this?" She halted, hoping the dragon's fire wouldn't spew.

"How could I? He would not understand." She sniffed and blew her nose.

"You've gotta. He's never said, but I figure he's purty sure you don't think a whole lot of him. You ride him mighty hard most of the time, and I don't reckon he knows if you love him or not. High time somethin' got done about it. Who knows, maybe this happened so you'd finally make things right with yer son."

"Do you think so? I should tell him right away then." Mrs. Montgomery wrapped a blanket around Jules's shoulders. "Get some rest, dear. I need to go have a talk with my son."

~*~

Drew couldn't explain how Jules had managed it, but somehow, she'd brought a transformation in his mother's heart. *I guess I have You to thank too, Lord.* He'd hoped but never believed it would actually happen, especially after all those years of distance. Drew couldn't wait to personally thank his wife. He'd been waiting for the opportunity for days. Mother sat in the kitchen, and he finally had some time to speak with Jules alone. He hurried to the bedroom. When he got there, she was fast asleep.

He eased his body onto the side of the bed, careful not to awaken her. The scent of wildflowers drifted to his nostrils. Sarah had helped Jules bathe and wash her hair earlier in the morning when she'd come for her daily visit. She'd insisted it wasn't good for the two women to constantly smell smoke in their hair, and high time they did something about it. His sister had ordered him to heat water and fill the tub, then shooed him from the house.

Jules stirred as he fingered the drying locks of soft hair. She whimpered, and her whole body trembled. Her eyelids fluttered and she thrust her arm forward. Her fingers gripped him like steel.

"Sweetheart?" He spoke softly so he wouldn't startle her.

She continued to thrash. "Careful, Josh. Appears like they're up ahead of us." She picked at her hip, as if trying to draw her six-shooter. She must be having the same bad dream again. "Those low-down, dirty varmints aren't goin' to hurt nobody ever again, just you wait and see." She growled the words. Her eyes darted back and forth beneath her closed eyelids. "I'll protect you." Sweat glistened on her upper lip. "Bad Bart and his brother aren't goin' to get the best of us."

Bart? Hadn't she mentioned Burt the last time she'd had this nightmare? His wife struggled to a crouched position in the bed. Surely she would awaken. She stayed in the pose for a good many minutes then finally settled down again. He thought the worst was past, until she groaned and rolled from side-to-side, mumbling about the flames and heat. Had her dream transitioned to her time in the house, attempting to rescue Mother? His heart constricted wishing he could somehow take the pain away from her.

"Flames. Hot. Alone…so alone. Everybody's left me. Drew come back." The words ripped from her lips as if from her very soul. Tears streamed down her cheeks but she remained asleep.

"I'm here, sweetheart." He thumbed away her tears. "Shh, Jules, you're safe with me. There's no need to worry."

She shuddered, sighing before her eyes fluttered open. "Drew? Where am I?"

"In our home, Jules, in your bed." He tucked a perspired strand of hair behind her ear. "You were having another nightmare. Do you remember what happened?"

The haunted expression in her eyes confirmed his question. Her lips trembling, she glanced away.

"I think you've had the same dream before, am I right? Perhaps you'd feel better if you told me about it."

"W-why would you say that?" Her gaze darted towards his then sprang away.

"Because the same things keep coming through."

She licked her lips. "L-like what?"

"You've referred to the name Burt or Bart. Whoever he or they are seems to have something to do with your brother. I believe you were dreaming about the fire too, because you mentioned the flames and being hot." He longed to take her in his arms. "There's nothing to worry about, sweetheart. You're safe with me. I promise to take care of you. There's no need to be scared of being alone anymore."

~*~

Jules's heart raced like a herd of wild mustangs. Her mouth went dry, and she couldn't speak. How had she talked about all those things in her sleep and not been aware of it? Why, oh, why, did Drew have to be the one to hear them? She shuddered. There was no way she was going to risk him learning more about her past. He wouldn't want her if he ever learned the truth.

"Sweetie, are you okay? You're face has gone white all of a sudden. Do you need something? A glass of water?"

Jules shook her head. She'd do whatever it took to get him to forget those dreams. She combed through her brain until an idea sprang up. Was it any better than what he was jawing about? *I have no other choice.* She swallowed. "Is it true?"

He raised his eyebrows. "Is what true, sweetheart?"

She gulped. "Yer mother said she believed me to be with child afore we married. Do you think the same way?"

He licked his lips and swallowed hard a couple times.

"There's been no other man in my life, Drew, and I'm not carryin' anybody's babe. Of all people, I thought you'd know that."

"Yes, Jules." He swiped his hand across his forehead.

Drew said the right words, but can I believe him?

21

The envelope had scorched his chest ever since Drew placed it in his pocket over two weeks ago. He had yet to break the seal and read its contents. Mother hadn't given him any explanation when she'd handed it to him. The picture of an eye and the words, 'we never sleep' confirmed it held a missive from the Pinkerton Detective Agency. His gut clenched. Did he really want to read the results of the inquiry into Jules's past? Would it do any good to stir things up when for the past two months they had enough halts and starts in their relationship?

"Drew, where's Pepper?"

He welcomed the interruption and forced a smile as Jules strolled toward him. How he longed for a real marriage, but she'd been distant since the day of the fire. He couldn't help but feel it had something to do with his kiss. After his apology for the kiss, she'd withdrawn. He mentally kicked himself each day for how he'd handled the situation, but he didn't know how to go back and change it either. Drew bit back a groan. *If only she'll soften her heart to the Lord. It'll make life so much easier.*

"What'd you ask about the pup?"

"I haven't seen him all morning. He loves to run all over the country, but I thought he'd be back by now." Jules scanned the horizon.

"I'll watch for him on my way to David's."

She bit her lip. "Can I come too?"

"Not today, Jules. I won't be long. I promise." He stopped himself from embracing her. Ever since she'd become more aloof, he found himself wishing more for her affection. It didn't make any sense. Would she ever have feelings for him?

She shifted her gaze away from him. "Mind askin' David and Sarah to lunch after church tomorrow? It's been a few weeks since we got together, and I miss her. Besides, I want to show her my latest sewin' project."

"Ah, the mysterious activity you've been working on. Could it have something to do with Christmas next week?" Drew clasped her hand.

A smile flitted across her face, but it wasn't reflected in her eyes. "I reckon this isn't the time of year to be askin' such a question."

She pivoted toward the house, and he fell into step with her.

"Hope Sarah will have the baby sometime soon. Sure would make a special Christmas gift, don't ya think?"

"Yes. It *would* be momentous if their child were to share a birthday with the celebration of Jesus' birth." What would it be like to hold a child of his own in his arms? *Will I ever have the opportunity?* He cleared his throat. A sudden urge to pull her into an embrace and kiss her until she molded herself to him surged. Picturing that almost overwhelmed him. She'd been as skittish as a newborn colt lately.

"Is somethin' wrong?"

Her words yanked him back to their conversation. Fire crept up his neck and into his cheeks.

"Drew, you comin' down with somethin'?" Her eyebrows rose.

"No, I'm fine, just fine. I'd best be on my way." He snapped his hat in place.

"Be careful, and don't forget to keep an eye open for Pepper. He's probably chasin' a rabbit or some other critter."

He stalled for an instant when she mentioned the word 'eye'. She hadn't caught a glimpse of the envelope, had she? "I'll be home soon." He kissed her forehead and hugged her, not giving himself time to think about it. He took off at a sprint toward the barn.

The ride to his brother-in-law's house went faster than he would've liked. He'd hoped to have more time to compose his thoughts before he shared them with his friend, but they continued to be jumbled when he arrived at the farm. Joyful and Pepper greeted him.

"So, this is where you've been, little scamp. Your mistress has been terribly worried." He knelt to pet them both.

"Pepper showed up earlier today." David stepped from the barn. "I guess he aimed for a social call." He chuckled. "It's been awhile since *you* last visited, long enough I'd almost think it was intentional."

Drew swallowed the lump in his throat. "Not exactly. Been busy is all." He darted a glance at his brother-in-law.

"Let's go to the house, and we can talk it over." He clapped Drew on the shoulder. "Sarah laid down for a nap a bit ago, so we'll have the kitchen to ourselves."

He bit back a sigh as they strolled toward the house.

"I think there's some leftover coffee on the stove. It must've been cold riding here." David tucked a rag into his pocket.

A few minutes later they sat enjoying their hot brew.

Drew chewed on the inside of his cheek contemplating how to start the conversation. He had yet to come to a conclusion when his brother-in-law interrupted his thoughts.

"Might as well share what's been eating you the past couple months. I don't understand what's taken so long."

Had he been *that* obvious? Had anybody else noticed? *Jules?* He squared his shoulders and took another sip of his coffee. "Actually there are a couple things on my mind." He slid the envelope out of his pocket and dropped it on the table in front of David.

"What's that?"

"When Jules first arrived, Mother contacted a detective to check into her background. Remember? She determined to find a way to end our marriage. Mother gave that to me two weeks ago." He nudged the envelope further away.

"What's it say?"

"I suspect it's the result of whatever the Pinkerton agent discovered. I haven't been able to bring myself to open it yet."

"Let me ask, are you afraid that what's inside will maybe change how you regard Jules?"

"I don't know." Drew jammed his fingers through his hair. "There's something she hasn't told me, and she keeps avoiding it whenever possible."

"How so?"

"She has recurring nightmares, and they always seem to center around two different things. One I believe is from the day of the fire, because she often speaks about the flames and being alone when she cries in her sleep. But the other, and the more bothersome of the two, concerns someone in Texas."

"Has talk of her past come up?" David lifted the envelope, tapping the corner of it on his hand.

"Not really, except for the things she's shared with all of us. Whenever she has the dream she appears to be aiming a gun at something or someone. She mentions somebody named Burt or Bart.

I'm not sure if they are the same person or not, but always she's trying to protect her brother Josh from whatever the danger is. At least from what I can gather." Drew ran his hand across his stubbled chin.

"What exactly does her brother do?"

"I recall her saying something to do with him working as a deputy for the U.S. Marshals, but I'm not sure, and I guess that's what's worrying me. It has to be bad if she's not willing to discuss it."

"What makes you suspect she's hiding it?"

"Every time she has one of those dreams she won't answer my questions. She changes the topic or comes up with a clever way of evading a direct answer. I suppose that's why it's taken me so long to work up the courage to open the letter." Drew leaned toward the missive.

"Wait. Are you prepared to deal with whatever it says? Will it change how you feel about Jules if she doesn't fit your expectations?"

Drew chuckled. "She hasn't been anything like I expected."

"How's that going? From what I've witnessed, your relationship had improved some there for a while, but lately she seems less comfortable. What changed?" His brother-in-law surveyed him over his cup.

Drew fidgeted with the envelope, running the edge along his fingers. How could he tell David he'd messed things up by kissing Jules prematurely and taken it back? He hadn't understood his actions himself. "I'm not sure." He avoided David's piercing glare.

David rubbed his chin. "I've heard all over town how you've been helping people, but how does that show Jules the kind of love she should experience from a husband? She's lost her glow, and I can't help but think it's not her fault. Is it the fact that she's not accepted Christ? It takes faith to believe she'll be saved. Sarah senses she's closer to it all the time." He lifted an eyebrow. "I've also noticed you've been holding something in and have wondered what it is."

Drew cleared his throat. "Actually, I've been meaning to discuss that. I-I've been seeking another preaching position." He glanced at his friend.

"And?"

"Nothing. I've sent out letters as far away as Topeka, but apparently no one has need of a minister. I don't understand it, David. I've done everything suggested, and yet, God has stayed silent."

"In what way?"

"I've helped anyone who's mentioned needing assistance, but my former job hasn't been restored. All my letters are returned with the words, 'we have no need of a new minister at this time.' The elders are no closer to reinstating me either. I'm trying to show affection to Jules and not work at changing her." His cheeks burned. "What else I'm supposed to do?"

"When's the last time you truly were still and quiet?"

"I don't see what that has to do with anything." He shoved back his chair and rose.

"Hear me out. Sit down, and don't get testy."

Drew reluctantly obeyed.

"I'd say you've probably been working *too* hard at helping people, and *too* hard at sending inquires for a position. Where does loving and showing love of Jules fit in that?"

Had he been loving his wife? Drew drummed his fingers on the table, not sure how Jules would answer that question. "It's what you advised me to do. Remember?"

David held up his hand. "Now wait just a minute. Recall what else I told you to do."

Drew refused to squirm and instead, scowled at his brother-in-law.

"Let me refresh your memory, it had something to do with a verse in Psalms."

"I know, I know. 'Be still, and know that I am God: I will be exalted among the heathen, I will be exalted among the earth.' But what good does it do me? I've been sharing my faith with Jules, and as of yet, she hasn't made a decision to follow God. What else am I expected to do? I've been praying, but God's not answering."

"Maybe He is, and you haven't been listening."

"What's that supposed to mean? I've not been deep enough in my faith? Is that it?" Drew slammed his fist on the table.

"No. Simmer down so you don't wake Sarah."

Drew lowered his voice. "Sorry."

"Forgiven. Drew, when's the last time you were truly quiet and were able to hear God? I think you've been so busy serving, the listening's been forgotten. What if He says He doesn't want you preaching but has another assignment in mind? Are you willing to obey a different set of plans?"

Has preaching been my plan instead of His? Hadn't that come from

God? The book of Psalms also mentioned delighting in God and how He promises to give man the desires of his heart. Drew longed to serve through preaching and leading a congregation. Surely David couldn't fault him for that. His aim was noble, in fact. Maybe he *needed* someone else's guidance.

"Wait just a minute. Listen without getting peeved. Drew, I realize you've been working hard and trying your best, but have you fully given the whole thing to the Lord?"

Drew winced. He'd been praying and asking for God's will in his life. He hated to admit it, but he also expected God to answer the way he wanted. Had God been showing him a different way the entire time? He dropped his head to his hands.

"God may restore you to the minister position at the church, Drew. I don't know. I believe the main issue is for you to be open and trust Him no matter *what* happens. Do you think you can do that?"

"Maybe God's called David Brown to preach instead of me."

"No. That's not my place." His brother-in-law patted Drew's shoulder. "You've only lost sight of the path where He's leading for a bit. It happens to all of us at one time or another. Don't take it so hard. That's why fellowship is so important. We can lift each other up when we're having struggles, because we all face them at one time or another. Believe me, I've had plenty."

"I've been so foolish."

"Don't allow Satan to win by discouragement and defeat, my friend. The important thing is, what's going to change, and how will you do things differently?"

"To begin with, I need to spend some time alone with God to see what His will is for my life and *listen* for His answer. I guess it wouldn't hurt to say something to Jules too. I haven't told her I've been searching for a position at other places."

"It's time to let her in on what's been going on. Maybe she's not sharing her thoughts or feelings because she senses you withholding something. Women have an uncanny way of knowing things. Drew, don't be afraid to seek her counsel too, even though she isn't a believer."

"What?"

David leaned closer, smiling. "Do *not* let on to Sarah, but there's plenty of times she's advised me and been right. I've learned to seek her wisdom when I have a decision to make, especially one that affects both of us. You'd be wise to do the same thing."

"I suppose."

"How about we pray now, Drew?"

"I'd appreciate it."

Both men bowed their heads. "Dear Lord, thanks for my brother and friend. Drew's mighty special, Lord, but You already know that. I pray for wisdom and direction as he seeks what to do. May he not be afraid to let go and trust You're going to be there for him. Guide and direct him to Your will. Help him to be patient as he waits for an answer. We pray too, Lord, for Jules. She needs to come to salvation, so we ask for a softening of her heart. Place her in situations that cause her to make a decision to serve and follow You. God, may Your love show through Drew so Jules can see it. Use the hard learning and growing times we face because it's in the midst of those times we realize our need to depend upon You. Thanks for Drew finally getting a glimpse of what You wanted to tell him. In Jesus' name, amen."

Drew wiped a tear from his cheek. "Thanks, brother."

"Glad I could help. Ready to open that letter?" David handed him a knife.

Drew slit the edge and pulled out the single sheet of paper with unsteady hands. The knife clattered to the table as he read the few lines scattered across the page. Raising his gaze to David, he dropped the paper, and it fluttered to the floor.

22

Drew hadn't been the same since he'd gotten home yesterday afternoon. He went to his study, came out long enough for supper, and then high-tailed it back to the room again.

Jules had waited for him to come out, but her tired body had given up. Too many sleepless nights had taken their toll. She'd gone to bed without seeing him. This morning, she stood in front of the mirror brushing her hair. How could she bring up whatever ailed him? A knock at the door halted her brush mid-air.

Drew stepped into the room and sat on the bed.

She fumbled the brush with nervous fingers, and it clattered to the floor.

"Here, allow me." Drew scooped up the brush and ran it through her hair.

She almost forgot how to breathe, it felt so good. What had caused the sudden change in him? Didn't matter. She lapped it up like a horse drinking after a long day with no water. "Mmm. That's right nice." She tipped her head, allowing him better reach. "Josh told me I used to love to have Ma brush my hair at night. I don't remember it though. Wish I did."

"You've not said much about your past." He cleared his throat. "I've been meaning to ask."

She groaned, stepped away, and missed his care at the same time. "I'm afraid it'll have to wait. We don't want to be late for church. I'll have our food ready in two shakes of a dish towel."

His arms snaked around her waist, holding her, his breath tickling her neck. "We do need to talk, Jules, but I know there isn't time this morning, or we won't make it to service."

"What will folks say if the preacher is late?" She bit her lip so hard it drew blood. "I'm sorry, I didn't mean to…"

"Don't worry, sweetheart. Think nothing of it. Let's get some breakfast." He smiled as his gaze fell to her lips.

Her stomach did a funny flip.

A short time later, she struggled to pay attention to the circuit preacher's sermon about a baby being born in a place called Bethlehem. The clock on the shelf didn't seem to be working. The minute hand had barely moved, and Jules felt as though she'd been sitting for an hour already. She shifted on her seat for the fourth time or more. She'd lost count.

Drew's brow wrinkled.

She stopped fidgeting, although it proved to be a mighty hard task.

When church finally got done, she leaned close to Sarah. "I need to say somethin' to you."

"Are you feeling all right?"

"No…yes…I mean…we've got to talk." She hoped Drew hadn't heard her.

"Perhaps we could go for a walk after our meal. I need to stretch my legs after sitting for so long. David hovers so, I can hardly move without being told to take it easy." Sarah rubbed the side of her swelled belly.

They broke away from the pack of folks and strolled toward the house. The two of them worked together to get the food on the table.

Jules's had a hard time keeping up with the talking as they ate. Things seemed a might uncomfortable between the men.

Drew smiled at her a lot while they ate, but she could tell something was eating at him. His face stretched in a smile, but it didn't reach his eyes. Something had happened while he'd been gone yesterday.

Once the dishes were washed and put away, Jules moved closer to Drew. She longed to run her fingers through his hair but held back.

"Drew, uh, Sarah and I want to go for a walk."

"I don't think so," David interrupted. "Sarah's too close to when the baby is due."

"Nonsense. The exercise will do me good, and there's no reason why I shouldn't walk. Doc says exercise is fine as long as I don't overdo. You worry too much." Sarah winked at her husband.

"Why don't we all go together," Drew said.

"We wanted time for woman-talk. If Sarah has trouble I can run for the doc. We'll take Pepper too." Jules held her breath.

Pepper barked and jumped at hearing his name.

"I don't know..." David ran his fingers across Sarah's shoulders.

Drew chuckled. "I guess we're out-numbered, David, especially with the dog chiming in too."

"We won't be long." Sarah's hand rested on her husband's chest, gazing into his eyes.

"I don't know for sure, Drew, but I think Sarah's using her feminine wiles to convince me to do what they want."

Sarah grinned.

Jules fiddled with the cuff of her sleeve.

"Go, have your talk." Drew tapped her chin, starring at her eyes.

What did he see?

"If you're not back within an hour, we'll be finding you." David hugged Sarah.

Jules follow her sister-in-law, and swung the door shut behind them.

"I reckon we'd never get to leave." Jules snapped her fingers when Pepper got too far ahead of them. "Stay with us, boy."

"What's so important you couldn't wait to tell me?" Sarah arched her back, walking at a slow pace.

"Did David say what the men jawed on yesterday when Drew came over?"

"Drew visited my place? I hadn't realized that."

"You sure he didn't say anythin' about it last evening or this morning? Maybe you forgot."

"No. You're making me nervous. What's going on?" Sarah pulled Jules to a stop and stared at her.

"I can't figure it. Drew left the house saying he had to talk to David. When he hugged me goodbye, I could hear a paper rustlin' in his coat pocket. I'm not sure if that's what he needed to talk on, or if it was somethin' else. All I know is when he got home last night he weren't himself and hasn't been since."

"He seemed fine to me." Her sister-in-law started her slow waddle again.

Jules shook her head. "No. I can tell. He spent the night holed up in his study like a jack rabbit too stubborn to come from his burrow. He wouldn't say what he was doin' neither."

"Maybe reading his Bible?"

"I don't think so. Every night he's been readin' it to me, and last night he plumb forgot because of whatever he was doin' in the study. I have a mind to ask him."

"Has he mentioned anythi—"

Jules yanked her sister-in-law to a halt. "You *do* know somethin', Sarah Brown. Spit it out."

Sarah wouldn't face her, and she wrung her hands. "I promised Drew I wouldn't share what he planned on doing."

"Say anythin' about what, Sarah?"

"I shouldn't, really. I promised Drew months ago…"

"Months ago?" She spat out the words. "He's been keepin' somethin' from me that long? I knew there was some kind of worryin' in him. Why not tell me? I've seen how David shares thing with you. I'm Drew's wife...I have a right to know." Jules paced back and forth.

"I told him he should tell…he wanted to wait...it happened right after the fire, and his concern then was for you and Mother." Sarah nibbled on her lip. "Ask Drew, Jules. He made me promise not to tell."

Jules sighed and linked arms with her sister-in-law. "I'm sorry if I'm being cantankerous." Her lip quivered. "I'd hoped he'd tell me about whatever's frettin' him so." *Wish he'd told me instead of David.* She scratched her head. Could *that* be what he'd wanted earlier?

"Don't be too hard on him. I'm sure it's been difficult for him to lose his pastorate."

"You're right. I reckon I need to work at being more helpful-like." Jules glanced at the horizon. "I aim to find what he's been keepin' from me. Guess for now, we best 'preciate our walk afore the fellas try to find us." She'd deal with her man later.

~*~

Drew tapped his fingers on the table.

"Have you said anything to Jules yet?"

"No. I made no plans since reading the letter from the detective."

"What happened when you got back home?"

"I spent time in prayer, had supper with Jules, and spent the rest of the evening reading my Bible, and begging God to show me how to respond." Drew sighed. "He hasn't given me an answer yet, and I can't ask Jules until I get some direction from the Lord."

"I'm thankful you're truly seeking His guidance now, Drew, but don't wait any longer to say something to your wife. Don't allow things to fester, or it might get nasty. Maybe the information in the letter isn't correct, or isn't all there."

Drew jabbed his fingers through his hair. "We both know the reputation of the Pinkerton Agency, David."

"There may be a simple explanation. Don't jump to conclusions until you hear the full story from Jules."

"How can you say such a thing?" Drew ripped the letter from his pocket, but he didn't need to read it again. The words were forever branded in his memory.

Dear Mrs. Montgomery,

After a thorough investigation, we have learned the

woman in question, one Julia Anne Walker, killed a man in Texas last December. If we can be of further assistance, please contact our office.

The Pinkerton Detective Agency

Drew ground his teeth together. *His wife* had murdered a man. No wonder she kept having bad dreams. His hands trembled. Things would never be the same between them. No matter how he worked at learning to love her, there seemed to always be a barrier. Maybe God had been trying to show him all along, and he'd been too hardheaded to understand it.

~*~

The women stopped to rest at a small grove of trees a quarter of a mile from town. Jules longed to ask Sarah questions to do with husbands and wives. She'd waited for months, and Drew had no interest in kissing her, unless one counted the peck he'd given her yesterday. She still didn't know if that was the right word for that kind of caring. Whatever folks called it, she could tell he'd done it without thinking it over… not as if it was special-like for them. She'd spent many restless nights trying to figure what she'd done wrong the day of the fire, but no answer had come.

"I don't know, Jules, but I'm exhausted. Who'd have thought carrying a baby took so much of a woman's energy." Sarah wiped her perspiring forehead.

Jules stifled a yawn and studied the sky. "I reckon we should head to town soon, or our men will worry."

"Yes, but I need to close my eyes and catch my breath a few minutes first." Sarah eased her cumbersome body to the ground.

"I suppose I could use a short break too." Jules couldn't stop her next yawn. "Come here, Pepper." She peered at the countryside. No soul in sight. She eased the kinks from her stiff body. It wouldn't hurt to rest a short while. They had plenty of time to get home, so the men wouldn't get riled.

Pepper bounded up and licked her face.

"I reckon we can sit for a spell." She sank to the ground beside Sarah who already looked as if she'd fallen asleep. Another yawn nearly split Jules's jaw. A few minutes of shuteye and they'd head for town. "Stay, boy." She issued the command as her eyes fluttered closed.

~*~

Something startled Jules awake. She sat up, searching for Sarah. Her sister-in-law slept beside her. The hair raised on the back of her neck. Something was *surely* wrong. That feeling always meant trouble was close by. She reached for her weapon at her hip out of habit, but it didn't hang at its normal place. Drew's worrying over what other people thought made her stop wearing and carrying any guns, 'especially on Sundays. He'd talked her into letting her guard down, and she sure was sorry. The knife she'd kept in her boot had been forgotten at the house in her hurry to talk to Sarah. She was helpless. Jules's gaze sharpened, as she looked around to get a bead on where the danger was hiding.

A sack went over her head, and the business-end of a gun was shoved into her back.

Jules screamed, struggled and kicked as hard as she could.

Rough hands grabbed hers, pinned her down and tied her wrists together.

"Shut yer face, or I'll kill you now."

Ice ran through her veins.

"Bart. What's yer sorry hide doin' outta jail?"

The bag ripped from her head, and he slapped her hard across the mouth. She stumbled backward, but he caught her as she fell. Blood filled her mouth as he gagged her with his filthy neckerchief.

"There. I don't want to hear yer whining no more." He jerked the sack back in place.

Sarah grunted and struggled beside her.

Pepper growled deep, followed by a yelp when something hard hit the dog.

Tears streamed down Jules's cheeks. *Please…God…I don't know You very good but please let Sarah and Pepper be all right.* Her mind went blank for a moment, there was something else. "Amen," she whispered around the rag in her mouth.

"Well, well, ain't this interesting. A pregnant whore and a—"

Jules ducked her head and plowed in the direction of Bart's voice before he could finish his sentence, only to stumble and fall headlong into the dirt. Pain shot through her gut.

Sarah whimpered.

There was the familiar creak of a saddle, and then Bart shoved her onto the back of a horse. She got her hands around the saddle horn, hanging on tight. A sourness from her stomach rose to the back of her throat. She quieted her raging thoughts and listened to the sounds.

Bart thrust Sarah onto the horse behind Jules. Sarah's whole body trembled against her. Her sister-in-law's fingers grasped the back of Jules's dress and held tight. Leather squeaked as Bart swung up onto his own horse.

He must've been planning her capture for a while. Her throat went dry. It'd been almost a year since she'd last seen him and his twin brother. Jules shivered. She'd never forget *that* day.

"Giddy up."

The horses clipped along at a fast pace.

The wind in her face sucked away her breath.

Sarah was weeping.

They rode hard for a long time. Jules figured they'd crossed at least one stream, maybe two. The first time the water stood high enough it splashed onto her dress, chilling her right away. Sarah must've gotten wet too. Was she doing all right?

Bart had stopped at the last stream for a few minutes to water the horses.

The further they rode, the heavier Jules's chest felt. How would Drew ever find them? The temperature dropped, and she figured it had to be close to nightfall. Bart would have to stop soon, or he'd kill the horses with this pace. Her legs throbbed from riding all afternoon, and her fingers were numb from clutching the saddle horn or the horse's mane.

Sarah slumped against her, and Jules wondered if she'd fallen asleep. If only she could somehow get word to Drew. She'd been so worried about her sister-in-law that she hadn't taken note of whether they'd traveled through the corn-stubbed field or stuck to the main road.

Too bad Josh isn't here. He'd know what to do. Without her weapons, she didn't have a way to defend herself or Sarah. Drew's words floated through her mind to haunt her. One day you'll find all your weapons won't be enough. The question is what will you do then? Jules shuddered.

23

Drew peered out the window for possibly the twentieth time. Jules and Sarah were nowhere in sight. He dropped the curtain back into place.

David rose. "We need to go after them."

"Surely nothing has happened, and they're merely late." Drew ran his hand through his hair.

"I don't doubt they got busy talking and walking and forgot the time. Pepper's with them, and he would've returned if something was wrong." David pulled on his coat and gloves.

"I reckon you're right."

David chuckled. "That sounds more like Jules."

Drew smiled. "Guess I do."

"Come on, old man. Let's check on our tardy wives. It's the last time I plan on allowing my wife to go for a walk without me." David held the door open.

"Me, too." Drew shrugged into his coat. "Happen to notice which direction they went?"

"I saw them heading north through town." David rubbed his arms. "Brr. The wind sure is picking up. Maybe we'll end up with snow in time for Christmas."

"Jules would love that. She's said they don't often get snow in Texas, and she's been hoping we'd get some soon." Drew examined the sky. "I don't like the way the temperatures have dropped the past hour. Surely the women would've returned once it started getting cold."

"We're sure to meet them on the way."

They walked fifteen minutes in silence.

Lost in his thoughts, Drew didn't want to waste time with small talk. He'd feel much better once he knew Jules was safe, and he could get her home, away from the bitter wind.

When they got to the outskirts of town not a soul could be seen.

Drew's gut roiled. He viewed the stand of trees just ahead.

"Think they went a different direction?" David scanned the horizon. "I don't know where they could've gone."

Drew shrugged.

They continued walking.

He pointed at a small mound just beyond the trees. "There's something lying there." Ice took up residence in his chest. *Dear Lord, don't let it be Jules.* He took off at a sprint.

"I can see from here it's bleeding badly." David panted at his side.

Drew's heart sank when he saw the mangled body. "It's Pepper." He bent to see if the dog was alive.

"He's barely breathing." David touched the dog's head. "Appears he's been kicked with the toe of a boot. He's hurt bad."

Drew gathered the dog into his arms. Jules's pet didn't move. Not even a whimper. His head lagged to the side, and he lay limp in Drew's arms. He cradled the mutt close while David inspected the ground.

"I'm not good at tracking, but it looks as if the women rested on the stretch of grass here by the trees. There are lots of hoof prints, Drew. I can't tell how many horses though." He moved a few paces away. His face drained of color when he stooped to pick up something.

"What is it?"

"I-It's the hankie your mother gave Sarah last year for her birthday. She's taken to carrying it all the time too. I'm sure they were here." David swallowed hard.

"They were taken, weren't they?" Drew's gut clenched.

His brother-in-law nodded.

~*~

If they didn't stop soon, Jules feared they'd both topple from the horse. Her body wasn't used to hours in the saddle anymore, and Sarah's never had been. *Lord, I don't rightly deserve You takin' note of my prayers, since we ain't acquainted-like, but could You send someone to help us? If not for me, at least for Sarah's sake. She loves You and talks about how good You are. Sure could use an extra dose of vinegar while You're at it,*

Lord, 'cause I don't think we can hold on much longer...'specially Sarah.

Her mind raced, figuring how best to get them unsnarled. Why hadn't her brother somehow warned her? How had Bart escaped from jail? Last she'd heard he'd been sentenced for life.

A coyote's howl echoed through the night. The blowing wind chilled her to the bone. With the steady drop in temperatures, she wouldn't be surprised if it started snowing soon. That'd be nice if they wasn't with Madman Bart, but it'd cover their tracks, making it harder to be found.

Jules tried to roll her stiff shoulders without knocking Sarah off the horse. Her muscles were stiff after sitting so long, and she had no idea how much time had passed. Uncontrollable shivers racked her body while other demands pressed at her too. When the horse slowed, she decided to take the risk. She let go of the saddle and leaned to the side, bracing as she fell off the horse to roll on her side. Sarah tumbled after her. Jules hoped her body softened the fall for her sister-in-law. Sarah's "oomph" didn't sound as though she was hurt. She huddled close.

"Fool women." Bart swore under his breath.

Delayed pain shot through Jules, and she tried to ease Sarah off without hurting her. A gun pressed against her forehead, halting her movements.

"I should kill you now, but I won't. It's too early. How does it feel knowing there's only four more days to live?" His laugh was low and guttural.

Four days. Her feeble mind took a while to figure the dates. *December twenty-third.* A chill ran through her. One year to the day from when she'd killed his brother. *Lord, this can't be happening.*

She struggled with the sack tied around her neck. Bart slapped her hands and yanked the rope, scraping her tender skin. He jerked the bag from her head. Her eyes had trouble focusing.

"What d'ya want?"

Her stiff fingers fumbled with the gag.

Bart untied it.

She motioned toward her sister-in-law.

"Spit out what ya want so we can get moving. Can't take a chance of anybody catching up." He cackled.

"We need to attend to, uh, private matters and could use some food and water." Jules stood her ground, not cowering to him. "Untie her."

"Yer not the one to be making demands, missy." He spat a stream of tobacco juice at her feet.

Jules shot him a glare.

Bart finally yanked the bag from Sarah's face but left the gag in place.

"Take care of business with yer hands tied. There ain't no way I'm budging on that." He motioned to a small bunch of bushes. "Be back here in two minutes, or I'm coming to get ya."

"Untie her bandana."

"No way. I don't need two hens squawking together. Get on with yer business. Time's a ticking."

~*~

Drew supported the dog as they ran toward town. He prayed while they sprinted. His thoughts were jumbled, and he couldn't formulate a plan of what they should do next.

"Let's drop Pepper off at Doc Adams' place." David panted by the time they entered town.

Unwilling to waste any energy, Drew didn't answer. Arriving at the doctor's residence, he kicked the door.

David raised his fist to pound on the wood slab, but it swung open.

Doc Adams squinted. "What do we have here?"

"Doc, I know it's not something you normally do, but my wife's dog needs immediate attention. He's been badly injured. Please take a look at him." Drew shoved his way into the house, not allowing the man the chance to say no.

"What happened?" The doc asked, puzzlement lining his features.

"He was kicked, I think." Drew eased the dog onto the doctor's examining table. "Thanks, Doc. I'm much obliged. I'll check in later, but David and I need to find our wives now."

"Find your wives?" The man's scraggly eyebrows bunched toward each other.

"The women went for a walk a while ago and haven't come home. We found Pepper injured in the road, and I found my wife's handkerchief in the same area where there were hoof prints." David ran a hand through his hair.

"Something happened to them?"

"It appears so. We need to get going, Doc." Drew shoved his hat on his head.

"Go on. I can't make any promises. The dog's chances of pulling through are pretty slim with how he looks, but I'll do what I can to take good care of the pup. I'll be praying you find your wives. Go on now so I can get busy." He motioned toward the door.

David and Drew went out to the street.

"What now? Where do we start?" Drew's gaze swiveled around searching for any movement on the landscape.

"Let's double check the house to make sure they didn't get there by a different route. Although I can't imagine Jules leaving Pepper in the middle of the road like that." David's worried tone didn't hide his fear.

There was *no* way Jules would have left Pepper, unless something was dreadfully wrong. *Dear Lord, what am I to do?* Drew's fingers fumbled with the latch at his door. The women wouldn't be inside, but he held his breath as he nudged the door open.

David ran through each room of the house calling for Sarah and Jules.

No answer came.

His friend sank to his knees. "What do we do?"

"We should rally the town. We can't find them on our own, we need help." Drew helped David to his feet. "And...we have to remain strong."

"Right."

They rushed out and crossed to the schoolyard.

Drew yanked on the rope. The bell clanged.

People streamed from their houses, donning winter coats while running.

Drew kept tugging on the rope so folks on the outskirts of town would also be alerted. His arms ached as did his heart.

The crowd milled around, waiting. David wove through the mass to the front, raising his hand for silence. "Thanks for coming. Drew and I need your help. We believe our wives were taken by someone sometime this afternoon."

Amid the uproar while everyone asked questions, Edward Miller stepped forward and placed a hand on Drew's shoulder. "Settle down, folks. Give the preacher time to talk." With a nod, he continued, "Go ahead, Pastor."

"We aren't sure what happened. Jules and Sarah left with my wife's dog almost two hours ago to go for a short walk. We haven't seen them since then."

"Maybe they walked back to Sarah's house, Pastor. Should've gone there first." Someone from the crowd interjected.

"No, we haven't gone there, but we have reason to believe they were taken." A sob choked Drew's throat.

David placed his hand on Drew's other shoulder. "We found Jules's dog left for dead at the grove of trees on the north side of town. There were also hoof prints, and I found Sarah's handkerchief, so the women had been there, and their tracks didn't lead away from the spot."

"Why would someone take two women? It doesn't make any sense." Murmurs ran through the crowd.

Edward held up his hand and the people silenced. "Now, folks, we're not getting anywhere if we keep on like this. Let's simmer down and come up with a plan. Henry, ride to the Browns' place and make sure the women aren't there. If they are, fire off a shot." Edward motioned, "Women, search through town to make sure they haven't been missed. Fellas, we'll split up into groups of four and head from town in all directions. David, did you say they were last seen on the north end of town?"

"Yes. Maybe we should concentrate most of the men in that vicinity. If we get moving, we'll have a few hours of daylight left to follow the tracks made by the horses."

"You heard him, boys. Saddle up, and let's go. Don't forget, if they're found, fire off a single shot. Let's bow in prayer, and then we'll get going." Edward tugged his hat from his head. "Dear Lord, we pray for wisdom as we search for these two women. Direct our paths so we can find them. Guide our steps and keep everyone safe. Amen."

The crowd started to disperse. Edward gripped David and Drew each by an arm. "I know you fellas want to take off right away, but I think someone should stay at your house in case the women make their way home."

Drew shook his head. He wasn't staying home when Jules needed him.

David tensed, and Drew suspected he was of the same mind.

Gertrude touched her father's arm. "I can stay, Papa."

The man smiled at his daughter. "Thanks, dear."

An arm wrapped around Drew's waist. "I will be here too, son. Do not worry, we will find them."

"Thanks, Mother." He kissed her forehead and smiled at Gertrude. "Thank you."

"Let's get going," David said.

"One more thing, Drew, I wanted to say something else." Edward Miller halted him.

"I'll go saddle the horses." David kissed Mother's cheek and sprinted toward the barn.

When they were alone, Edward clapped him on the back. "I realize it isn't the best time to say this."

Drew shifted his weight back and forth, wishing the man would hurry.

"The elders have been noticing how much you've helped the town's people the past few months, your treatment of the younger Mrs. Montgomery, and we've come to realize how wrong we were to make such a hasty decision regarding the pastorate. We'd like to reinstate you to the position as Pastor whenever you're ready." Edward held out his hand. "I wanted to be sure to rectify matters right away. I should've said so a long time ago. My Gertie's been pestering me something fierce. Please forgive me for jumping to conclusions rather than allowing you an opportunity to defend yourself."

24

Drew paced the kitchen. Lord, it's been two days, and nobody has found anything to indicate where Jules and Sarah have gone. Now, we've a foot of snow, so David and I can't find any potential tracks.

"We haven't slept since they disappeared." David's hand shook as he brought a steaming cup to his lips. "I say we take a break to rest and resume our search in a few hours. We won't do Sarah or Jules any good if we're injured because we're too exhausted."

"Stay and sleep then, but I'm leaving."

"Don't be foolis—"

Someone pounded on the door.

Drew swung it open. A stranger stared at him. "Can I help you?"

"Invite the man in from the cold." David's mug thudded on the table.

"Forgive my lack of manners." Drew stepped aside. "Come in." He shot a glance at David. The man could be the one who'd taken Jules and Sarah.

"Drew Montgomery?" His gaze shot from Drew to David.

"Yes, I am." Drew straightened to full height.

"Where's Jules?" The stranger's gaze darted about the room. "Tell me she's been kept safe."

"What concern is Jules to you?" Drew peeked at Jules's rifle propped in the corner.

"Forget making any move for it." The man's six-shooter suddenly aimed at Drew's heart.

David raised his hands up above his head. "Don't know what's going on but put that thing away. Sit down and talk calmly. We'll sort through whatever the problem is."

~*~

Jules had to admit it. They were on their own. Any hope of rescue would have to come from her. *Think, Jules, think.* She tapped the side of her head, but no plans formed. Her body hurt and was tired from riding in that saddle for two full days with only a couple hours of rest each night.

The threadbare blanket she and Sarah shared didn't do much to keep them from the howling winds slicing through their clothes. She shivered and shook the snow from the cover. "Come on, Sarah." She jiggled her sister-in-law's arm with her elbow.

The woman groaned and stirred. "I-It's freezing." Her teeth chattered.

"Stop yer yapping or I'll put the gags on ya again." Bart tossed a piece of jerky in their direction and laughed when it fell into the snow. "Eat up, yer in for a long day of walking."

"Walkin'?" Jules snatched the food and handed a piece to Sarah.

"'Cause my horse came up lame. We'll have to leave him behind." Bart spit a stream of tobacco juice near their feet. He crossed to his horse, grabbed his rifle, and shot the animal.

Jules winced, the shot echoing in the morning air. The thud of the horse falling to the ground made her heart thump harder. They needed to get away. Somehow. She only had a day and a half—

"Don't just stand there, get moving." Bart pointed the gun at Sarah, who whimpered.

Her whole body shook.

Jules covered her friend as best she could. "Shh, it's gonna be fine, just wait and see."

Bart swung onto his saddle.

They stumbled through the knee-high snow drifts, their tied hands slowing their movement.

"I'm scared." Sarah sank to the ground, her chin wobbling.

"There's no reason to fret none." Jules awkwardly patted her sister-in-law's arm with her bound hands. Her gaze flitted across the terrain searching for a way of escape before she helped Sarah up.

"Stop yer yammering." Bart pointed his rifle at Jules's ribs. "I didn't say ya could stop. Move it, or I kill ya right now."

Sarah's face lost its color, going paper-white.

Jules had to make the outlaw quit jawing so at Sarah. "Bart, how'd ya get yer sorry hide outta jail?" Jules moved in between him and Sarah.

"I broke free with one thought in mind. To get even with ya." Bart cackled. "Yer brother thought he could hide ya by changing yer last name, but he couldn't fool me. I'm gonna make ya pay for what ya done to my brother."

So that's why Josh made her marry Drew. Lord, help me. I reckon I don't have a right to ask, Lord, but I'd be much obliged if You show me how to get us away from Bart. Jules licked her chapped lips. I don't deserve Your help, Lord, but could You save Sarah and her baby? Drew can do better without me, but David loves Sarah. Amen, Lord.

"Never figured ya to be the marrying type." Bart's eyes raked over her body. "Yer brother never let anybody get close to ya. What happened? Finally sell ya to the highest bidder?"

"What an uncouth man! How dare you speak to my sister-in-law that way?" Sarah rallied, her eyes blazing as she headed in Bart's direction.

Jules nudged Sarah before she got too close to the man.

"Wellll…isn't that interesting? Sister-in-law, huh?" Bart doubled over in laughter.

Jules clenched her fists tight together, so she wouldn't be tempted to slug him. She'd fought with tied hands before, but Josh had been there to help.

"Might be I can have some fun with ya before I kill ya day after tomorrow." Bart moved closer. "Maybe yer friend here too." His dirty hand grazed Sarah's cheek.

Jules stepped in front of Sarah. "Keep yer filthy hands off her. Leave her be, and I'll do whatever you want."

"Jules. No. You can't." Sarah's face, already white, matched the snow they tromped through.

"Can't never make up for killing my baby brother." Bart's eyes darkened.

"W-What's he talking about?" Sarah's voiced warbled. "You wouldn't hurt anyone."

"Don't be believing her lies." Bart shook his head. "Missy, she got ya fooled good. She killed my brother in cold blood, giving him no chance."

"Now who's lyin'?" Jules couldn't meet Sarah's stare. She didn't have to see it to know it begged her to say Bart was wrong.

"Jules?"

She bit the inside of her cheek, tasting blood. "It isn't like he said."

"You shot someone?"

"Yes." Jules glared at Bart. Telling her side of the story would make him act like a wounded mountain lion. Somehow she had to distract him. "How'd you break out of jail, Bart? You never did share the particulars." Narrowing her gaze, she watched him, trying to figure his plans. If she could keep him talking, maybe he wouldn't see her searching for a way for them to break free. She needed a sturdy tree limb.

"Knocked off the deputy when he brought a meal. He thought I took sick and opened the cell door. I stole his gun and bashed his skull open."

"Right clever." Jules swallowed the bile that rose to her throat. "When was that?"

"Been out for a week. Yer brother's been trying to track me." Bart darted a glance over his shoulder. "But I'm smarter than he is."

Jules stared at the flat ground but didn't see nobody. Maybe they'd have a chance if Josh was nearby. *Please, Lord.*

A piercing scream ripped from Sarah.

Bart slapped her hard across the face. "Shut yer mouth, woman."

"The baby." Sarah doubled over, her dress getting wetter. "I-I think it's time. My water broke."

Jules had seen enough animals give birth that she knew what that meant.

"The baby is ready to be delivered," Sarah gasped out. "I've been having pains all night."

Oh no, please, Lord, not that. Jules helped Sarah straighten, drawing her close to her side. Could things get any worse?

A frantic look flitted across Sarah's face.

Jules didn't need no answer. That baby was fixing to show up.

~*~

Drew's heart raced.

"I don't know where Jules is, but she'd better show up soon, or I'll start shootin'." The man's expression turned to stone.

"Sister? Did you say sister?"

"I did. Now where is she?"

"S-she's…" Drew sank to a chair and dropped his head to his

hands.

"You were supposed to marry her." The man's face could've been chiseled in granite. "That's why I wrote those letters."

Sister? Letters? That meant he had to be Josh.

David pushed a chair from the table. "Let's sit down and start over? I'm David Brown, Drew's brother-in-law, and I'm guessing you're Jules's brother?"

The man eyed them, eased his finger from the trigger, and put the gun in its holster. "Name's Joshua Walker." The fellow gave a firm handshake to both of them.

"Did you marry my sister or not?"

"Yes, but you should've known that since we were married by proxy before she even arrived." Drew stared at his newly-introduced brother-in-law, refusing to let the man get the best of him.

"I reckon I owe you an apology." The man had the decency to duck his head. "I had a reason for answering those letters and not telling Jules I'd done it."

"Such as?" Drew cocked an eyebrow.

"Keeping my sister safe." The man paced the small room. "Will you let me see her? I need to make sure she's unharmed."

"Drew's been trying to say...Jules isn't here. She's been taken, along with my wife, Sarah." David pounded the table.

"What? Didn't Jules get my letter? I heard a rumor a while back that Bart swore to get even with her if he ever escaped from jail. She's been taken?" Josh halted. "Jules can hold her own. I've never seen anyone who can outshoot or out track her. She's the best." A smile spread across his face.

"Only problem is she doesn't have her guns or her knife, and she's traveling with my sister who's expected to deliver a baby any day." Drew's hand scraped across the stubble on his chin.

"Why would she go off without her weapons? That's a fool thing to do. I taught her better than that." Josh shoved his Stetson on his head. "You've changed her, haven't you?" His brown eyes, so like Jules's, bored into Drew.

"It isn't appropriate for the wife of a minister to be carrying a gun to church now, is it?" David came to his rescue.

"I suppose I didn't consider that when I responded to yer letters, but she sure has a way with a gun. She cooks a mean coyote stew too." Josh laughed, apparently lost in memories, but then his face changed, and his gaze settled on Drew. "Jawing about the past does us no good, so tell me what's happened."

"There isn't much to tell. The two women went for a walk on the north side of town. We suspect they rested by a grove of trees. Whoever took her left our injured dog behind. We found Sarah's handkerchief and some hoof prints. The whole town's been searching the past two days, but we haven't come up with anything. They've vanished." Drew traced his fingernail along a groove in the table.

"It's gotta be Bart Thomas. I've been tracking him for over a week. Left as soon as I heard he broke out of jail. His lone ambition has been to get vengeance on Jules. It's why I sent her the letter a few months ago so she'd be ready for him. It's not like her to be so careless."

"She never had the opportunity to read the letter once she received it. It was lost in a twister on our way home." Drew cleared his throat. "Who *is* Bart Thomas?" His hand shook. He wasn't sure he was prepared for Josh's response.

"She hasn't said anything? I'm not surprised, I reckon. Ending a man's life tends to do something to a person. I could see it rubbed her raw like a constant rope burn. She needed to live a life she's always longed for, something I'd hoped you'd provide for her, Pastor. She never put it into words, but I could read it in her eyes. Jules wanted a home and family. I'm glad she's found it here."

"Yes, but what about Bart?" Drew leaned forward in his chair.

"He plans to get even with Jules for killing his twin brother Burt. My guess is he'll seek his vengeance soon."

So, the letter from the Pinkerton Agency was true, his wife *was* a criminal. A block of ice formed in his heart. How would he ever feel safe with her again?

25

"We need to find somewhere to stop, Bart." Jules stumbled, trying to support Sarah in the heavy snow as they trudged along. "She's fixin' to have this baby soon."

Bart spewed a stream of curses. "I should shoot her, so we can keep moving." His hand rested on the butt of his rifle.

Jules stepped in front of Sarah. "You don't want to do such a thing, Bart. They'll hang you for sure if you kill a woman, 'specially one with an unborn babe."

"I don't aim to get caught."

"If I know Josh, he isn't far behind." Jules squinted into the distance around them.

Bart's gaze darted back and forth, and his hand jerked when he yanked back on the reins.

She hid her smile. Good, let him fret over Josh for a while and keep his mind off the two of us. Three of us.

"What's that ahead?" Sarah panted in between pains and pointed.

Jules caught a glimpse of a mound looming off to the right. "I can't rightly say."

"It's a sod house, ya fool." Bart spit a wad of tobacco juice at Jules's feet. "Stay put while I go check on it. And don't get no ideas about fixing to escape." He dismounted and crept toward the hill, tugging the horse to follow him.

"We aren't getting away, are we?" Sarah sank into a snow drift, her face etched with pain and tiredness. "We're going to die here. Aren't we?"

"Now, don't be talkin' like that. We'll find a way, if I have to make one myself." Jules gently tugged Sarah to her feet. "You'll feel better once we get some shelter."

"How are we going to escape with my babe on its way? We can't tell which direction home is from here. It's hopeless." Sarah groaned, clutching her stomach. "We don't have much time."

"I'll figure us a plan. Trust me." Even as Jules spoke the words she knew they weren't true. Unless help came, she had no way of changing Bart's mind. She wiped her sweaty hands down the sides of her dress, wishing she'd worn her britches. *No, they wouldn't have a chance of running, not in Sarah's condition.* She'd have to think of something else.

Bart plodded towards them, "Ain't much, but at least it's dry." He swung onto his horse. "Don't appear like it's been used in years. Get moving."

"Thank You, Lord." Sarah gripped her belly.

Jules urged her tired body to move forward and help Sarah to the house. Bart wouldn't aid anyone, except for maybe his own kin. Jules wanted to crawl in a bed, sleep, and wake up to find it had been a bad dream. If only.

~*~

"W-what did you say?" Drew forced his roiling thoughts back into control, trying to concentrate on Josh's words.

"If I know Bart Thomas, it gives us about a day and a half before he'll make his final move."

"What do you mean *final*?"

"Like I said, Bart came here with one idea in his head. To kill Jules. I reckon he aims to do it on the anniversary of his brother's death, December twenty-third." Josh's boots scraped the floor. "If you could spare some grub, I'd be much obliged. It's time I got moving."

"We're going with you." David shoved his chair away from the table. "Those are our wives." His face blanched. "If this Bart fellow plans to kill Jules, w-would he do the same to Sarah?"

"He and his brother already killed a bunch of men and have robbed a lot of stagecoaches and banks. It's why they were wanted dead or alive when we were hunting them. Jules protected me a year ago, and I reckon it's my turn to return the favor." Josh peered at the men. "If you plan to head on the trail with me, you'd better get moving. We're leaving in five minutes."

Josh's words reverberated in Drew's mind. Jules had shot in self-defense trying to protect her brother. She *wasn't* a cold-blooded killer.

Peace settled upon his heart. He should've never doubted her. *Forgive me, Lord. No wonder she's struggled so much with trying to safeguard those around her. Protect her. Help us to get to the women in time. Lord, help Jules see her need to rely upon You, instead of her own strength.* While he prayed, Drew gathered food and blankets, packing them in Jules's knapsack. The sight of it brought moisture to his eyes when he remembered her stepping down from the stagecoach with the pack slung over one shoulder and a rifle over the other. He smiled at the memory.

~*~

They trudged into the dark room, and Jules wrinkled her nose at the smell. Something must have died there. Once her eyes adjusted, she could see a cot on the side wall. She forced her frozen feet to move toward the bed, despite the pain.

"Come on, Sarah, only a few more steps."

She huffed, easing the laboring woman onto the bed. Every bone in her weary body cried for rest, but Jules kept moving. She sneezed as she draped a musty blanket over Sarah.

"Lay there, and rest a bit, and tell me what I need to do to get ready for the baby." Jules wiped perspiration from her forehead.

"You'll need to boil some water." Sarah panted.

She glared at the small cook stove on the opposite wall. Another beast to tame. She squared her shoulders determined not to be defeated.

"Bart, you have to untie our hands so we can get this baby out." Jules stood and kept her voice as firm as she could make it.

Bart studied her for a few minutes before he came over and cut the ropes on both her and Sarah's hands.

Both women rubbed their wrists, massaging life back into their frozen hands.

"Bart, scour up some firewood for us, unless you want to help birth the baby." Jules turned her back, not waiting for his answer.

The man grumbled but closed the door behind him.

"Why do we need hot water?" Jules darted a glance at her friend.

"I have no idea." Sarah groaned when a tremor racked her body, and then her piercing scream filled the small room.

Bart stepped inside, leaving the door wide open.

A cold wind blew through, chilling the small space.

Jules shivered.

"Stop yer caterwauling." Bart's face darkened, and he glared at them before he dumped a load of firewood onto the floor. He aimed his gun at the laboring woman. "Keep her quiet, or I will."

Sarah's eyes widened in her pale face. Her fingers clenched the blanket. She moaned when another pain gripped her body.

"Why don't you make yerself useful, Bart, and start a fire for us." Jules crossed the room and lifted the damp hair from Sarah's cheek. "Give us some privacy when you're done there."

Bart loomed closer and slapped Jules on the side of her head. She sank to the floor holding her ringing ear. Tears welled in her eyes and scorched their way down her face. She swiped them away, determined not to appear weak in front of him.

"Jules? Are you hurt?" Sarah's small voice sounded from the bed.

"Don't worry none for me." With tremendous effort Jules thrust herself to a standing position. "There isn't much that slows me down." She forced a smile for Sarah's sake.

"Why aggravate him so?"

"Because she never learned no manners with that brother of hers." Bart spat on the floor and shoved a piece of wood into the stove. He cackled and raised a hand as if to strike Jules once more. "I heard tell he's a lawman on account he's afraid to be around folks. Won't live in a town or nothin'. The only thing he does is goes after wanted men to keep his baby sister safe. He ain't here to help you now though, is he?"

Jules decided not to let Bart rile her. She could only come up with a plan to escape if she stayed calm. Her breath came in bursts, her heart raced. She tried to slow it down. Spotting a bucket sitting by the door, she crossed the room to retrieve it. "I'll be right back. I need to get snow to melt so we can heat some water."

"Not so fast there. No way I'm letting you to explore on your own. Stay here. I'll get it." Bart slammed the door, ripping the bucket from her hands. "Fool woman. Your time's coming."

The door banged shut behind him.

Sarah pushed herself up on her elbows. "You knew he'd never let you get that on your own, right?"

Jules smiled and waggled her eyebrows.

Her sister-in-law chuckled, the lines in her face easing up.

"I think it's time." Sarah's breathing came in short bursts. "I feel the urge to push."

Jules lifted her friend's skirt and removed her pantaloons. She crouched at the foot of the bed and gasped at the sight of a small, rounded head of hair. "I reckon you can go ahead and push 'cause I can see the babe."

Sarah thrust her shoulders against the wall, then squeezing her eyes shut, she heaved with all her might. She collapsed against the bed panting.

"It's comin', Sarah. Do it some more when that pain hits you. You're doin' great."

Long minutes later, and a lot of straining on Sarah's part, finally the baby slid into Jules's hands. She used the undergarment to wipe the baby clean. "I-it's a boy."

"The cord needs to be cut and tied off." Sarah's voice grew weak. "Is there a knife here?"

"Sarah?"

She lay quiet on the bed, not moving.

Jules's heart pounded.

~*~

They'd been traveling for hours, and Drew was frigid. The snow had grown heavier and thicker. He breathed on his palms, and then eased his gloves on his near-numb fingers. They'd ridden over miles of endless, frozen prairie. With no tracks to follow, he wondered how Josh knew which direction to go. Drew prayed they were heading the right way. His stiff muscles complained of the unusual abuse to them from days in the saddle. He arched his aching back.

Ahead, Josh dismounted and studied a heap under the snow. Jules's brother swung his boot through a drift.

"What is it?" David called.

"I'm guessing they made camp here one night." Josh toed his boot further into the mound. "We're going the right way."

How did Josh know it was Bart's campfire? Drew didn't have the strength to ask. He clung to the hope of seeing Jules and Sarah alive. David's haunted eyes mirrored Drew's thoughts. *Lord, I've been such a fool to keep things from Jules. I wasn't honest with her, and I'm sure she didn't feel free to share her past with me. If only we'd not lost that letter, we'd have been prepared. Forgive me, Lord, for being so caught up with my own problems I failed to notice the needs of my wife. You've given me a precious jewel, Lord. Help me never to take her for granted again. Bring her to salvation, so she may learn of Your love and mine.*

He didn't know when it had happened, but his heart had become forever intertwined with feisty Julia Walker Montgomery…his Jules. Regardless of her spiritual state, Drew cared unconditionally and wanted the opportunity to declare his love. *Please, Lord, give me the chance to tell her.*

~*~

Jules stared at the baby. She'd never seen anything so tiny and special. A nephew. Her heart swelled as she wrapped him tight in an old shirt she'd found on a shelf. It seemed clean enough to use on the little fella. She wished there'd been a soft blanket to warm him. Jules tucked him into Sarah's side where she slept.

Surprisingly, Bart had taken charge when he'd returned to the hovel. His gleaming knife had cut the cord, and he'd agreed to hold the baby while Sarah delivered the afterbirth.

Jules cleaned everything up. She shivered. There'd been so much blood, and she wasn't sure if that'd been normal or not. She couldn't shove the sight from her mind. Her hand lay on her flat stomach. Would she ever get the chance to bring a babe into the world? *It were a might slim likelihood since Drew don't love me.* She squared her shoulders. *Best to think of something else.*

Her coming to Burrton Springs had risked the lives of all she now loved. Bart's thirst to get even could splash onto all of them. It wouldn't be enough for him to kill her. She guessed he'd only be satisfied by making them all suffer. Somehow, she had to get him away from the sod house and end everything. She'd have to make him want to leave Sarah and the baby behind. If only she could find a way or some kind of tool…there'd be an opportunity then of knocking him over the head.

Her blood ran cold. It wouldn't be enough. The only way to stop him was to kill Bart like she had his twin brother, Burt. A shudder rippled Jules's body. Could she do it? Last time when she squeezed that trigger, her only thought had been to save her brother. That'd almost done her in…killing Bart would most likely do that again. She'd have to give up all she'd ever wanted. A home and family.

Drew. Tears trickled. She'd do anything to keep Sarah and the new babe safe. Even if it meant risking her own neck.

Sarah shifted, opening her eyes. She licked her lips.

Jules took her a cup of water and helped her sit up in the bed.

Sarah lay on the pillow, careful not to bother the baby. "I don't understand why I'm so weak."

Jules tucked the covers around her. "You just gave birth. Even animals along the trail had to sleep-off givin' birth."

"He came fast, didn't he?" Sarah smiled and grazed the babe's forehead with a kiss. "David will be pleased."

"What are you fixin' to call him?"

"I'll wait until David sees him." Her face paled. "He'll get to, right?"

"He will." *Lord, if You could see fit to let David see them alive and not killed, that'd be right helpful of You. Amen.* Jules hid her thoughts from Sarah. "Rest 'cause we're gonna need to get you outta that bed here soon." Jules touched the palm of her hand on Sarah's forehead. "Don't like how warm and red your face is. I'm affeared there's a fever. That can't be right. Why'd you have that after giving birth?"

Sarah yawned, her eyes blinking several times. "I'm terribly tired."

Jules dropped into the one chair in the hovel. "Get some rest. I'll wake you when the baby needs to feed."

Her sister-in-law's eyelids fluttered before closing.

Bart had left a long time ago and hadn't returned yet.

Her weary body sagged, and she closed her eyes.

She dreamt of walking through a field of blue flowers, her flowing green skirt blowing around her feet. A laughing little girl danced about, a circle of wildflowers in her golden hair.

Pepper barked and trotted back and forth between them.

Drew held Jules's hand, walking by her side. His eyes glowed with his love for her. He leaned forward to whisper in her ear, "My precious jewel."

She cradled her swollen belly with her other hand as the babe kicked inside. Her heart swelled with love for her husband, the little girl and the unborn child.

Drew chuckled, moving to support her other side with his free hand.

The wind picked up, and Jules could see angry clouds swirling where the sun met the land. She dropped Drew's hand and gathered the girl close to her. She wrapped her other arm around her husband to keep them safe.

The clouds got dark, bunching together in a wild rolling mess that touched the ground as it raced their way. Dirt shot up, blinding her for a bit. The funnel dipped again, eating everything in its path.

Jules's feet were planted to the ground. She couldn't move. Jules screamed and dug her fingers into Drew's arm, as he and their daughter were tugged from her grip. They, along with the babe in her belly, were sucked up into the gray, wild winds. Pepper was yanked up there too.

The tornado lifted and disappeared as soon as it had come.

She stood alone, everyone she'd loved gone forever.

A spark lit the grass on fire at her feet, but she couldn't move. Jules screamed again when the flames licked their way up her body.

26

"Wake up. You're having a bad dream." Sarah's voice came from nearby.

Jules rubbed the sleep from her eyes and yawned. "What're you doin' out of bed?" She stood, stretching as she worked to get the kinks from her neck and back. Once she stopped her body from complaining some, she helped Sarah settle in the bed again.

"You aren't getting away with it that easily." Sarah propped herself against the wall, positioning the baby at her breast. "What's been bothering you? It will help to share it."

A sudden chill filled the room, and Jules ran her hands up and down her arms, trying to warm herself. She crossed to the cook stove, opened it, shoved a piece of wood inside, and stirred the coals.

Bart snored in a corner of the room.

"Pull the chair closer, so we can talk," Sarah whispered.

A sharp pain sliced through her hurting body as she dragged the chair closer to the bed, doing her best not to wake Bart. She twisted side-to-side to get rid of the pain, rubbing her fist against her lower back. Then she settled into the chair. "C-can a body get to Heaven if they've killed somebody? C-can God forgive them?" She wrenched the words from deep inside, waiting and holding her breath, not sure what Sarah would say.

"The Bible says for all to come to Christ who are burdened and heavy laden, and He will give them rest. In His eyes, one sin is no different than another." Sarah shifted the babe to her shoulder and patted his back.

"Don't seem right. Surely it matters between a lie and a killin'." She rubbed the side of her nose.

"Not in God's eyes. A sin is a sin. He loves and forgives us when we choose to follow Him and ask Him to be the center of our lives." The baby burped softly then Sarah tipped him down to feed some more. "Perhaps it'd help to share what's been troubling you, Jules…h-having to do with the shooting."

Bart breathed a soft sigh and kept sleeping.

Jules' thoughts whirled, and her heart raced. "It was a cold December mornin'..." A day forever etched in her memory. She licked her lips and inhaled deeply. "Josh got his new assignment—to hunt down the Thomas brothers. The posters said they were wanted in three different territories for their outlawin'. The twins had shot lots of people durin' a bank robbery and had hurt a heap of folks in their round of stagecoach thefts. They were dangerous, so Josh was told to bring them in, dead or alive. I looked the wanted poster over real careful-like when Josh handed it to me. The men were no different except for the dent in Bart's chin." She rubbed her finger along her own to show Sarah what she meant. "Josh set his Stetson on his head and asked me, "'Are you ready for this? We've never tracked two men at the same time before. I reckon it won't be easy.' He stared off at the land then said, 'I heard those two high-tailed it to the hill country.'"

"I pulled my collar around my neck to buck the cold wind that'd come at us overnight. I did what Josh had taught me and read the ground as we rode. Blue picked his way over the rocky soil, goin' around the agarita bushes on our left. For some reason, I caught the call of a turkey off a-ways." Jules closed her eyes remembering the next part. "We spent the better part of the day workin' our way along their trail when we finally came across tracks of two gallopin' horses.

"Josh told me it was pretty foolish of them to push those horses so hard over the terrain we were in. We slowed our mounts when we got to a section of dangerous limestone. I figure them brothers weren't too smart, though, with the crimes they'd been committin'. They had to know the law would catch up with them one day." She swallowed and straightened in her chair.

Bart still snored in the corner.

"I got off my horse, bein' careful when I hunkered down to check the ground, not to sit my backside into a cactus. I told Josh if the hoof prints were from them two, they likely were heading to the Narrows." Jules swiped a hand down one side of her face, her heartbeat picking up speed. "The Narrows would make a good place to hide 'cause of all the crags in the rock there. We figured we should head there, followin' the tracks. Didn't talk as we rode since Josh and me had learned to know each other's ways, 'specially when it came to trackin' criminals. Through the years, I recognized what his head-tilts and such meant."

She tugged her sleeves tighter around her wrists, trying not to shiver. "We rode a short while then sighted two horses ahead of us. The hair kinda stood up on my neck, when we closed in enough to see it were the men we were huntin'. We saw them split off from ridin' together, one headin' north. I followed him, and Josh headed after the other fella. Sweat was beadin' on my face and upper lip. I kept one hand on the reins and the other rested on my six-shooter." Lost in the memory, she stopped talking.

"Jules? What happened?"

"I got a couple hundred yards away from the river. I couldn't see it yet, mind you, but I knew it were there 'cause I could hear it rushin' through the canyon part. The ground leadin' up to the water was uneven and jagged. I got off Blue and tied him to the nearest scrub oak. Didn't want to take a chance on injurin' the fella. I got my rifle from my scabbard beside the saddle. "She swallowed past the lump in her throat and continued, "As I got closer I could see that no trees could take root with the limestone the way it was in that area, so I had a hard time findin' cover since none of the bigger rocks were near me. I crept low to the ground, inchin' my way forward, tryin' to get close enough to see which brother I was trackin'. The man ducked into an outcrop of rocks about twenty yards ahead of me. I couldn't tell what it was for sure since there were some bigger rocks a fella could hide behind.

"Josh'd taught me better than to just rush into someplace like that, so I went real slow-like and felt it was takin' forever until I found the hole where he'd disappeared. I had to stop and slow my breathin' way down or he would've heard me as soon as I entered. My heart was beatin' somethin' fierce."

Sarah gripped Jules's hand and squeezed.

"Before I stepped inside, I made sure I had my rifle ready. I scooted around the edges of the cave openin', being careful with my footin' on account of the jagged rocks. Sure didn't want to break an ankle. Once I was inside, I shouted, 'Put yer hands where I can see them.' My words yelled right back at me, bouncin' off the walls and all. I kept walkin', once I got my eyes to work in the dark, but the place was empty. I sure couldn't figure where he'd gone. I went a bit further and heard the call of a killdeer from up top of me. Buffalo bosh, if there weren't a hole in the roof rock there. Big enough for a man to crawl through. I tripped on a big stone and nearly fell. The fella was a crafty fox to've gotten himself outta there like that. He'd had plenty of time to escape through the gap, since it took me so long to sneak up to the cave without bein' shot."

Jules rubbed her hands against her upper legs, wiping her palms. "All I could think about was findin' Josh. For all I knew, they had him cornered. I remember the goose bumps raisin' on my arms under my sleeves. Whenever that happens I know somethin' troublin' is about to happen. Fear tore at my gut so bad, but bein' on the trail so long with my brother, I knew I had to see it through, makin' sure he was all right."

Sarah squeezed Jules's shoulder.

"I-I snaked along the wall of the cave, holdin' up near the entrance and checked the countryside for any kind of movement. I strained to hear over the gurglin' water. The glare of a rifle flashed in the dimmin' sunlight, a short distance away from me. I edged forward, that limestone scrapin' my hand somethin' awful as I crept low to the ground. When I raised up a bit, I could see the back of one of the Thomas brothers, hidin' in a dip in the boulders…facin' Josh, who was in the open. I could see the whites of my brother's eyes from where I crouched…" Her hands shook, but she forced herself to continue the tale. "My heart skittered and scampered inside my chest when that outlaw cocked his gun, aimin' at Josh's heart. Time stopped. I don't know when I lifted my rifle or aimed it."

Tears ran free, and Jules swiped at them. "I knew I'd released the trigger when I saw *my* bullet rip through Burt's coat, and he slumped over a rock. I saw his blood soak through the cloth and all over the ground."

"Jules?"

She blinked, forcing herself to stare at Sarah and not think about the sight of Burt's blood. The telling of the tale had taken its toll on her. She'd never told it to anybody else. Her fingers shook when she tucked a piece of hair behind her ear. She licked her lips.

"It must've been horrible." Sarah quickly looked to the man slumped on the bedroll. "What happened to Bart?"

"He got away from us that day. Another deputy caught up with him later and arrested him. We'd hoped he wouldn't hear I'm the one that killed Burt." Jules gathered her sleeping nephew into her arms.

"Apparently he did though." Sarah rested her hand on Jules's shoulder. "If you hadn't shot him, it would've been Josh who'd died.

Isn't that right?"

She nodded. Knowing didn't make it any better. She'd killed somebody… bad guy or not. There wasn't a day that went by she didn't see the slumped body and the blood in her mind. She shuddered, closing her eyes for a minute. *Please, Lord, don't let Drew find out. He'd never forgive me or look at me the same. I couldn't stand to see the ice in his eyes if he learns the truth. He'd never come to love me or forgive me if he discovers what I done.*

~*~

The men stood around the dead horse the next evening.

"Lame." Josh examined the horse. He looked around in the snow, his gaze obviously seeing a story Drew and David didn't know. "The women are a-foot. We'll not stumble around in the dark. Time to set up camp for the night. No fire."

Drew chafed at the delay. The next day was the twenty-third of December. They needed to do *something*. "I'll take the first watch." Drew doubted he'd sleep. He hadn't since Jules and Sarah went missing.

Josh yawned. "Wake me when you need a break."

He paced the perimeter of their campsite, peering into the gathering darkness. Nothing appeared out of order. He gripped the rifle and wondered if he'd have to pull the trigger when they'd come to the actual rescue. Did he have what it'd take to protect Jules? He swallowed around the lump in his throat. *Dear, Lord, help it not to come to that. I don't want to shoot anyone, but I can't stand the thought of losing Jules either. Help me.*

The air soon filled with loud snores.

Drew heaved a sigh and started pacing again. It kept him warm. It didn't calm his thoughts. Nothing would help until he saw Jules with his own eyes—that she was safe…and he could hold her. He glanced at the stars overhead. It looked to be a long night. Drew prayed for the safety of Jules and Sarah. Hours passed while he pleaded with the Lord to protect the women and for Jules to turn to God.

~*~

Jules rocked her nephew.

"Did your nightmare have to do with the shooting?" Sarah propped herself on an elbow. Her face grew shadowed.

"Not this time."

"There've been other times though?"

Jules nodded. "I-I haven't been able to tell Drew. I reckon he's been s'picious though, since he asks questions every time after I've had one of my bad dreams."

"Afraid it'll somehow change his love for you?"

"I *wish* he loved me, but how can he when I took a man's life? He's already not happy with me."

"Oh, Jules, he *does* love you. I'm sure of it."

"No, and even if he did, he won't once he learns everythin'."

The baby squeaked, and she loosened her grip. "Sorry, little boy." She kissed his sweet cheeks.

"What else do you dream?"

Sarah was like a never-tirin' dog, snapping at her heels.

"In this one I walked in a field with Drew and Pepper, and we had a two-year-old daughter with us. I was swelled with child too. We were laughin' as we strolled along, when a storm came up. I screamed and tried to hold on, but they were all sucked into the swirlin' wind, even my unborn babe. I was all alone. A fire burned at my feet, but I couldn't move or get away. The flames were lickin' their way up me when you woke me."

"How terrible." Sarah nudged her way to the edge of the bed and leaned to give Jules a hug.

"T-this isn't the only time there's been fire in my dreams. Storms and flames, and bein' left alone happens over and over." Jules hugged her nephew tight to her chest. "Everythin' I love is ripped away." She grew silent for a moment. "I don't get why I keep havin' the same thing happenin'. I reckon it's because of fightin' the fire a few months ago at yer ma's place."

"Maybe." Sarah shifted on the bed. "Or perhaps God has given you a glimpse of what your life *could* be like."

"What's that 'sposed to mean?" Jules thrust the baby into Sarah's arms. "Why would I choose to be alone or to burn in a fire?"

Bart grunted in his corner, rolled over, and went back to snoring.

Jules lowered her voice and sat again. "Why would you say somethin' like that?"

Sarah held up her hand. "Simmer down and hear me out. The last book of the Bible talks about Judgment Day. It's a time when all of us will stand before God, and we'll be held responsible for what we've done with our lives…whether or not we've chosen to accept Jesus and follow Him. God has something called the book of life, and in it, is the name of every person who's turned to Him. Their reward is eternity in Heaven with God."

"What's eternity?" Jules scooted her chair closer.

"It means forever."

"A long time then. What happens to the folks who don't have their names in that book?"

"The Bible says those whose names aren't found in the book are cast into the lake of fire, where they'll be tormented day and night forever and ever. I think *that's* the dream you've been having, Jules."

Could Sarah be right? A tear trickled its way down her cheek. She gripped the arms of the chair and breathed in short bursts. "What do I have to do to get my name in the special book? I reckon it's time I met this God I keep hearin' about."

"In the book of Romans, it says we're all sinners. Our sin separates us from God and leads us to death. The only way to eternal life is through Jesus Christ. He died on the cross to pay for all of our sins and provided a way for us to go to heaven."

"What do I need to do?" She gripped her sister-in-law's arm.

Sarah smiled and took hold of Jules's hand. "You need to confess Jesus as Lord and believe in your heart God raised Him from the dead and you'll be saved."

"That's too easy." Jules paused. "Wait, Jesus is our Lord, the God Drew talks about all the time and the one from the Bible? He's been readin' me the stories, tellin' me about how Jesus was born and came here to save us. I think Josh tried to 'splain it to me, but I wasn't understandin' back then. I thought Jesus was a friend of Josh's from before our parents died."

"Yes, He is the One both Josh and Drew have told you about. And it's both simple and hard. You're giving up the right to control your life and asking Jesus to be in charge."

"You mean to have God tame me instead of Drew tryin' to?"

Sarah chuckled. "Kind of like that, although we must submit to our husbands, but we've discussed that several times before. Ready to choose to have God direct your life instead of trying to do it alone?"

"You're sure He can forgive my shootin' Burt?"

Sarah nodded. "All you have to do is ask Him."

Jules sank to her knees beside the bed and folded her hands.

Sarah laid the baby on the bed and slipped into place beside Jules.

"Lord, I reckon it's time I get to know You better. Sarah says if I ask, You'll forgive me of all my sins, and You probably guessed they're plenty of them." Her voiced choked, and she couldn't go on for a while. "I didn't mean to kill Burt, but I couldn't let him hurt Josh. I'm powerful sorry, Lord. Please forgive me. I wanna live the way You want me to. I a-accept Jesus. I reckon it's time to let You tame me, but it probably won't be easy. Drew's havin' an awful time doin' it on his own, so I'm sure he needs the help. Amen." Jules swung her teary gaze to meet Sarah's. "I feel right good."

Bart sat up and growled, his face going all red-like.

27

"I ought to shoot ya dead now." Bart spat out the words as he stomped closer. He rammed the end of his gun into the side of Jules's head with one hand, and yanked her by her hair with his other. He dragged her to her feet.

The room swayed and dipped then righted itself.

He shoved her into the chair and wrapped her arms behind it, securing them with a rope.

Sarah cowered on the bed, her arms snug around the baby.

"Ya didn't give my brother a chance but shot him in the back. Only a coward does such a thing." Bart hoofed back and forth in the small space.

The room got quiet except for the whimpering from Sarah's little guy.

"Answer me." Bart roared. He skulked closer and backhanded Jules across the face.

Her head tilted to the side, and she tried to think. "W-what'd you wanna know?"

"Why'd you shoot him in the back?"

"H-He had my brother pinned down in the Narrows. I saw him cock his gun, and I pulled my trigger. I didn't mean to kill him. I-I was tryin' to save my brother." She forced herself not to wince when he stomped toward her again.

"Where were you that day, Bart?" Sarah's voice stopped him in his tracks.

Jules let a breath go she hadn't realized she'd been holding.

Bart spun and walked to the other side of the room. "I escaped through the roof of the cave and doubled back to our arranged meeting spot." His grip on the rifle shifted. "I waited and waited, but Burt never showed, and I knew something had to be wrong. Didn't figure on a woman shooting my brother." He pulled out a pocket watch. "It won't be long now, and you'll pay for your crimes." He ripped the door open, clomped out, slamming it shut behind him.

"Oh, Jules, what will we do? He's going to kill us, isn't he?" Tears streamed down Sarah's cheeks.

"Not if I can help it. Quick, get this rope untied."

"What if he comes back?"

"If you hear him, scamper onto the bed."

Sarah laid her son on the cover and hurried behind Jules's chair. Her fingers fumbled with the knots for a good while.

"It's no use. They won't budge. Didn't you have a knife when you cut the cord after the baby's birth?"

"I didn't cut it. Bart did. It's his knife, and I'm sure he has it on him. He wouldn't leave it lyin' around for us to use on him." Her mind raced, trying to figure a way to escape. If she could get him away from the sod house, Sarah and the baby, maybe they'd have a fighting chance. Her dream reared up then went quiet inside her sudden-like. Maybe saving those she loved meant she had to be willing to give up something in return. She swallowed. *Lord, make me strong, and help me save them.*

~*~

Drew startled. He stretched the kinks from his neck, lifted his head, straining to hear. There. He heard it again…footsteps in the distance. He gazed at the sky, estimating it'd be dawn within an hour or so. The snap of a branch reverberated in the cold, still air. Drew peered at the other two men wrapped in blankets. He'd let them sleep through the night so they'd be fully rested.

Awaken them or investigate the noise on his own? He hated to rouse them if it was just an animal. *No need to further prove my inadequacies to Josh.* Drew pushed to his feet, dusted snow from his backside, and grasped Jules's rifle. His fingers tingled at the touch of cold metal. *Lord, please keep me from having to actually use it.*

He picked his way over branches and snow, keeping a sharp eye on the area ahead. His heart hammered in his ears. Could the other creature hear him? He stopped for a few seconds to control his ragged breathing. *Lord, help me to remain calm.* He continued to pray as he proceeded in the direction where he'd last heard movement.

A cold perspiration broke out on Drew's brow. He could be

following the escaped criminal. Perhaps he *should've* awakened the other men. It was too late now. Determined to stick with his decision, he pressed onward. Each time when he thought he'd lost the man, a twig would snap, or a string of quiet curses would fill the early morning air. He remained a safe distance behind the fellow. Drew guessed he'd been following the stranger for a half hour or so. The first streaks of dawn spread across the horizon. He'd have to take cover, or he'd be spotted.

A small clump of trees loomed in the distance. If he could get to those, he'd be able to find protection behind them. Drew clenched his teeth, moving into position. The fellow stood a mere twenty yards from the hiding spot.

The man's words carried across the snow-covered field. "Who does that fool woman think she is?"

Drew cringed when a slew of curses followed.

"As soon as it's sunlight, I'll finally get even for Burt's killing. I'll shoot them all—her sister-in-law, the baby, and I'll hunt down her husband and brother too. They all need to pay for her crime."

Baby? Had Sarah given birth? The hair raised on his arms. What kind of man would kill a woman and a baby?

The man continued to rant about his own troubles and Jules.

Drew *had* to find a way to get to her before that cold-blooded killer ended her life. *Lord, guide my steps. Keep Jules, Sarah, and the baby safe.* Time was of the essence. In a few moments the sun would be above the horizon. He was so intent upon coming up with a plan of rescue, and his prayer, that he failed to hear the footsteps behind him. But he did feel the cold, metal tip of a gun shoved into the back of his head. He closed his eyes. He'd failed.

"Well, well, well, what do we have here?" The man spit a stream of tobacco juice, staining the white ground.

Drew clamped his teeth together.

"Wouldn't be here to try and rescue that pesky creature, would you?" The man's steely-blue eyes bored into Drew's gaze as his fingers closed around Jules's rifle. "What's your name?"

"Andrew." Maybe giving his first name would keep the man distracted of who he really was.

"Andrew, huh? What're you doing snooping around so early in the morning?"

He gulped. Drew didn't want to lie to the man, but he didn't want to help or infuriate him in any way either. Perhaps silence was the best answer.

"Not willing to talk, eh? Guess ya might as well join my party, although I'll warn ya, it'll be ending real soon." The man chortled and gripped Drew's shoulder, shoving him forward.

His mind raced as they trudged across the terrain. A slight hill loomed ahead of them. Drew prayed David and Josh would soon awaken and find him missing. He bit his lip to keep from shouting. He should've known better. *Forgive me, Lord, for being proud and thinking I could take care of things on my own. You, David, and Josh are my only hopes of surviving.*

~*~

Jules's shoulders ached from hours of being in one position.

Sarah and the baby slept peacefully in the bed.

It had taken some doing, but she'd finally made her sister-in-law rest when her fever came back. Jules could no longer feel her fingers as she continued to work at the knots. *Please, Lord, help me.* She struggled with the rope for a few more minutes, they finally loosened. Needles pricked their way up her arms as feeling returned. She bit her lip to stop from crying at the pain.

She *had* to get away. Her only hope of saving Sarah and the baby was if she was gone when Bart showed up. He didn't care about them. The outlaw only wanted to make *her* pay for killing his brother. If she could lead him away, maybe the two would have some hope of being saved. Surely somebody had to be searching for them.

She stepped beside the bed and gazed one more time at her nephew and Sarah. Jules blew them a kiss before creeping her way across the dugout. She held her breath and eased the door open, praying it wouldn't make a sound. If she could get outside without being heard, then she'd have a chance. Jules forced her breathing to slow and stepped through the doorway. The cold air made her wish she'd taken time to pull on her coat. Light colored the sky. She studied the area, but she didn't see Bart anywhere. *Lord, guide my feet.* She headed in the one direction she remembered from a couple days earlier.

All the years of training from her brother came to her in an instant. She struggled to stay low to the ground. Her arms and legs were stiff as she hurried to get as far away from the soddy as possible.

Her body didn't bend the way it had when tracking Bart's brother. She was outta practice. Her dress was soon soaked as she crawled her way through the snow. Soon she couldn't feel her fingers.

Her head throbbed where Bart had slapped her, blurring her sight. Jules slowed a few seconds, praying the pain would let up. A grove of trees stood off to the left. If she could get to them, she could rest for a few minutes.

Ten. Five. One yard to go. Her trembling body took forever to cover the distance. She sank to the ground with her back against a tree trunk. Her lungs cried for air and her chest heaved. Jules allowed herself to rest for a few minutes. She searched the area, straining to hear something other than birds.

There. Something was just up ahead of her. She tensed when she heard voices in the distance behind her. Which way should she go? The flatlands of Kansas didn't allow for many hiding spots like Texas had. She debated. Should she go back? Did Sarah need help? No, her best hope was to keep pressing forward, away from Bart. At least she prayed it was so.

Jules pushed her body to move. She'd stay in the cover of the bushes and trees for as long as possible. She crawled along, trying not to make a single sound. Not an easy task for a woman in a dress who had barely slept the past few days. Two more feet and she'd be exposed to whatever lay ahead of her. She writhed her way through the undergrowth and peered around it.

Two men stirred to her left. A horse snorted and pawed the ground. In the dim light, she saw two more horses. Where had the third man gotten to? She glanced in all directions, but she didn't see anyone else. Was there another bunch of outlaws trying to catch up with Bart? Maybe the murmurings she heard belonged to the extra fellow. What hope did she have if there were four? Her heart raced. If there were that many, then maybe she'd be able to steal a gun from one of them. Then what? Would she kill again if she had to? *Dear God, don't let it come to that.*

Jules forced her shivering body to hold still. The men weren't fully awake yet. If she could sneak into their campsite afore they roused, she might be able to find one of their weapons. *Yes.* It was her only source of attack and would give her an edge over her enemies.

She urged her sluggish legs to move. The men faced the other way, giving her an advantage. At least they couldn't see her coming, and she did her best to make sure they didn't hear her. Years of training allowed her to move without a sound, despite months of living in town. Controlling her breathing was a harder task.

One man's hand twitched. She waited but soon he snored some more. When she crept within five feet of their camp, she could make out a gun belt lying at the side of one of the men. She saw no other weapons. Too bad it lay between the two of them. She'd have to walk soft-like if she didn't want to be caught snatching it.

Jules edged her way closer inch-by-inch. The foot-high snow helped to hide the sound of her footsteps. Finally, the belt was within her grasp. She bent to grab it when one of the men snorted. Jules froze. She didn't move or breathe. Pain thudded in the side of her head. She held in a gasp. In one swooping motion, she grabbed the gun, and took two steps backward.

The man furthest from her was moving.

Her hand shook as she cocked the six-shooter and aimed it at him. "Put yer hands up where I can see them, mister. I don't want to shoot you, but I will if need be." She struggled to keep her voice from shaking when he sat up with his hands in the air, facing away from her.

"Jules?"

She knew that voice.

"Is that you?" He turned his head and glanced over his shoulder.

Josh? What was he doing here? Was the morning light playing tricks on her eyes?

The other man stirred. "What's going on?"

She blinked her eyes and would've rubbed them if she hadn't been holding the gun. David sat up, his gaze darting back and forth between the two of them.

"Lower that thing before it goes off from all your shaking." Her brother drawled the words. "I've never seen you so rattled, Jules."

"Josh? Is it really you?" She lowered the gun and flung herself forward. She wrapped her arms around his body, silent sobs shaking her shoulders. She struggled to get her emotions under control. Bart was loose. They wouldn't be safe until he'd been captured.

"Where's Sarah?" David's words broke through her fog of tears.

She swiped her nose on her wet sleeve and pointed back in the direction from where she'd came. "They're back at the sod house in the side of the hill."

"You left her alone?" David grabbed hold of her arm. "Why would you do something so foolish?"

"I figured she and the baby'd be better off if I could get Bart away from them, which is why I left when she slept. Bart's been gone for a long while."

Jules's gaze wandered in the direction of the horses. She counted them again. There were three, but why if only Josh and David were here? *Wait.* Champ stood with the others. That meant Drew was too. The hair stood up on the back of her neck. "Where's Drew?"

28

Drew's eyes were slow to adjust to the dim light in the sod house. He noted a cot near one wall, and it appeared someone sprawled there. His heart skipped a beat when he heard a soft, mewling sound coming from the same corner.

Bart motioned for him to sit in the chair beside the bed.

Drew hastened to comply. He studied the room, seeking something he could use to defend himself or in some way take the criminal unawares. Nothing presented itself.

A string of curses rent the air. "How did that ornery woman escape?" The man stomped around the room like a caged beast.

The whimpering increased.

Something small writhed on the bed. Dare he lean closer? Bart's back momentarily faced him. He decided to risk it. The squirming infant quieted once Drew picked it up, gathering it close. Big blue orbs scrutinized his face.

"Drew? Is that you?" Sarah blinked, sat up, and rubbed her eyes as if she thought he might disappear.

"Ya two know each other?" Bart spun around. "Isn't this a cozy get together? Thought your name was Andrew." He poked the rifle into Drew's ribs.

Drew shielded the baby in his arms. "My name *is* Andrew. Andrew David Montgomery."

Bart scratched his head. "Montgomery, huh? Wouldn't happen to be married to Jules Walker, would ya?"

Sarah's eyes begged him to deny it.

He winced when Bart jabbed the gun deeper into his side. Drew wouldn't lie. "Yes."

Sarah lunged for her baby when the outlaw loomed closer. She shrunk nearer the wall.

What atrocities had she and Jules been subjected to? Drew

cleared his throat, refusing to give in to the fear threatening to engulf him. He needed to maintain a calm head. Their safety was at stake.

~*~

Jules didn't like the look the two men gave each other. "Where's Drew?" She repeated, hoping he'd show up any minute.

"He agreed to take the first watch last night and was supposed to wake me when he grew tired." Josh wrapped his coat around Jules's shaking shoulders.

"And?"

"I reckon he never woke me." Josh shrugged his shoulders. "Sorry, Jules. Maybe he just wandered off for a bit."

"I don't know—"

"Look, I understand your concern for Drew, but how's Sarah?" David gripped her arm. "Is she injured?"

"No, she and the baby are doing fine."

"B-baby? She had it?" David's voice warbled.

Jules nodded. "A son. Sarah did a good job birthin' him."

"They truly are doing all right?" The man swayed a bit.

Jules grabbed his arm to hold him up.

"Sarah's been runnin' a fever some, but they're both doin' good."

"W-what did she name him?"

"Sarah is waiting until you could have a part in it."

"I hate to interrupt and all, but we've got a problem here, folks." Josh waved his hand. "Appears as though Drew possibly got himself captured. If he were checking the perimeter, he'd be back by now. We need a plan to get your family out of there. Jules, how many weapons does Bart have?"

"He's got a rifle, six-shooter, and a knife. I reckon it's possible he has a derringer too, but I've never seen one if he does."

Josh gazed at the unused bedroll. "Then I suppose it's a likely possibility Bart stole your rifle from Drew."

"Drew carried a gun?" She swung her head in David's direction to confirm Josh's words. "W-why would he do that? He hates weapons."

"Because he loves you and is willing to fight to save you." David smiled at her.

She choked up. *Could he be right?* But now wasn't the time to worry about whether Drew loved her. She *had* to focus on the task at hand. "Does he even know how to shoot?"

David frowned. "No, but it won't stop him from trying to protect you."

Jules bit her lip to keep from crying. If only she could wake up from this bad dream. It was her fault. Somehow, she had to find a way out of the mess. She squared her shoulders and stepped forward. "It's me Bart wants. He'll leave the rest of you alone if he has me."

"We don't know that for sure, Jules. I'm not willing to risk taking that chance with your life." Josh tilted her chin up, peering at the side of her face. "Especially not when he's done something like this. There'll be another way. Let me think."

In her hurry to get away, finding the men so close, Jules had forgotten the painful bruise to her cheek. "There's *no* other way, and you know it, Joshua Walker. We can trade me for Drew, Sarah, and the baby."

"There's no surety he'll go for the idea. He's a heartless killer, and there's no telling what he'll do when cornered. Wouldn't put it past him to try killing all of us." Josh slammed his hat against his side.

"He doesn't know you and David are here, so maybe it's worth the risk. You two could hide out, and I'll give myself up only if he'll release Drew and Sarah," Jules said.

"You don't have any leverage." Josh jammed his hat back on his head.

"So let me use yer gun, and keep yer rifle ready."

"How're you going to explain going back in with a gun all of sudden? It's not like you can say one appeared on the trail." He glared at her.

"I can say Drew left it with his horse."

"I don't like it." Josh rested his hand on her shoulder. "There's too many ways your plan can go wrong. He won't hesitate to kill you, especially since today is..."

"I know what today is—believe me—but I say we don't have a choice. Besides, it's my life, and it's my husband with that crazed criminal. I'll do anything to keep him safe."

"Even if it means giving up your own life?" Josh dropped his hand, scowling.

"Yes." Jules reached for the six-shooter.

"We need some type of signal or something." He studied her.

"You can make yer move after Drew, Sarah, and the baby are

safe. Not before, is that clear?"

Josh grumbled. He might not like her plan, but he'd go along with it. She knew he'd not let her down.

Jules kissed his cheek while handing him his coat. He started to fuss.

"Bart'll believe I got the gun off Drew's horse, but not him havin' an extra coat. It's better this way."

"Take care of yourself, Jules."

"I love you, Josh." She hugged her brother tight. *Dear, Lord, don't let this be the last time I see my brother.* She turned and made her way back the way she came, this time not hovering close to the ground. Jules set her jaw and steadied her grip on the weapon. There was no time for female emotions. She had a job to do. Saving her husband's life.

~*~

Bart stepped closer.

Drew braced as the man got nose to nose with him.

The outlaw snorted, pulling back with a chortle.

"That whore of yours killed my brother. I'm surprised you'd be interested in second-hand goods." The man had the audacity to wink.

Drew clenched his fists, wanting to beat the insolent man for making such horrid statements regarding Jules. *Lord, keep me calm.* Sarah's hand on his sleeve provided the strength he needed. "I'm aware my wife shot your brother, while defending hers."

Bart slapped his hand against the table. "Is that the lie she's spreading? She shot him in the back. Never gived him a chance. Had nothing to do with her brother. He weren't even around."

Sarah's eyes pled with Drew. He patted her hand.

"Bart, give some thought to what your life could be if the thirst for revenge were to be taken away. What good will come of killing Jules? It won't bring Burt back, will it? It won't erase the pain of having him lost either. Unfortunately, none of us can go back and change those hurtful things in our past. We each have those types of regrets." *Lord, reach him, and save us, especially my Jules.*

"Like a preacher man has regrets. Ha. No. What do ya know about real life? Ever had someone ya loved snatched away?" Bart spat on the floor.

"Yes, but not the way you have. My father died when I was a young boy."

"What happened?"

Good. If he could keep the man talking, maybe Drew could diffuse the volatile situation. "He died in a train crash. I lost my mother's love the same day."

"How? Did she die in the crash too?" Bart perched on the edge of the bed.

"No, but she shut herself away from me, at least emotionally. I reminded her too much of my father."

"Is she still living?"

"She is and as a matter of fact, we reconciled recently because of my wonderful wife." Drew hesitated, unsure how much of the story he should share.

"What good could that fool woman do? She's nothing but trouble."

Drew chuckled. "I thought the same thing when she first arrived, but God has shown me even with her rough and uncultured ways, she's a precious jewel in the making. I'm grateful the Lord brought her into my life. Jules is exactly what I needed."

Bart studied him, and Drew wondered if his words were starting to penetrate the outlaw's heart. If he could keep the man's mind off wanting to kill Jules, there might be hope for a future for all of them. He smiled. He was making progress.

Someone pounded on the door of the sod house. A muffled voice filtered through. "Bart Thomas, get yer ornery hide out here."

Jules. Of all times for his wife to make an appearance. Drew bit back a moan.

Bart leapt to his feet, extracting his six-shooter from its holster. A gleam filled his eyes. His fingers twitched as if eager to finally retaliate. The man crept to the door and pressed his ear against it.

Drew's mouth went dry. Bart's back was to him. Had he time to make use of the opportunity? His gaze darted about searching for anything he could use to knock the man unconscious. A cast-iron skillet on the cook stove snagged his attention. How had he missed it? His pulse thudded as he rose. Sarah's eyes widened when Drew's fingers closed around the handle. He inched his way closer to the outlaw. Only two feet to go. He raised the cookware above his head.

~*~

Jules had given Bart long enough to respond. Time to take the situation into her hands. She kicked open the door with the six-shooter drawn and aimed straight at Bart's head. "I said to get yer ornery backside out here, Bart, and I don't like havin' to repeat myself."

He spit a stream of tobacco in her direction and slid his gun from its holster. "What makes ya think I'd do your bidding? Ya maybe can order your man about, but not me."

"You may think otherwise since I'm willing to become yer prisoner again, but only on one condition." Jules cocked the gun.

Bart swore. "Which is?"

"Let them go." Jules nodded toward the inside of the house. "We both know it's me you really want. Killin' them won't give you any satisfaction. Only killin' me will."

"How do I know it ain't some kind of trick?"

"You'll have to trust me."

Bart chewed on his tobacco and appeared to be considering it. He spit a long stream before he spoke. "You're willing to give up yer life for them?"

Jules nodded. *Dear, Lord, make Bart agree to my idea.* "Once they're free, I'll give myself over."

"No, Jules." Something *thunked* on the floor. Drew's head poked close to the door.

She blinked back tears when she spied her man. Her throat choked up. *Now's not the time to go all female.* She dragged her gaze away, knowing her grit would waver if she continued to look at his pleading face. *Lord, help me do this.*

Bart glared at her before peering back in the house.

Jules struggled to keep her body straight and keep a steady hand on the gun. The long, tiring days had plumb worn her to bits.

"Deal." Bart glanced over his shoulder "Get that woman out of bed and get going. Take that squawking baby too." He motioned toward Jules's gun. "Drop that there and kick it aside."

She shook her head. "The gun stays right here until they're a long ways from here."

~*~

Drew's heart splintered. He'd dropped the skillet when Bart scampered out of his reach. Now, he helped Sarah to stand. He gathered the infant in his arms and handed a coat to his sister. Jules's jacket lay across the back of the chair. He wrapped it around the child. *Dear God, don't let it end this way.*

Sarah trembled head-to-toe as they made their way across the small room. He couldn't believe Josh and David hadn't come to their rescue. *Where are You, God? What can I do to save them?* Drew's head thudded a steady beat. Would he ever see Jules alive after they left?

"Don't try anything funny," Bart said.

What could he possibly do? He wouldn't risk Sarah and the baby's lives. Lord, now's a good time to do something. I never got to tell Jules what a precious jewel she is.

Drew longed to touch his wife as they shuffled by her, but he didn't dare do anything to rile Bart any further. He yearned to kiss her one last time.

"I love you," she whispered the words for his ears alone when he lingered for a second.

If he'd thought his heart splintered earlier, it broke wide open at her declaration. Drew's leaden steps guided Sarah in the direction of the campsite and the other men.

"I kept my end of the bargain. Now it's your turn." Bart sneered. "Drop that gun. Get your back to me…nice and easy-like. Don't be no hero."

Drew's eyes flickered shut, a groan ripping past his lips.

~*~

So that was it. She'd killed Burt, no reason she shouldn't die the same way. Jules took a few steps back, stooped, and set the six-shooter on the ground.

She stared at Drew's and Sarah's retreating backs. At least they'd gotten away. Her death was worth it, if it meant they'd be safe. A movement at her right snagged her attention.

Josh crouched behind a bush. His gaze flitted to hers.

"Goodbye." She mouthed the words to her brother, hoping he could read her lips across the distance separating them.

"Keep your back to me." Bart cackled like a hen.

She could hear each of his steps as the snow crunched under his feet, and his gun jabbed into her back.

"Any last words? I'll give you what you didn't give Burt." The barrel dug into her ribs, and he stood off to the side.

Her mind raced. "I'm sorry, Bart, for the pain I've caused you. I never planned to kill yer brother." She halted when her throat clogged with tears. "I pray one day you'll forgive me." She gulped, trying to stop the blasted sobs and rein in her boiling feelings.

The cock of a rifle across the clearing took her to the same scene from a year earlier. Her heart stopped.

"No!" Jules jerked in front of Bart. Hot, searing pain rammed through her body. She grabbed him as they both fell to the ground. Everything went black.

29

"Jules!" The word wrenched from Drew's throat. He thrust the baby into Sarah's arms and sprinted toward his fallen wife. He bent, cradling her limp body in his arms. Sobs wracked his frame. Why had she stepped in front of the bullet meant for Bart?

"Careful." Josh rested a hand on Drew's arm. "We've gotta get inside and see how bad it is. Carry her, and I'll check on Bart. He's not moving."

David hurried over. "Should I ride to get the doc?"

Josh shook his head. "No. Bart's alive…barely. Can't wait for the doc. We'll have to take care of it ourselves."

Drew carried his wife into the dim interior, placing her on the cot.

Sarah followed with the baby and fell into the chair, her face pale. She bent over her baby, lifted her skirt and started ripping bits of petticoat. She handed the shredded cloth to Drew.

Josh and David transported a groaning and cussing Bart, gently putting him on his bedroll, his chest soaked with blood.

Drew staunched the blood coming from Jules's shoulder with a wad of Sarah's petticoat. His wife's head moved, and he leaned toward Jules. He studied her pale face. "Jules, sweetheart?"

Her beautiful, chestnut eyes fluttered open, and a smile flitted for a second, before a flash of pain splashed across her face. "How's Bart?" Her voice was so weak he had to lean close.

"He's alive. Why?" he growled, wanting to ask more.

"Needs to know God can tame him." Her eyes pleaded. "Tell him."

His mind raced. What had she meant? "I don't understand, sweetheart." Drew ran his finger along her bruised cheek.

"God…can…tame him…like me." She visibly forced the words through cracked lips and gripped his hand tight as if trying to get him to comprehend.

Sarah sat at his side, patting the baby.

Jules's gaze flickered to her sister-in-law. "Tell him." Her eyelids drifted shut.

"What did she mean?" Drew wanted to pound something—hard.

"She's trying to tell you to share with Bart how to find salvation before it's too late for him." Sarah squeezed his shoulder. "Jules doesn't want him to die without having the chance to make a commitment to the Lord."

"How would she even know what that is?"

"She made *her* decision yesterday." A tear ran down Sarah's cheek.

He glanced at Jules and back to Sarah. "You mean…" Drew's throat clogged.

"Yes, Jules became a Christian. Or as she worded it, 'allowed God to tame her.'"

Drew chuckled. "That's what she meant by taming?"

Sarah joined him in laughter. "Yes, she prayed and said she reckoned it was time she got to know God better." She smiled down at Jules. "Is she going to make it?"

"I don't know." He rubbed Jules's uninjured arm.

Her lashes fluttered open, and Jules struggled to speak. "Talk to Bart." She yawned, and her eyes closed.

Drew moved to the floor where David and Josh huddled over the injured man. He knew the right thing to do was to share about God's love, but he didn't have any love for Bart Thomas right then. It could easily have been Jules lying there on the brink of life and death. He shuddered to think of it. *Lord, help me to forgive him enough to be able to share Your hope. I can't do it in my own strength, but let me lean on You and be able to do it for Jules.*

"He doesn't have long," Josh muttered when Drew knelt beside them.

Bart's gaze settled on Drew. "Why'd she do that?"

"Because she didn't want you to die without knowing God and how much He loves you." Drew rubbed a hand across his whiskered chin.

"Why?"

That's exactly the kind of woman she is. His heart surged with love for Jules. He whispered a prayer for both his wife and the wounded man.

"How?" Bart's fingers dug into his arm. "How can He love me?"

"He loves each of us no matter what we've done. God loves you, Bart, and desires a relationship with you." Drew cleared his throat. "Tell him you're a sinner and ask Him to forgive you."

"Too late."

"No, even when Jesus was dying on the cross the criminal beside Him cried out for the Lord to remember him, and Jesus said the man would see Him that day in paradise. As long as you have breath, it's not too late, Bart."

The room grew quiet except for the man's ragged breathing.

"It's Jules's desire for you to understand what it means to be tamed by God." Drew glanced at his wife.

A muffled yelp came from the cot.

Josh held a bottle upright from his sister's shoulder and then eased her on her side. He took strips of Sarah's petticoat and wound them around Jules's shoulder and under her arm before tying it off.

"Sure it's not…too late?" Bart wheezed. "Done…bad…things. Don't know much about God."

"God's already aware of each sin, but He loves you enough to have died for those sins."

"Would've kill…ed…her."

Drew swallowed the lump in his throat. "I suppose so, yet she was willing to give her life to save us…and *you*."

"Like Jesus?"

Drew nodded when moisture filled his eyes.

Bart grew quiet, and Drew wondered if he'd died. He pleaded silently for the man's salvation.

"Pray?" The word was difficult to distinguish as Bart gurgled, his breathing shallower and more labored.

"Do you want to join me as I pray?"

The man's head moved a fraction of an inch.

"Pray in your heart, Bart—I'll pray aloud." Drew covered the man's hand with his. "Dear Lord, I pray You be with Bart as he cries out to You. Forgive him of his sins and all the wrongs he's committed. Help him to give his life to You. Ease his pain, in Jesus' name, amen."

"A…men." A peace settled upon the man's face as his heart slowed its beating. The gurgling slowed to a stop.

"He's gone." David lifted the blanket up over the man's face.

~*~

Drew crossed the room. "How bad is it?"

"Bad enough. At least the bullet passed through and we don't need to dig it out, but the biggest concern is infection."

"Will she survive?" Drew clenched his hand tight.

"Hard to tell. There's not a whole lot we can do. I cleaned the wound best I can."

"What'd you clean it with?"

Josh reached in his coat pocket and held up a small bottle. "Whiskey, of course."

"What now?" Drew asked. He'd heard of the whiskey thing, but never seen it applied.

"Now we wait. Jules is tough. She should pull through." Josh's words didn't correspond with his drawn face. "Keep her warm and as comfortable as possible." He shifted his attention to the body on the floor. "I'll take care of Bart. Let me know if her condition changes. I'll be outside."

"Need some help?" David stepped forward.

Josh shook his head. "No, spend some time with you wife and that new son of yours." He lifted Bart's body to his shoulder and headed out the door.

David moved the chair to the opposite wall for Sarah and probably to give them some privacy. He took Sarah into his arms and kissed her, the baby cuddled between them.

A twinge sparked in Drew's heart. He dragged his gaze away from the reunited couple. Will I ever be able to share in such a way with Jules? Dear Lord, allow her to pull through. I want a real marriage too.

"What shall we call our son?" Sarah's soft murmur carried across the room.

"Joel William Brown." David responded. "After our fathers."

Drew closed his eyes for a second. How he hoped for the chance to help Jules name a son or daughter. He lifted Jules's listless hand and kissed it, his heart squeezing with longing.

~*~

Jules wiggled and squirmed on the uncomfortable bed. Somebody had placed too much wood in the beast. Sweat poured off her skin, and she pushed the covers, but her arms wouldn't do what she wanted. Her right shoulder felt like a hot poker stabbed it. She groaned and struggled to move it. Why couldn't she do something so simple as moving a blanket? She got her eyes to flutter open, but the room was dark and had a funny smell. Somebody was close by. *Bart?* How'd she get in the bed, and where was Sarah? Had something happened to her?

Jules tried to yell, but words stuck in her throat messed up with a gurgling sound. A face loomed closer. She blinked in the dimness. *Drew?* How'd he get in there? Or was she dreaming? *I gotta get up—tell him to run so Bart won't see him.* Nothing worked.

Drew rubbed his cool hand across her forehead. Why was his hand so cold in the blistering hot room? Was he really there? She shut her eyes, worn out from the effort. *I'll just rest a minute.* It was dark as night and with no more thought, she lay still, the dream overtaking her…

Bart killed Sarah, and the baby. She screamed, begging him to stop, but he snarled at her and shot David and Josh. Drew ran over and tried to fight Bart while she hollered for him to get himself outta the line of fire. He wouldn't listen. Bart laughed as he aimed and fired at Drew.

Jules cried, jumping in front of the bullet. She'd been too late. The bullet had ripped Drew's chest apart.

~*~

Drew agonized as Jules thrashed on the bed.

"We've got to hold her down." Josh's words were clipped as he stepped forward. "She'll open up that wound again if we can't get her calmed."

"Shh, sweetheart." Drew's heart throbbed as he secured his wife's limbs. "You're safe… everything will be just fine. No one can harm you."

She continued to toss and cry in her sleep as if she'd lost all she held dear. Perspiration emanated from every pore in her body. Heat flushed her skin.

It seemed Drew's heart would beat right out of his chest if he couldn't find a way to calm her. He leaned forward and captured Jules's lips with his own.

She immediately calmed under his ministrations.

A smile split Josh's face. "I wouldn't have guessed something like that would've worked, but at least she's quieted some. We've gotta get her cooled."

"How?" The word wrenched from Drew's throat. He closed his eyes for a second and ran his hand across them. Jules had been in and out of consciousness for nearly a day and a half and had shown no signs of improvement. He feared they would lose her if the fever didn't break soon.

"You'll need to get her out of those clothes. They're soaked through from sweating." Color washed across Josh's face. "Use snow and rub it on her bare skin. It's the only thing I can think of to cool her down."

I can't. Drew's neck and cheeks heated. *Wait.* Jules needed him. It wasn't the time for propriety.

"I'll help." Sarah stepped forward and squeezed his hand. She settled Joel on a coat nearby.

"We'll get the snow." David picked up the pan, and Josh followed him through the doorway.

Drew groaned as he lifted Jules's hot body and helped Sarah remove the sodden outer garments. He turned his back while his sister divested Jules of her union suit. His quaking legs took a while to calm.

"It's all right now," she assured him.

He pivoted and sat on the cot next to Jules. We need a miracle, Lord. Make the snow bring her fever down. I want to be able to spend time with my wife and let her know how much I care about her. Please don't take her away from me.

A knock hit the door.

Sarah retrieved the pan of snow from the two men.

Together they used Jules's already sodden dress to sponge her face, arms, and legs. Jules shivered as the icy snow touched her skin. But when they finished, she appeared to rest easier.

Drew stripped off his shirt and handed it to his sister.

Sarah gently turned Jules, putting his wife inside his garment to cover her.

Drew kissed Jules on the cheek, covering her with a light blanket. He went to let the other men into the warmth.

David and Josh stepped inside, blowing on their gloved hands.

Drew sank to the floor at the foot of the cot, his blurry eyes struggling to stay open. *How many days has it been since I truly slept?*

"Try and rest, Drew." Josh placed a hand on his shoulder. "I can wake you if anything changes."

"No. I need to be awake."

His family huddled around him, getting as close to the cot as they dared without disturbing Jules.

David's hand rested on Drew's shoulder. "Lord, we come on behalf of our dear sister, Jules. Only You can break her fever. We need a miracle, Lo—" David's voice broke.

Sarah picked up the plea. "She's special to all of us, Lord. We ask You to spare her life. Protect her and bring healing to Jules."

"W-we pray her wound doesn't become infected." Josh sniffed and audibly clenched his teeth.

"Help us to understand how to help her, Lord." Drew rested his hand on her foot. "P-please spare her, Lord. I need her..." His voice broke.

They remained gathered close, all of them silent.

Drew prayed as he'd never prayed before.

The baby broke the tense silence with a mewling cry.

Sarah broke free from the group to feed her son.

The men stayed with Drew, their strength supporting him.

David flipped his pocket watch open. "It's only a couple hours until Christmas." He closed the timepiece with a snap.

"She's resting easier." Josh touched his hand to Jules's forehead. "She's a bit cooler too."

Thank You, Lord. His wife's chest rose and fell at a slower rate than it had been. Maybe God would perform a Christmas miracle after all. He needed the gift of Jules. Desperately.

~*~

Jules licked her cracked, dry lips. Her whole body ached. She searched the room, trying to remember where she was. *The dugout.* It was slow in coming back to her.

Bart.

Josh shooting.

Stepping in front of the bullet.

Then nothing.

She had no idea how much time had passed. There were no

noises in the room, but someone sat in the chair beside her cot. Jules didn't know who it was; it was too dark to tell. She cleared her throat and the person immediately stood, struck a match, and lit a small lamp. He set it on the table.

Drew's whiskered face came into sight. "What a relief to see you awake." His hand rubbed across her forehead. "Praise God, the fever's gone. How're you feeling?"

"Thirsty."

Drew chuckled, crossed the room, and brought her a cup of water. He wrapped his arm around her back, lifting her from the bed, helping her to drink. The movement caused pain to sear through her shoulder. She clenched her teeth to keep from crying out.

"I'm sorry. I didn't mean to hurt you."

She lay on the cot again, now able to take small breaths through the receding pain. "What day is it?"

"It's Christmas, sweetheart." He leaned forward, touching his lips to hers.

Her cheeks nearly flamed as much as her shoulder. *What's gotten into him?* "Nice." The word left her mouth before she could snatch it back.

"There's plenty more when you're up to it, Jules." His hand caressed her face. "I thought I'd lost you."

"Bart?"

He didn't answer her right away. "He, uh, didn't make it."

She closed her eyes, and a tear escaped.

Drew wiped it away with his thumb. "He came to know the Lord before he died, and all because you were willing to die in his place." His eyes sparkled with something she didn't recognize. "I shared how God could tame him, if he let Him."

"Y-you did?"

"Yes, Sarah explained what 'taming' meant, and sweetheart, I'm so excited that you'll have the experience of knowing Jesus as Lord and Savior." He kissed her again. "I thought about holding off on kissing until your body heals some, but I think maybe you wouldn't mind the second one…as a way of celebrating your decision to follow Christ and…and…the only gift I can give you right now."

She could get used to this. "Don't hear me tellin' you to stop." Jules studied his face. Color rose to Drew's cheeks and she grinned. He leaned in and gave her a longer kiss. When he pulled back, her pulse raced. She stared at him. Muscles corded beneath his union suit.

She whispered, "Where's yer shirt?"

He nodded toward her, his gaze on her body, not her face.

She looked down at her chest. *His* shirt showed above the blanket covering her. Her face got hot again and her heart stampeded inside when he leaned in, capturing her mouth with his. She used her good hand to touch his hair, and she tugged him closer. His kiss got deeper, and she warmed all over.

A cough from the other side of the room made Drew stand up.

She didn't like it. Not one little bit.

"I reckon you're doing better." Josh stepped beside the bed, his hair standing on end as he shoved the tails of his shirt into his pants. "Always did have a hard time keeping you out of trouble."

"She does have a knack of finding her way into disturbances." Drew grinned.

Josh crossed his arms. "I suppose she keeps your life exciting."

"Never a dull moment." Drew touched her face, his fingers brushing her lips.

Jules's heart thudded in her head. She twisted on the bed, sucking in a sharp breath when her shoulder seared with pain.

"I wouldn't want it any other way," Drew said. "She's the best thing that's ever happened to me."

30

"What's that?" Jules shook her head. Surely, she'd heard Drew wrong.

He smiled, and wrinkles showed at the corners of his eyes. "I told Josh you're the best thing that's ever happened to me. God has shown me over the past months what a precious jewel you are."

"I reckon you two have some reacquainting to do, as much as you can with all of us in the same room." Josh grinned, squeezed her hand, and walked away.

Jules nibbled on her lips, staring at Drew. "I don't get it. I thought you regretted marryin' me, since I've been nothin' but trouble."

Drew took her hand in his. He kissed the tip of each finger, sending delicious shivers up her spine.

He chuckled. "I admit you weren't what I'd expected in a wife. But you're what I needed, even though it took me a while to see it. I thought I had to tame and change you into what I assumed was best."

"I don't tame easy-like." She looked away, trying to hold back the tears wanting to let loose. "God has an awful job ahead of Him too, I reckon."

"My precious Jules, I was so wrong to think or act that way. Please forgive me. It wasn't *you* who needed to be different. God used you to speak to my heart about areas where He wanted me to grow and mature. I'm sorry I haven't been very honest with you at times."

"How so?"

"I've been seeking another job." Drew cleared his throat. "I should've told you sooner."

"Did you find one?" She held her breath.

He put his hand under her chin, bent, and kissed her. "Yes. Edward Miller came to me the day you and Sarah were taken. He said the elders wanted me to preach again. They offered back my position."

She ran her hand from his cheek to his chin. "Oh, Drew, that's wonderful. I'm so happy…for us both."

"I praise God for allowing us to stay in Burrton Springs. I never should've kept things from you, Jules, and I'll make sure it's the last time I do it."

She loved the way he looked into her eyes.

"My life has changed in so many ways since you've entered it."

"I'm sorry I didn't tell you about Bart and Burt." Tears spilled from the edges of her eyes and into the hair on the sides of her face.

He squeezed her hand. "It's forgiven. I, uh, I'm sorry I doubted you. Those letters…"

"Josh wrote them, Drew, but it could've been me just as easily. I wanted a real home for a long time." She smiled at him. "A husband too."

Drew's cheeks flamed.

"I reckon it may take me a while to figure how to be a proper wife, but I'm willin' to keep learnin'. I want to be a woman yer not ashamed of bein' with." Jules ducked her head. "I'm tryin' to be someone genteel, honest, and a first-rate homemaker like that piece of paper said in yer Bible. I may not have learned it all yet, but I sure got a hankerin' to serve God with you."

"What matters most, sweetheart, is your desire to follow Christ. Those other things will come in time. Besides, I already see a lot of those traits in you." Drew lifted her chin and kissed her neck.

Her body shook at his touch. "I can't promise if I'll ever be a good homemaker, 'specially when it comes to that beast of yours. It sure is a burr in my side when it comes to cookin'."

~*~

Drew chuckled. It was the middle of the night, and he should be exhausted, but he wanted to wrap his wife in his arms, gather her close, show her his love, and never let go. His heart nearly burst with that desire. He sighed. *Patience has never come easy to me, Lord.*

Jules frowned, unwilling to meet his gaze. "I reckon my cookin' must still be a disappointment to you."

"Believe me, cooking is the furthest thing from my mind right now, sweetheart."

"I couldn't figure out for the longest time what awful disease I had," she said, fiddling with the blanket edge.

"What do you mean by disease?" He traced the curve of her neck with his finger.

Her breathing came in short breaths against his hand.

"I reckoned there was somethin' fearful wrong with me. My belly flopped and twisted in a knot, and my heart pounded whenever you were near. I couldn't sleep at night when I listened to you breathin' in the other room. Couldn't think straight neither." Bright spots of color tinged her pale face.

"So what do you think it was?" Drew leaned forward.

"I weren't sure. None of the sicknesses in your medical book described my symptoms. It's taken me a long while, but I finally figured what it was." She stopped.

He didn't move, waiting for her to continue.

"I-I'm afraid it's a condition I'll have the rest of my life." She peeked at him from beneath her thick lashes.

"What? Is it serious?" He nearly choked on the words. He couldn't lose her now that he finally had her back again. *Oh, please, Lord, no. Give me strength.*

"It's fatal, Drew. There's no way I can ever recover from it."

"But..." He couldn't finish. A sob caught in his throat.

Jules's hand rested on his arm. "I hear it might be catchin'...at least...I sure enough hope so."

Drew's mind raced. Would he ever understand his wife? Could it truly be something contagious?

"I reckon I don't want to recover though either. I kind of like it. It's somethin' I've never experienced before." A smile spread across her face.

"I don't see how you can be happy at a time like this. You just told me you aren't going to live." Drew bit out the words.

"Nope, didn't say no such thing. I said I have a special condition."

"And what might it be?" He rose.

She tugged him back to her side. "Being madly in love with you." She pulled him closer and claimed his lips with hers.

~*~

Their lips touched, and Jules knew nothing could be sweeter in the whole world. Her heart threatened to explode when Drew deepened the kiss, running a hand through her hair, touching her face in a special way. She didn't know how long their hearts entwined together in that single kiss. Or was it multiple ones? Her heart sang and danced within her.

"I *love* you, Jules Montgomery, and I want you to be my wife." Drew sat straighter for a bit.

Jules giggled. "In case you hadn't noticed, I already *am* your wife."

Epilogue

January 1, 1876

Jules stood at the mirror, staring one last time. Her hand shook when she pushed an escaped curl back in place. Her stomach fluttered as she met her sister-in-law's gaze.

"You're absolutely beautiful, Jules." Sarah stroked Pepper, who rested on his side on the bed.

"You think?" Jules smoothed the skirt of the deep blue dress Gertrude had made for the special occasion. "I'm guessin' I look some different than when Drew first laid eyes on me. Do you reckon I should wear my gun belt today, for old time's sake?" She grinned and waggled her eyebrows.

Sarah laughed. "I'm sure Drew wouldn't mind, but perhaps it's best if you leave it here at home. Are you ready?"

"I 'spose so." Jules hugged her friend. "I don't know why I'm so nervous. It's not like he's gonna say no or somethin'."

Sarah laughed and kissed her on the cheek. "I'll head on over to the church. See you in a few minutes."

Jules darted another quick look in the mirror before she headed toward the kitchen.

Josh stood as she entered the room, letting out a low whistle.

Her cheeks were on fire, she could feel it.

"You're mighty pretty, Jules. I don't think I ever noticed before."

"I wish you didn't need to leave this afternoon." She sniffed and wiped her nose on the back of her sleeve.

"Don't you worry none about me. I'll be back to check in on you every once in a while. I need to finish up my commitment as deputy. I've been thinking about finding something closer, so we can see each other more often." Josh fiddled with the hat in his hands.

She ran into his arms. "Oh, Josh, that'd be wonderful."

"Before we go over, I wanted to tell you something." Josh

swallowed hard and ran his finger along the collar of his shirt.

Jules met her brother's eyes. "What?"

"I should've told you about the letters I wrote to Drew. I figured if you knew you would've put up a fuss and refused to come."

"You're probably right."

"Killing Burt took its toll and was changing you. I needed to do something drastic." Josh slapped his hat back on his head. "Drew's a good man."

"He most certainly is." Jules smiled. "I'll be forever thankful for what you did for me, Josh. Someday I hope to return the favor."

"We'd better get over there, or Drew will think you stood him up, and we can't have that." Josh held out his arm and they walked the short distance to the church.

The unusually warm air matched Jules's mood. When they stepped into the entrance, a hush fell over the assembled congregation. Everyone turned toward her. Smiling faces shone as she and her brother walked down the aisle.

Drew stood beside the circuit preacher. His eyes shimmered with unshed tears, and his face beamed as he watched her. It had been his idea for them to 'officially' marry again, a special time with all their friends and loved ones.

The preacher said the words that Jules barely heard. She repeated what he told her to repeat, and then looked at her husband, drowning in his gaze. Her heart throbbed. *Thank You, Lord, for bringing me to this place.*

The music swelled as she stood beside her husband.

"Thanks for tamin' me. You, and the Lord," Jules whispered in Drew's ear.

He leaned close.

And she kissed him full on the lips.

A Devotional Moment

Hear my cry, O God; listen to my prayer. From the ends of the earth I call to you, I call as my heart grows faint; lead me to the rock that is higher than I.
~ Psalm 61:1-2

Sometimes, due to circumstances beyond our control, we are thrust into an overwhelming situation. We have to adapt and cannot go back to where we once were. In these times, we feel all alone, but rather than sink into a pit of despair, we can place our trust in God. When we are devastated by losing everything we hold dear, we can hand our heart to God so we can learn all we need to know.

In **Taming Julia**, the protagonist is thrust into a situation for which she has no skills. While she tries to manage within the framework of what society expects, she is exposed to the Presence of God, a development she neither expects nor understands. With gentle grace, God leads her to the person most able to help her learn and grow, not only in His loving arms, but in the world she now inhabits.

Have you ever felt overwhelmed and alone? It is a scary place to be, feeling as if you have no one who understands or who can or will help you. In these situations, remember, it is OK to lean on other people—even new people who have the experience, expertise or insight you lack. And always, always lean on God. He is there backing you up even if no one else is.

LORD, WHEN I AM ALONE, UNCERTAIN, UNSTEADY AND FEELING LOST, I ASK FOR YOUR GRACE TO HELP ME COPE. IN JESUS' NAME I PRAY, AMEN.

Thank you

We appreciate you reading this White Rose Publishing title. For other inspirational stories, please visit our on-line bookstore at www.pelicanbookgroup.com.

For questions or more information, contact us at customer@pelicanbookgroup.com.

White Rose Publishing
Where Faith is the Cornerstone of Love™
an imprint of Pelican Book Group
www.PelicanBookGroup.com

Connect with Us
www.facebook.com/Pelicanbookgroup
www.twitter.com/pelicanbookgrp

To receive news and specials, subscribe to our bulletin
http://pelink.us/bulletin

May God's glory shine through
this inspirational work of fiction.

AMDG

You Can Help!

At Pelican Book Group it is our mission to entertain readers with fiction that uplifts the Gospel. It is our privilege to spend time with you awhile as you read our stories.

We believe you can help us to bring Christ into the lives of people across the globe. And you don't have to open your wallet or even leave your house!

Here are 3 simple things you can do to help us bring illuminating fiction™ to people everywhere.

1) If you enjoyed this book, write a positive review. Post it at online retailers and websites where readers gather. And share your review with us at reviews@pelicanbookgroup.com (this does give us permission to reprint your review in whole or in part.)

2) If you enjoyed this book, recommend it to a friend in person, at a book club or on social media.

3) If you have suggestions on how we can improve or expand our selection, let us know. We value your opinion. Use the contact form on our web site or e-mail us at customer@pelicanbookgroup.com

God Can Help!

Are you in need? The Almighty can do great things for you. Holy is His Name! He has mercy in every generation. He can lift up the lowly and accomplish all things. Reach out today.

Do not fear: I am with you; do not be anxious: I am your God. I will strengthen you, I will help you, I will uphold you with my victorious right hand.

~Isaiah 41:10 (NAB)

We pray daily, and we especially pray for everyone connected to Pelican Book Group—that includes you! If you have a specific need, we welcome the opportunity to pray for you. Share your needs or praise reports at http://pelink.us/pray4us

Free eBook Offer

We're looking for booklovers like you to partner with us! Join our team of influencers today and periodically receive free eBooks!

For more information
Visit http://pelicanbookgroup.com/booklovers

How About Free Audiobooks?

We're looking for audiobook lovers, too! Partner with us as an audiobook lover and periodically receive free audiobooks!

For more information
Visit http://pelicanbookgroup.com/booklovers/freeaudio.html

or e-mail
booklovers@pelicanbookgroup.com

www.ingramcontent.com/pod-product-compliance
Lightning Source LLC
Chambersburg PA
CBHW030411310726
48979CB00002B/370

* 9 7 8 1 5 2 2 3 0 2 7 2 8 *